CRIMSON DESIRE

SIENNA DEAN

MILTON & HUGO L.L.C.
4407 Park Ave., Suite 5
Union City, NJ 07087, USA

Website: *www. miltonandhugo.com*
Hotline: *1- 888-778-0033*
Email: *info@miltonandhugo.com*

Ordering Information:
Quantity sales. Special discounts are granted to corporations, associations, and other organizations. For more information on these discounts, please reach out to the publisher using the contact information provided above.

Library of Congress Control Number:	2025904673
ISBN-13: 979-8-89285-395-8	[Paperback Edition]
979-8-89285-396-5	[Digital Edition]

Rev. date: 02/10/2025

To all my Good Girls who dream of being railed
by the Bad Boys ..... Giovanni awaits you.
"Beg me for it"

Below is a list of songs I listened to while
I wrote certain special parts ..
Enjoy!
-Sienna <3

Crimson Desire
No Mercy by Austin Giorgio (chapter2)
Me and The Devil by Soap & Skin (chapter 12)
Pain is my only home by Zevia (chapter 13)
Addicted by Jon Vinyl (chapter 22)
Belong to You by Sabrina Claudio (chapter 24)
Turning Page by Sydney Rose (Chapter 27)
Paint it black by Ciara (Chapter 28)
Women by Emmit (Chapter 29)
I feel like I'm drowning by Two Feet (Chapter 29)
Like you mean it by Steven Rodriquez (Chapter 33)
Jokes on You by Charlotte Lawrence (Chapter 40)
Love is Gone cover by Camylio (Chapter 41)
Noble Blood by Tommee Profitt, Fluerie (Chapter 41)

CHAPTER 1

IRIS

I wanted to be anywhere else other than The Amethyst Room on a Friday night, but here I was—all thanks to Lexi and Avery, my two best friends, more like sisters. After the two months I had between my college law finals, studying for the BAR exam, and walking in on my boyfriend—sorry, ex-boyfriend—Kyle in bed with some skank, yeah, I needed to relax and let loose. Avery and Lexi always knew just what to do to get my mind off anything.

I had been going to college for eight years to get my law degree. I graduated top of my class in a little town in the middle of nowhere, North Dakota. I got into my dream college, the Fletcher School of Law, here in Massachusetts. So I packed my bags and came to the big city. Got in way over my head with my college boyfriend, found my best friends, and, better yet, found myself.

I had to dig into the deepest part of my closet to find the skimpiest dress I owned: an emerald velvet number that barely covered my ass. It matched well with my copper-colored hair that falls into curls and my mismatched eyes—one bright blue and the other bright green. All finished off with black strappy heels. My name may be Iris O'Malley, but nobody ever calls me that, not even my own parents. I went through life with one nickname after the other—Penny, Ginger, Soul Sucker, Fire Head—but I preferred, and only answered to, Izzy.

1

Lexi and Avery never had to try this hard to be attractive or worry about ugly nicknames. Lexi is a 5-foot-3 Asian American with curves to die for. Her hair was down to her ass, straight, and a silky blue-black color. Her eyes were the color of sapphires. What I would do for her straight hair and curves. Avery a Latina about 5-foot-5 with tan goddess skin, brown wavy hair that went to her mid-back.. She could hypnotize anyone with just one glance of her amber eyes.

I had never been to The Amethyst Room before, but I was told it was a classy club where most college kids go. College kids and classy are two words that should not go together. The walls were as black as night with purple lights strobing against the white leather couches, eggshell chairs, and black tables. The floors were a nice shade of light gray, almost white ash. There was a stage at the front with the DJ set up and two big speakers on each side of the stage. I could almost feel the rumble of the sound waves vibrating against my spine from the bar. Most people in the club were wearing gold or white. I felt like a sore thumb in a green dress, but in this light, it looked black.

I must have looked younger than normal tonight. At 26, I don't get ID'd much. After ordering my vodka and lemonade, the bartender looked at me like I had two heads and asked for my ID. I'm not complaining. Believe me, no woman wants to look older. I found Lexi and Avery on the dance floor, dancing to a song I don't recognize, but I jumped in and danced with them anyway. Feeling the beat, my worries started to drift away—that is, until some jerk bumped into me, making me spill half of my drink down the front of my dress. He apologized and tries to clean it up with a napkin but lingered a little too long on my breast.

"Hey, can you get your hands off my tits?" I said, loud enough to be heard over the noise of the club.

"Don't be a bitch. I'm just trying to clean you up," the drunk slurred.

"Did you just call me a bitch?" I looked at the man in disbelief. "My name is Iris. Now leave. I can clean myself up," I glared. "Thanks thought"

"Cool. My name is Riley. Nice to meet you," he said as he held out his hand, expecting me to shake it. "You're pretty hot. Wouldn't mind taking you home tonight." His hand connected with my ass cheek. In such shock, I looked at him just as a fist came flying at him from my left.

"I don't think she wants you to touch her," a deep voice came out of the dark. I made eye contact with a six-foot man with dark curly hair to the top of his ears, a jaw that could cut ice, and a dark suit that hugged every muscle just right. Dark tattoos covered his tan skin from the top of his shirt to his chiseled chin.

Riley just laid on the floor as I looked at the other man.

"Um, thank you for that," I said, pointing at the knocked-out Riley on the floor. "My name is Iris. Can I buy you a drink to thank you?" I asked breathlessly.

"No, but I can buy you a drink," he said as he held out a hand. "My name is Giovanni, but you can call me Gio," he added as he adjusted his sleeve, twirling his cufflinks.

When Giovanni and I got to the bar, I noticed that he didn't just have tattoos on his neck—they were also all over his hands, and I bet they wrapped up his arms and around his big biceps. Looking at him in the light of the bar, I could see he had eyes the color of silver. I didn't even think silver eyes were real, but I can't deny that what I just saw was the most beautiful thing I had ever seen—just like how he was the most handsome man I had ever laid eyes on. Living in Boston, there were many handsome men of either Italian or Irish descent. My guess? Giovanni was most definitely Italian and just my type.

Grabbing my hand, he led me to the dance floor, spinning my back to his chest. My body moved to the rhythm of a Rihanna song, grinding against the length of his manhood. The lights shining on his face revealed his eyes tracing every move my body made. Dancing the night away with Giovanni, I learned he worked in his family business, lived in the tallest skyrise in the city, and wanted to take me home. Well, the last one was more of a guess, but the way he kept looking at my chest and touching my shoulder as his arm draped behind me, it was a good guess. He turned to me, running his finger down my arm in a circular motion. "Should we go somewhere quiet?" he asked. I shook my head in agreement, while my lower half flooded with the heat of a thousand suns.

I finally found Lexi and Avery while Giovanni got his car from the valet. The girls were not mad at all that I was ditching them. Lexi had told me once that the best way to get over a guy was to get under the next, and that's all I planned for this to be—fun, nothing serious.

I walked outside The Amethyst Room to the sidewalk, where I saw Giovanni waiting for his car. I took my place to his left. My jaw dropped as a black-on-black Mercedes pulled up, and the valet worker handed Giovanni the keys. His big, warm hand landed on the small of my back as he opened my door. He took my hand to ensure I was seated properly in the car. My center was on fire from just the slight touch of this man's hand.

We drove through the city to his apartment building. Soon after, we pulled into the parking garage and headed into the lobby, where a well-dressed man greeted Giovanni and me. "Good evening, Mr. Benedetti." I gathered that Giovanni's full name was most likely Giovanni Benedetti.

"Good night, Julius," Giovanni replied quickly as the elevator doors closed behind us. Giovanni reached over and hit the button marked "PH." When I looked down, I noticed the elevator floor had "Benedetti Tower" inscribed.

"You told me you lived in a skyrise, not that you owned one," I said, pointing to the floor that clearly displayed his last name.

"I don't tell people I own a building right off the bat. They tend to look at me differently. Plus, most people freak out when they hear my last name—but not you." He turned to face me. In this position, he seemed to tower even taller, at about 6-foot-3. He tilted my head up with his

4

index finger so I was looking directly into his eyes. "I like that," he growled.

Why would people freak out about his last name? I may not be from Boston, but I've lived here for eight years, and I've never heard of this man's last name before—at least I don't think I have.

The door opened to a small foyer with a door leading to his penthouse. Mirrors on each wall reflected a blank space. As Giovanni opened the front door, he started taking off his suit coat, and that's when I saw it: he had a gun strapped under his shoulder and another in the waistband of his pants. How did I not notice them before now? I was literally grinding on this man. Was he going to kill me?

He walked over to a black buffet cabinet, put in a code, took out his guns, and placed them inside. A small sigh of relief left my mouth. As he closed the cabinet, he glared at me through his long eyelashes from across the room. He stood to his full height, licking his lips. His home was decorated in a modern, luxurious style, with a white and gray color palette.

Giovanni's apartment is by far the nicest home I have ever stepped into. A mix of artwork envelops the white walls. A large mirror hangs above the black cabinet, across from a wall full of floor-to-ceiling windows. The floors are a natural wood color that pops against the light gray sectional in the living room. I turn to see the large white kitchen with a navy blue island. To the right of the kitchen, there is a door to the patio; to the left, a hallway leads to what I presume are the bedrooms.

"You can take your shoes off, you know. They don't look that comfortable, Iris," he says, starting to unbutton his white shirt. My earlier assumptions were true. The man is ripped and tattooed everywhere. Heat rushes to my core, making me drip. "I want you to be comfortable. Would you like a drink?"

"The only way I'm getting comfortable is if this dress goes away. And yes, I'll take a drink. Thank you—whatever you have is fine," I say jokingly.

"I can help you with that," he says with a grin, looking me up and down.

"With the drink or the dress?" I laugh, looking at him with doe eyes and parted lips.

"With whichever you choose, Iris. Everything that happens here tonight—or any night—will be your choice," he says as he steps closer, tilting my chin up so I try to meet his gaze.

"I think you know what I want, and I'm pretty sure you want the same thing, Giovanni," I mutter breathlessly, looking up at him through my eyelashes as heat fills my core, leaving me even wetter for the man standing in front of me.

"Then allow me to make myself clear, if I haven't yet." His hands trace from the nape of my neck to the zipper at the back of my dress. "I fully intend, if you allow me to," he continues as one hand tugs on my zipper while the other traces my jaw and wraps gently around my throat, "tie you to my bedpost and fuck you until your sweet pussy tightens around my cock and your juices run down the length of me, LEaving you dripping on the floor" He finishes his statement by crashing his lips against mine.

CHAPTER 2

GIOVANNI

"Tie you to my bedpost and fuck you until your sweet pussy tightens around my cock and your juices run down the length of me, leaving you dripping on the floor" I say as I plant a claiming kiss on her lips. It will be the only time I am sweet to her tonight—at least when it comes to the bedroom. Her dress hits the floor, and there she is in all her glory. The beautiful red hair that flows past her shoulders, the rarity of her eye colors, the pull of this woman's curves—everything about her does something to my throbbing cock. To put it plainly, this woman is so fucking gorgeous, and I want her. No, I need her. I need to devour this woman.

"Actions speak louder than words, Giovanni," she says, running her smooth palms up my chest. "Prove to me that you don't just talk a big game. I approve of anything you want to do to me tonight or any night." She speaks in the absolute sexiest, most seductive voice I have ever heard.

"God, I fucking love how you say my name. I'm gonna make you say my name when you cum on my cock." Her eyes light up the instant the words leave my mouth.

"Why do you still have your clothes on, then, Gio?" she asks as her hands go to the waistband of my pants and undo the belt buckle. With one hand, she takes my belt off and throws it onto the couch. The other hand unbuttons my slacks, which quickly find their new home next to

7

her dress. I fist her hair at the nape of her neck and thrust her mouth to mine. She lets out a small moan, which is devoured by our heavy breaths.

Desire fills me as I lift her, and she hooks her legs around my waist. I've always been able to control my need or the urge for anything—except when it comes to my work. That's the only place I let myself lose control. Other than tonight, I haven't brought a girl home in the last two years. The other women were just hookups in a club bathroom.

The desire takes over, and before I know it, I'm carrying her down the hallway to my room, tossing the delicate woman onto my bed. I never have sex in my own bed. I can feel her watching me as I walk over to the closet and grab my two favorite ties. A big smile grows across my face as I turn and see the goddess on my bed, fully naked, spread out, and ready to take all of me.

"I don't always go easy, but if you need me to—"

"No," she cuts me off. "I can take whatever you can give me, Giovanni. I trust you," she says, looking up at me with the most beautiful, devious fucking smile. What a fucking mistake.

Play: No Mercy By Austin Giorgio

I tuck a piece of her red flowing hair behind her ear and press her against the mattress. I travel up her body with kisses as I tie her wrists to each of my bedposts. I don't blindfold her—I want to see what those beautiful siren eyes do as I make her cum. I walk to the end of the bed and crawl until I'm perfectly positioned in front of her sweet, juicy pussy. Looking into her eyes from between her legs, I give her a wicked smile.

"Are you ready to scream my name, Mia fiore?"

Iris looks down at me with fire in her eyes at the nickname I've just given her. "Yes "a breathy moan leaves her lips.

I dive my head between her legs, giving her one full lick across her pussy lips as she lets out a hiss. She spreads her legs even wider, opening herself for me. I play with her clit, alternating between sucking and licking as her moans grow louder.

"Yes, please, just like that—keep going," she begs.

I kiss her thighs, teasing the sides of her sweet spot with small, playful licks as she squirms under my tongue. I thrust two fingers into her soaking pussy while pushing down on her pelvic bone. She is so tight.

"Oh fuck, Gio," she cries out as her pussy tightens around my fingers. I dip my head down and start sucking on the apex of her clit, working my fingers over the spongy part of her inner walls. She lets go, her orgasm combusting around my grip. I look up at her, my mouth still on her clit, as the biggest grin spreads across her face. Her chest rises and falls, her perky tits moving up and down, just within arm's reach. Somehow, I'm even harder than I was when my fingers were inside her. How is it possible that this woman can turn me on so much?

I shove my fingers into her mouth so she can taste herself. "You taste good, don't you, mia fiore?" She nods in agreement. I pinch one of her nipples between my index finger and thumb. I take the other between my teeth as she hisses and shudders at the mix of pain and pleasure I provide.

"God, it feels so fucking good," Iris moans breathlessly.

I move my body over her, standing at the edge of the bed as she pulls at the ties on her wrists. Unable to break free, she opens her mouth, and I slide my cock in, inch by inch, until she gags at my size.

"Your throat is so tight, it might make me cum right here, right now," I whisper as I push deeper. Slowly at first, then quicker, I thrust as her throat adjusts to my size. Tears run down her face as I go harder and faster. Finally, I pull out of her mouth and shoot my warm load onto her chest.

"Please untie me, Gio! I don't want to be bound anymore—I need to touch you!" Iris begs.

"Promise me you'll be good, fiore."

Iris looks up at me with sin in her eyes. "I promise," she says, licking her lips. Untying her, my shirt is the only thing between us, And it won't be coming off anytime soon.

Iris gets on her knees in the middle of the bed, drawing shapes in the gift I've just left on her chest. She trails her fingers up her body to her full lips, sucking them clean. I don't know how this woman does it, but once again, I'm as hard as a rock. I fist her hair in my hand and pull her closer as I whisper, "You are so fucking seductive, fiore. I might have to punish you for teasing me."

"Do what you have to do, Gio," she replies.

I pull her hair with such need that Iris follows my lead without hesitation. As if she can read my thoughts, she turns and falls onto the bed, her face pressed against the mattress, with her round, bare ass in the air.

I position myself on the bed behind her and make my entrance. Her pussy is so tight I would have thought she was a virgin.

"Oh my god, Gio, you're so big—holy fuck!" she says rapidly. Just hearing her voice in a moan makes me want to cum.

"Are you going to cum on my cock, fiore?" I ask as I run my hand up her back, fisting her hair and making her back bow.

"Fuck, yes!" she screams, bunching the bed sheets in her hands as if trying to mute her cries of pleasure.

I flip her onto her back and start to play with her nipples while thrusting into her as deep as her body will allow me to go. Iris takes my hand from her nipples and guides it to her throat. She looks at me with a mix of worry or disappointment. I don't think anyone has ever given her what she truly wanted in bed before. I'll give her everything she wants—this isn't just about me. I want to please her, too.

I tighten my grip on her throat, and she starts to ride my cock as I thrust into her. Her pussy tightens, and my dick begins to throb. We release at the same time. I look at Iris just as she cums.

"Fuck, Giovanni—god," she cries out, biting into my forearm.

"That's my girl," I hiss as the pain from her bite sears through my arm. New kink unlocked.

CHAPTER 3

IRIS

I must have fallen asleep last night after Giovanni and I finished our marathon—he made me finish four times. I woke up in a bed that wasn't mine, with no clothes on and a huge smile. I heard the shower running and quickly debated whether to continue the fun with him. But before I could make a decision, the shower turned off, and out walked Giovanni, wrapped in a towel.

From here, I could see things I hadn't noticed last night. Not only was he covered in tattoos, but he was also covered in scars and bruises—some looking fresher than others. He caught me staring as he glanced up at the mirror that hung above his dresser, he turns pulling a black t shirt over his body as if he is a kid who just caught stealing.

"Good morning. Did you sleep okay?"

"Yes, I did. Thank you. What time is it?" I asked, looking around.

"It's 7:35. I have to go take care of something at the office, but I should be back by noon if you want to stay," he said, leaning against the dresser behind him.

He walks into the closet with the towel still around his waist and came out wearing one of the sexiest navy blue suits I had ever seen. Giovanni started looking around the floor, clearly searching for something. I quickly realized what he was missing—a tie. I reached over and grabbed the maroon tie he had used on me last night. With a smile, I held it up in the air.

"Looking for something?" I teased.

"You're going to make me late, fiore," he said with a smirk.

Giovanni saved my number in his phone before he left for work.

"Last night was amazing. You were a god," I told him, walking toward the bathroom and putting a little extra sway in my hips.

"I am anything but a god. Have a good day. See you around noon," he murmured as he shut the bedroom door behind him.

What could he have meant by that?

I did my best with what he had in his shower for shampoo and body wash—it would have to work for today.

CHAPTER 4

GIOVANNI

What the fuck was I doing? Was I really going to leave a girl I didn't know in my house by herself for four hours? You'd think with my line of work I would know better. I stopped at the cabinet by the front door to get my gun, holster it, and headed to the elevator. What is it about her that makes me want more of her? Her eyes? Her hair? Her pussy? All of it? Either way, I'm still drunk on that woman, and I want the hair of the dog. I don't even remember driving to the mansion, but I was there before I knew it.

The mansion is where the business—or, as we in the family say, the *business*—happens. It's where we go to pitch ideas, sharpen our skills, and strengthen our minds. I only come here when my father requests my presence or someone calls on me for a job. My father is the head of the family, and when he dies or retires, the role falls to me. I was born for that role and trained for it. My father ensured I specialized in a unique role within the family. Not many people want to do it, but for me, it's just another day. I'm their hitman. High-ranking members come to me and pay me to eliminate their competition. That means I have dirt on 99% of the men who work with or for my father.

The driveway is at least a mile long from the main road, hidden behind a nine-foot iron gate. I pull around the three-tiered fountain surrounded by a mix of grass and white cobblestone. The house itself is a glorious sight to see: a 1900s brownstone with white accents and a bright red door covered by a white overhang held up by large white columns. The home is so vast that if you were to stand at one end, you'd never see the other side of the building.

My uncle and two cousins greet me at the front door.

"Yo, Giovanni, a little late today," my cousin Angelo laughs.

"Angelo, don't be a bitch. Nobody notices when your ass gets here," his brother Vinny barks back.

"Both of you shut up already," their father—my uncle Sam—yells at them.

We were always close growing up. Being an Italian family came with expectations, but being in an Italian mafia family raised those expectations even higher. Slowly we grew apart, now we only see eachother for family business.

"He in his office, Sam?" I asked my uncle.

"Yeah, he's been in there all morning."

Great.

I knock on my father's office door.

"Come in," he calls.

I slowly turn the doorknob and walk in, taking the seat across from him at his desk. He's a man in his late 50s with white hair cut much like mine and blue eyes. Tattoos cover his body, and his knuckles read *FAAE*—identical to mine. *Family Above All Else,* our family motto. He's dressed in a polo and khakis, which is unusual; he always wears suits. Today is the day for the debriefing on my last job.

"Where did you go after the hit, Giovanni?" His eyes narrow on me like a human lie detector.

"I went to The Amethyst Room. Why?" I say, sitting back in my chair and staring him straight in the eyes as sweat drips down my forehead. Why was I nervous? It wasn't a lie.

"Did you take care of the rat infestation?" He raises a questioning brow at me.

"Have I ever not finished a job for you? I've worked for you for twelve years and no complaints yet." I angrily bark, standing to leave.

"I didn't mean to upset you, Gio. I know you do great work, and I'm thankful to have you on our side," he says, laughing the last few words. "I was just making sure that nothing will come of this later—for the family's sake," he adds, staring at me with a raised brow.

"No, the rats are gone," I say, shutting the door to his office behind me.

I pull out my phone and text Iris to see what she's doing. She still has two hours left alone at my house.

ME: *Hey, sorry I had to bail this a.m., but I hope you stayed.*

Shit. Was that too formal? Too hopeful? Maybe even clingy?

IRIS: *Hey, yeah, I stayed. I don't have any clothes—you broke my zipper on my dress... so I did steal a pair of your sweatpants and a shirt after my shower. #notsorry.*

Just the thought of her in my house, lounging on my couch or bed with no makeup and messy hair, seems sexy as hell, and I can't wait to see it when I get home. God, one night with this woman and all of a sudden I'm addicted—I need more. I need my fix

ME: *I did. I'll pay to replace or repair the dress.*

I'm not sorry I ripped the dress. I wanted no barriers between her skin and my touch.

IRIS: *No, it's okay. It was an old dress, and besides, I'm not sorry you broke it.*

A smile spreads across my face as I slide my phone into my front pocket. My uncle puts a hand on my shoulder.

"What's got you smiling like a fool, Gio?" he asks with a grin.

"I wasn't smiling," I protest.

"Does it have anything to do with a certain redhead your cousins saw you with last night?" he says, raising an eyebrow.

My breath catches in my throat, and I swallow hard. I don't let my family know when I meet a girl—they tend to go full stalker on her. That's why I haven't brought a girl home in over two years.

"What? No! You know I don't get attached to girls, especially when I have too much work on my plate. I do have to get going, though—I've got a lot to do," I say, standing and heading for the front door, where my car waits.

FUCK. FUCK. FUCK.

What the hell am I supposed to do? I have a small panic attack in my car on the drive home. If my uncle and cousins know about Iris, it's only a matter of time before my father knows about her. He's the true boogeyman, haunting the dreams of children and adults alike.

Lorenzo dragged me out of bed at the ripe age of 12 and made me watch from my balcony as his men shot and killed a woman in our backyard. My screams were muffled by the loud sound of the gun. At the time, I had never even held a gun. It only took me two minutes to realize the woman he shot was my mother. He sat me down on my bed and told me my mother wasn't fulfilling her duties as his *mob wife* and needed to be "put down like the bitch she was." It wasn't until I was 18 that I learned all she had done was try to divorce him. She wanted to escape the dark shadow he cast over everything good.

I can't let what happened to my mother happen to Iris. Even though I barely know her, I already feel she's going to be special to me. I just don't know how special—or in what way. My hands tighten around the steering wheel as I pull into the parking garage. I scroll through my contacts and slide my thumb across his name.

"Zane. Hey, listen, I need men who aren't owned by my father—two who are trained to protect someone without being seen by her," I demand.

"Yeah, I got two. I can have them at your penthouse in 20 for an introduction," he replies.

"No, keep them out of sight. I'll give them the rundown. I'll send you an email," I say quickly, disconnecting the call. I send the email as the elevator doors open to my foyer.

When I walk in my front door, I'm shocked to see Iris sitting at my kitchen island, eating something. I take my gun off and put it in the cabinet, as I have for the last 12 years. I walk over to her, wrap my hands around her waist, and kiss the top of her head.

"Sorry I had to leave early this morning. Did you find anything to keep you occupied while I was gone?" I whisper in her ear.

"Yes, I made lunch. Do you want some? I made plenty for you. I thought you'd be hungry since you probably didn't eat breakfast," she says, looking up at me with the sexiest glare.

Seeing her in my clothes makes me realize I find her even sexier in "lazy day" clothes than in her skimpy dress. She isn't just pretty because of makeup. She has a natural kind of beauty—one you can't buy. Her lips are full and plump, the perfect shade of pink. Her curly hair fits perfectly in a messy bun on top of her head. Her eyes are the perfect shades of my two favorite colors: bright blue and dark green.

She looks comfortable and absolutely seductive at the same time. If I believed in destiny, I'd say this woman was made for me and me alone.

"Hey, have you ever had Temple of Wok? It's a Chinese place down the street. I was thinking we could order dinner and watch movies tonight." I stare into her perfect eyes as her lips part to reply.

"I would love to, but I do have to get home. I have one last final paper to write. I'm sorry," she says, and a frown creeps across her face. "But I'll text you when I'm done, and we can definitely grab dinner, if that's okay?" she adds with a smile.

"I didn't know you were still in college. What are you studying?" That was a lie—I knew everything I could find out about this woman.

"Actually, it's my last year. I just have to take the BAR exam, and when I pass," she says, crossing her fingers and looking up at the ceiling, "I'll be a criminal defense attorney," she finishes, rubbing her hands together.

The irony hits me like a brick. A hitman casually hooking up with a criminal defense attorney. What were the odds?

"Wow, that's very impressive. What made you want to study law?" I ask, though I'm more focused on her lips than her eyes.

"Well, my mom was a teacher in a small town, and I didn't know my dad. I realized I didn't want to live in a small town anymore. So, I settled on Boston—and that takes money. I knew I was good at arguing and finding loopholes, so it was kind of an easy choice for me." She looks up at me as if she's waiting for judgment, as if I might think less of her for following her own path.

If only she knew. I wish I had that kind of freedom, but as the heir to the family, I can't. I have rules and traditions I'm bound to follow.

"Wow, I thought you were sexy before. Now, I find you not only sexy but also smart, determined, independent, and powerful. I like that about you, mio fiore. Don't change that for anyone," I say as my lips brush against hers. I fist her hair, pulling her closer, and crash my lips onto hers. She parts her lips, letting my tongue invade every inch of her mouth. Needing more of her, I place my hand on her lower back and pull her even closer. Her curves fit perfectly against my body, as if we were made from the same piece of cloth.

A small whimper escapes her lips, met by a low moan from mine.

"Fiore, we have to stop, or you'll never be able to write that paper," I say as we peel ourselves apart. "Let me grab my keys—I'll drive you home." I glance at her, smirking. "Keep the clothes." I turn to grab my wallet as the cheesiest smile creeps across my face. God, I'll never get tired of seeing this woman in my clothes.

We step into the elevator, and before I realize it, my fingers lace with hers. I feel like I'm in way over my head. This woman doesn't even know anything about my family or the things we do, yet here I am, trying to start something with her. I don't even know if this will turn into anything, but the thought of her running when she finds out the truth—that thought hurts more than I expected.

Are these feelings real? Or are they just because I've been watching her for the past two weeks?

Two weeks ago, I was following a target that one of the board members assigned to me. He was a low-circuit judge here in Boston who had started asking too many questions at a poker game. He was one of the keynote speakers at a convention I tracked him to. During his presentation, he began talking to a stunning redhead. They seemed friendly with each other, but I couldn't take my eyes off her—even if I tried.

I knew what I had to do. During my "interrogation," I made sure to ask him about the redhead—her name and any other information he had on her. He gladly squealed like the pig he was.

CHAPTER 5

IRIS

Giovanni is different from the men I've slept with in the past. With them, sex was all about their pleasure. They didn't care if it was good for me, and they definitely didn't want me to stay the night. But not Giovanni. He cared if it was good for me, wanted to make sure I came—multiple times—and even did aftercare. It seems like he actually cares, but maybe I'm overthinking it.

Now, he takes my hand and proudly walks me through the lobby to the car. I've come to a conclusion: this is a man. The others were boys. Giovanni opens the car door for me, placing a light kiss on my lips. I can't get enough of this man touching me. Even as he navigates the chaos of Boston traffic, his hand rests on my thigh, like he can't get enough of the feel of my body either. I, for the life of me, can't figure out why this man is single. He has plenty of green flags, and I haven't seen any red ones... yet.

When we reach my front door, Giovanni walks me too.

"Well, this is me. The girls are in there. If I were you, I'd run, but I'll text you for sure," I say, looking up at him.

"I'll be waiting, mio fiore," he replies, leaning down to place a hand on the door. He grabs my chin and plants a kiss on my lips. I part them, letting our tongues slide against each other's, just before he bites my bottom lip. Fire burns through me as the sting from the bite sends heat straight to my core. His eyes darken.

"You opened a new kink for me last night," he murmurs, leaning into my ear. "Biting is my new turn-on," he whispers, pressing his thumb to my bottom lip. When he removes it, there's blood—I must have been nicked hard enough to bleed. He sucks on his thumb.

"See you later, Iris," he says as he walks away.

Why did that turn me on so much?

I live in the Fletcher dorms, but as an RA, I have a single room, unlike most students who share doubles. My dorm has its own bathroom, a decent-sized closet, a desk, and a small table for collecting my junk. I can already hear Lexi and Avery talking inside as I turn the knob, letting out a deep breath.

Lexi is sitting on my bed holding a bag of seaweed chips. Avery, on the other hand, is at my desk with a pen and a piece of paper, clearly ready to play investigative journalist about last night. I walk in, place my purse on the table, slide off my coat, and hang it up. Then I sit next to Lexi on my bed and smile.

The girls go crazy, bombarding me with rapid-fire questions in unison:

"Was the sex good? How big was his dick? Did he do anything weird? Does the guy have money?"

And, of course, the most important question: "Are you going to see him again?"

I answer them to the best of my ability without giving away too much detail. Smiling and giggling, I finally respond, "Of course I'm going to see him again. I just have to finish writing my final paper, and then we're going to dinner."

I kick the girls out so I can finish my paper and see Giovanni faster. Just as I shut the door, my phone dings.

Giovanni: *Remember our promise, mio fiore.*

I hold back a smile.

ME: *To behave or to text you? Also, what does "mio fiore" mean?*

Giovanni: *Both, unless you want a spanking. I would hate to punish you knowing you'll like it...*

Giovanni: *My flower.*

My core tightens. Does this man know I'm not as innocent as I seem? I would try anything once, but to be honest, I've always liked the idea of BDSM. I've just been too scared to ask someone to try it with me.

ME: *What makes you think I'd like that? Also, I like the nickname.*

My hands are shaking as I type, hoping he picks up on the flirting.

Giovanni: *I saw it in your eyes as my cock filled your throat.*

Just the thought of his cock doing anything to me sends heat to my core and wetness to my pussy.

Giovanni: *Plus, you put my hand on your throat. People only do that when they like being punished.*

Thinking of what to say, I watch the bubbles pop up on my phone as he types.

Giovanni: *And yes, I'll try anything. I like playing with fire. Remember, though—you found my new kink.*

My hand instinctively goes to my lip as I remember the pain his bite brought—but, more importantly, the pleasure. My core instantly heats again.

ME: *That might be a new one for me, too.*

I briefly contemplate playing with myself, but decide against it. I have to get that paper done, and besides, I can't do it like he does, so what's the point?

Giovanni: *Bite you later, fiore! Now finish your paper.*

A smile creeps across my face.

ME: *Yes, sir!*

I pull out my laptop to finish my paper, just as there's a knock on my door. I don't think much of it—students knock on my door all the time with stupid problems. It ranges from "my roommate stole my shirt" to "my roommate just had a baby in our room." I wasn't expecting anything crazy, though; most people are focused on finals and studying.

But when I open the door, I'm taken aback. Standing there is Kyle.

I haven't seen him in a months.

"What the fuck do you want?" I snap.

CHAPTER 6

IRIS

"Who the hell was the guy?" he says as he grabs my arms hard enough to make me wince, pushing me back into my room.

"What the hell are you talking about, Kyle?" He just stares at me blankly and doesn't say anything.

"Who was the guy who dropped you off this morning? Are you fucking him? I knew you were a whore who asks to be choked " Kyle screams. That's when I notice he smells like booze.

"You need to leave now."

Just then, a tall white man in a black suit, much like what Giovanni wears, pulls him out of the dorm room to the courtyard. Kyle tries to come back into the building, and the man throws a punch that connects with Kyle's jaw and knocks him out cold.

What the fuck just happened? WHo is this guy?

"Hi, who are you?" He just stares above me at the wall, says nothing and just walks away. I chalk it up to campus police.

Eleven pages later, and my final paper on nature vs. nurture of criminals is complete. I hit the big green submit button at the bottom of the screen. I look at my phone, and the time reads 23:43. I contemplate texting Giovanni; I don't have class tomorrow, but I'm sure he has work, so I decide against it. I close my laptop and put it on my desk as I grab my towel and head to the shower in my bathroom. It's nice to have my own shampoo, conditioner, and body wash back. I like smelling like my stuff—green apple and passionfruit—but I loved smelling like Giovanni. I dry my body and wrap my hair in a towel. I slide on the T-shirt I brought back from Giovanni's with me. It smelled like him, and I liked the way I slept last night, so I was hoping I would sleep well tonight with just the scent that lingers on the clothes.

I wake up the next morning to the sun already peeking through the window. When I grab my phone, the time reads 07:15. I try to roll over to go back to bed. My phone dings. I look at it with crusty eyes.

Giovanni: If you're up and done with that paper, I can bring breakfast over.

I read it three times, trying to focus on the words while I rub my eyes over again.

ME: Morning, yes, I just got up.

Just like that, there is a knock on my door. God, I hope it isn't Kyle again, and if so, I hope that guy is around. I open the door with my hand in a fist just in case. To my surprise, it's not Kyle or some annoying student. It's Giovanni in a T-shirt and jeans. He is good looking in a suit, but he is hot as fuck in jeans.

"How did you get here so quickly? I just texted you." I am confused. Was he some type of superhero?

"Would you believe me if I said I was in the neighborhood?" he says, lifting an eyebrow.

"No, I wouldn't." I cross my arms.

"Okay," he says, putting one hand up. "I have been waiting at your door since 7 o'clock with breakfast, waiting for you to get up." His eyes get bigger. "I brought breakfast to help get the juices flowing to finish that paper," he says, holding up a cup and a brown and green bag.

I take the cup and the bag and turn into my room. "I finished my paper late last night," I say as I let out a yawn and take a sip of the coffee. My shoulders relax. I turn and see Giovanni standing against my door, eyes black as they focus on me. I feel like I shrink as he stares at me.

"You said you were going to text me, Mia fiore, and you didn't. Do you know what that means?" he says as he pushes off my door and stalks to my bed where I sit. "Is that my shirt?"

Both of us look down. I swallow hard.

"Yes. I finished the paper late last night. I didn't want to bother you in case you worked this morning."

He fists my hair. "You are never a bother to me, fiore. Do you understand?"

I shake my head slowly as he forces a kiss to my lips.

Giovanni works his hand under my shirt—his shirt—and cups my breast. Just like that, he rips the shirt over my head. I stand and pull his shirt off, exposing his toned chest. He looks into my eyes and caresses my waist as I reach between us to unbutton his pants—no belt this time. His gaze darkens as I drop to my knees. I slide his pants down his hips, freeing his full length. It looks even bigger than it did two nights ago.

I start with a lick up his length, swirling my tongue around the tip. Glancing up through my lashes and hair, I see Giovanni throw his head back.

"Fuck," he hisses.

He fists my hair, pulling my mouth closer and forcing his cock deeper down my throat. I work his shaft with one hand, pumping him in an unsteady rhythm. His cock starts to throb in my hand, and I quickly take him fully into my mouth, cupping his balls as he thrusts deeper. I gag as he shoves further, his body trembling. With one final thrust, he spills himself onto my tongue.

Giovanni grips my chin, tilting my gaze up his perfectly sculpted body.

"You look like a goddess taking my cock," he says breathlessly. "Now be a good girl and let me make you cum."

He lifts me off the ground, and I wrap my legs around his waist. His cock rubs against my clit, teasing the entrance to my sweet spot. With one hand, Giovanni reaches between us, his fingers competing with his cock for dominance over my arousal.

"Your pussy is so wet for me. You want to be fucked, don't you, Fiore?" His lips brush mine as he speaks.

"No, sir. I want you to punish me. I didn't keep my promise," I reply, holding his intense gaze.

"Good girl. Now tell me how you want me to punish you," he says, his voice darkening. He starts to kiss my neck, his lips igniting every nerve.

"I want you to choke me while you fuck me from behind in the shower," I whisper.

"Speak up, Iris. Don't be afraid to say what you want," he murmurs into my neck.

I fist his hair and pull him back, my voice firm. "I said I want you to choke me while you fuck me from behind in the shower." I bite his jaw, and he growls.

"Good God, woman, you're going to be the death of me." he says, carrying me toward the bathroom. With each step, his cock brushes closer to my entrance, teasing me. I ache to feel him stretch me, to take him fully.

Inside the shower, I turn the knob to the perfect temperature. Giovanni takes a seat on the bench. Though my shower isn't as luxurious as his, it's big enough for the two of us. He lowers me onto his cock, and I take his full length inch by inch. The sensation is exquisite. Letting out a deep breath once he is fully in.

Giovanni takes my nipple into his mouth, the contrast between the heat of the water and the coolness of his tongue sending shocks through me. I throw my head back, the water cascading down my body. He reaches up, wrapping a firm hand around my throat while his mouth remains on my nipple. I buck against him, but he grips my hips, holding me still.

"Slow down and enjoy yourself," he whispers in my ear, leaving kisses along my neck. He tilts my head forward so our foreheads touch, then kisses me softly. "Turn around and sit on my cock."

I stand, feeling empty as he slides out of me. I go to turn, but he grabs my arm, his eyes darkening when he notices the bruise Kyle left yesterday.

"What happened here?" he asks through gritted teeth, his jaw tense. He tucks my hair behind my ear, pulling my forehead to his.

Looking down at the shower floor, I reply, "My ex came by yesterday. Apparently, he saw you dropping me off and wanted to know if we were fucking." I take a deep breath, then meet his eyes. "Then someone who I think was campus police, grabbed him and threw him out."

Giovanni's eyebrows twitch. "Oh my god did you get me a bodyguard, Gio?"

"Yes, Iris, I did," he says angrily.

"Why?" My lip quivers.

"It's a dangerous world out there. I can't keep you safe all the time, and yes, you are mine to protect."

My brows knit together. "Who do I need protection from?"

His gaze hardens. "My family and apparently your ex"

The seriousness in his voice silences me. I decide not to press further.

"Gio," I look up at him. "Can you fuck me now?" I ask breathlessly.

"Of course, beautiful."

I turn so my back is to his chest. He guides me back to him and lowers me onto his cock. I lose my breath as it enters me inch by inch. He fills me, and I let out a moan.

"Good God, Gio."

His hands trail to the front of my body. He grabs under my knees and lifts my legs so my feet are on his knees. I have never had sex in this position before. He thrusts slowly and lightly as his hand moves to my clit, rubbing frantically. I whimper.

"Fuck yes, Gio. Don't stop, please."

I throw my head back, feeling his chin rest on my shoulder.

"I'll never stop pleasing you," he whispers.

Just then, his free hand reaches around and grips my throat. My vision begins to blur as he thrusts with a need and desire to make me cum. I feel searing pain in my shoulder. I look over and see Giovanni's teeth sinking into my skin. I don't say anything because I like it, and so does he.

"Oh my God, I'm going to cum, Gio," I scream.

"That's right, baby, you scream for me."

It's the first time he's called me *baby*, and it sends me over the edge. My walls start to contract around his cock. He grips my throat even tighter, and I cum. But I've never cum like this before—it rushes out of me like a waterfall.

I lay back against Giovanni, trying to catch my breath. "What was that? That has never happened before."

He rubs my arm as my legs shudder with pleasure.

"Fiore, you just squirted, and it was the fucking sexiest thing I've ever seen," he says, kissing my back from one shoulder to the other, stopping at the nape of my neck and releasing small breaths on my sensitive skin.

CHAPTER 7

GIOVANNI

Iris and I spent the rest of the day lying in her bed, cuddling and napping. I don't cuddle, but she was tired from her shower, and I didn't want to do anything today except be with her. She naps while I try to figure out what to tell her when she inevitably asks the obvious questions: *Why is your family dangerous? Why do I need security? What does your family do? What do you do for your family?*

With all these questions running through my head, I debate being honest with her. But honesty won't do us any good. Maybe I should let her go. She's too good for the world I tiptoe in. That thought gets shoved to the back of my mind. I can't do that—I'm addicted to this woman already. It's my duty to keep her safe, even if it means telling her part of the truth. Maybe not all of it, though—definitely not what I do.

I wrap my arm around her waist and roll her over so I'm closest to the door. Eventually, I doze off with my nose buried in her hair. I'm obsessed with the way this woman smells.

Iris stirs. At first, I think she's just waking up, but then she lets out a whimper—not a sexual one, but one that sounds scared or sad. I wake up fully and tighten my grip on her waist.

"It's okay, baby. I've got you," I whisper in her ear.

It seems to settle her for now, but it makes me wonder what she was dreaming about. My phone buzzes, snapping me out of my thoughts. I grab it and read the message on the screen.

DAD: *Meeting called today for 1430. In my office at 1400. FAAE.*

I glance at the time: 1:08 p.m. It takes about ten minutes to get to Iris's dorm, but I need to swing by my place and change before heading to the mansion. I give myself five more minutes to take in this woman's beauty and scent. Then I shake her lightly.

"Hey, work just texted. I have to go in for a last-minute meeting," I say, kissing her forehead. "I'll text you when I get out. Sleep tight, baby."

Her nose scrunches, and she gives me a cute smile. "Okay," she murmurs.

I slid out of her bed keeping my back away from her, pulling on my pants, followed by my shirt and shoes by the door. I grab my keys on the way out. I don't see the two guys I hired for her security detail, but that's exactly how I wanted it.

I quickly change into a dark suit—my wardrobe consists only of dark suits. They hide the blood better. I grab my gun and slip it into the waistband of my pants. Before leaving, I make sure to lock the door.

When I step out of the elevator, I notice Julius isn't there to greet people like usual. I arrive at the mansion at exactly 1:56 p.m.—just enough time to get to my father's office by 2:00 p.m. sharp. If I'm even a minute late, he'll flip his lid.

I knock on the door.

"Come in," he says.

"Afternoon. You wanted to see me?" I ask, confused.

"Yes. Have a seat." he points to the black chair across from him,

I walk to the chair I always sit in during these meetings.

"Do you think I'm stupid or naïve, child?" he says, his voice rising.

"what are you going on about now?" I reply, slumping further into the chair.

He turns his laptop to face me. On the screen is a video of Iris and me holding hands in the elevator of my building and kissing in the parking garage.

Fuck, fuck, fuck. Play it cool, Gio. He doesn't know much—if anything.

"You're mad that I don't tell you about every bimbo I hook up with?" I try to pass Iris off as a one-night stand.

"So, you're telling me she's just a hookup? You're not going to see her again? Is that what I'm hearing?" His eyebrows knit together as he stares at me.

I take a deep breath. "Yes. Just some chick I met at the club."

He stands, walking around his desk with his phone in hand.

"Oh, really? Then what is this, Gio? Don't you dare lie to me," he says, thrusting the phone toward me.

On the screen is a picture of Iris and me *this morning* inside her dorm room. How the fuck did he get in without me waking up. Rage flares in my chest. I see red. I want to lash out, but he has far more leverage than I do.

"How the fuck did you get this?" I demand, standing to face him.

"Well you see, Gio," he says as a smile sneaks across his face, "it wasn't that hard to get past the security guys you hired, and they were pretty cheap too." He rubs his thumb and index finger together."All this picture proves is this WHORE," he starts yelling, "is distracting you from your job and the main focus should be your family." He sits back in his chair.

"So, how are we going to fix this problem of yours?" He waves a hand at his phone. "Because you know the rules, the one woman you are allowed to fall for and put precedence over your family is your wife. As you do not have one of those, and she is not, a decision needs to be made."

Flashbacks of my mother lying out in our backyard with blood everywhere flood my mind. I need to sit. I'm still enraged as he continues his speech.

"Look what she has done to you! You can't even have a conversation with your father about how we are going to fix this little problem. That is what this meeting is about; the family will be part of making the decision," he rubs his hands together, "but don't you worry, you both will have a say in it as well."

I look up at him and stand. "What do you mean, both?"

He hits a button on his desk and before I know it, Iris is standing in front of me, the tears running down her face and shaking. She runs to me falling into my arms. I push her behind me to shield her from the monster that is my father.

"She will get a say in her future. Whether she has one or whether her mother will need to fly a body back to North Dakota for a funeral." He stands and leaves the room.

Iris looks at me and starts to hysterically cry, "What is going on, Gio? I was sleeping and two big men came into my room, grabbed me, and threw me in the car and now I'm here and some man is threatening to kill me. The two men kept saying that their boss wanted to see me, and they had guns, and and and," she starts to hyperventilate.

"Slow down, breathe baby. I sit her down on the couch and kneel at her feet I will tell you everything, but you need to understand something." My hands find her arms and they slide down to her hands. "Once

35

I tell you, your choices become even smaller. Do you want to know everything? Think carefully." She shakes her head while I put her hand on my chest to help her slow her breathing.

"The two men who grabbed you work for the mafia, specifically the Italian mafia," I take a deep breath in to stop my voice from shaking. I have never had to tell anyone this news. The girls I would sleep with in the past were active members; they knew everything already.

"I also work for them. But it is more than that," I take another deep breath, "not only do I work for them, I am the heir, and the man that forced you here, the man that was in that chair is my father. The head of the family and the mafia on this coast. He says because of you I am distracted and can't do my job."

She looks up at me, "What is your job, Gio?" I start wiping the tears away from her cheeks. I am going to regret telling her the truth, she will never look at me the same way again.

"I am his fixer. I carry out the jobs he needs done under the table," her eyes go wide and she leans away from me a few inches. Shit, this isn't what I wanted to happen.

"I'm sorry I didn't tell you, it's not something you just drop on somebody you just met," I frantically look for her hand to grab. After moments of silence with her pushing my hands away, cowering from my touch. She finally lets out a few tears and a sigh followed by the questions I am not ready to answer.

"What did you mean that my choices are limited now that I know?" she whispers out, trying to hold back a cry or a yell Tears flowing from her eyes.

I put my hand on her face, "You either choose to not stay with me and they kill you," she looks up at me tears burst out of her eyes rolling down her cheeks, "or you marry me and take the Family oath, you become one of us." She looks at me not as I am a monster but as if I am a man that had to make the same choice. I had to make this choice when I was 18 to stay and head the family or die and be replaced by someone.

"How do you know that they still won't kill me?" Tears break free but she wipes them immediately. She takes a deep breath, "Or my mom to make sure I stay in line," her hands start to shake as she wraps them around her chest to steady her rib cage from rattling. She stands and runs to the trash bin next to my father's desk. She began to disgorge the contents of her stomach.

This is all my fault if I would not have told her to stay. I should have just left her alone, dropped her off and not gone back. My father would believe that she was just a one night stand.

"Even though we have rules, killing our own or the family of one of our own is strictly not allowed. None of us would carry it out even if the order was given." I look into her eyes as something changes in her eyes. It's a fire I recognize from my one. It's rage, she's angry whether it's at me or the situation. I want to ask her but she cuts me off.

"Well then," she stands and runs her hands down her front, "I guess I'll be your wife if you're still offering that?" I'm taken back by her choice.

"Under one condition, this will be a marriage of safety and safety only." She takes a seat on the chair I normally sit in.

"Yes, Mia Fiore, I understand, and I will work my hardest to earn your forgiveness. That is my promise to you," I say as I stand behind her and place a hand on each of her shoulders. She doesn't pull away. She is either an amazing actress already learning how to play the role, or she's not mad at me enough to avoid my touch.

"What does it mean to be your wife? What will I have to do after the marriage?" she huffs out.

"Well, they will expect us to have an heir and—" she cuts me off.

"No, that is not what I meant, damn it. If you are in the mafia, I won't be able to practice or use my law degree. So I just did all of that for fucking nothing?" she says with a bite to her words. She stands walking away from me.

"Well, no," I walk up to her and stop her from pacing. "You could represent the family in any legal action."

"Oh, yes, I always dreamed of protecting the mafia. Sounds fucking great," she turns to face out the window across the office from me.

She took it better than I could have imagined. The strength of this woman has my chest in knots; she is stronger than any of us know. Had I been in her position, I would have been hunched over, crying in a corner. I just began the journey of snuffing out her light.

CHAPTER 8

IRIS

I had no choice, well, I did but not good ones. Die or marry Giovanni. I meant what I said when I told him I wanted space. I needed time to myself to deal with these feelings. My life was over. I was now going to be a wife to a killer. I would never see my family. From the things I know about the mafia, which is practically nothing, I am going to be a slave. I'm going to be expected to clean the house and cook for him, oh yeah, let's not forget I'm going to be expected to have kids—at least one. Although Giovanni doesn't give me those vibes. I want to cry but I know I can't. I don't let people see my weaknesses; they tend to use them against you. Kyle knew how I felt about my body and did everything he could to make me feel like shit. I don't love that I have love handles or stretch marks on my ass and legs. One time at a pool party, Kyle told me to go put on pants because nobody wanted to see "whale legs." I'm not small, but I'm not a fucking whale.

Giovanni left me in the hallway outside of what I assume was a meeting room. The hallway is like much of the house from what I have seen of it. White marble floors, white walls, and black trim. I can't seem to see any actual personal photos, just artwork ranging from landscapes to abstract. The tall ceilings, easily 15 feet, make this hallway much bigger than it is. I start to hear voices raising behind the door. It was Giovanni's voice, yelling that his father made him tell me everything and that is the only reason an outsider was in the meeting house. Is that what this is—a meeting house? Is that why there are no personal touches to the space, or does everybody in the mafia decorate like this? Even Giovanni's house is decorated like this.

Ten minutes later, Giovanni opens the door. The room is covered in white walls and dark brown wood panels on the bottom half, the same marble flooring, and a dark brown oak table surrounded by nine high-backed leather chairs that match the table. There are six men, plus Giovanni and his father, sitting around the table. All eight men wear dark-colored suits—must be a mafia thing. They all had short hair, if they had any at all. They all look very similar in the way they dress and sit. I stand by the door that I just walked through, my hands clamped together so hard they are turning white. I look at Giovanni. Even though I am mad at him, he is the only person in this room I know. He takes a deep breath, reminding me to breathe.

"Ms. Iris O'Malley, please tell the board," the man looks around, "when you first learned of the family business," he picks up a pen and connects it to the paper in front of him.

I take a deep breath. "When I was pulled out of my bed in my dorm and brought here against my will by this man," I point at Giovanni's father.

"When did you find out what Giovanni's job was, Ms. O'Malley?" a different man asks as he looked at me so hard he could have broken me if I was lying.

"When I was brought here, Giovanni told me everything, when he told me what my choices were," I swallow again.

"And what was your choice, Ms. O'Malley?" he asked, as if he didn't already know. No person would choose to die willingly.

I look directly into Giovanni's eyes And back at the men. "Well, I'm not going to choose to die. I will marry Giovanni."

The men all start looking at one another. The man directly to the left of Giovanni stands. "Ms. O'Malley, I'm glad you made that choice, but the final decision will be left up to the boss, Lorenzo," the man says, putting his arms out to point at all of the men, "and the board. We will vote on it after you pass the test for the family. Until then, you are not allowed to go anywhere except Giovanni's penthouse and the mansion in which you stand. This is for your safety and ours. Do you have any questions?"

They all look at me, these men have a way of making someone feel small. "Yes, what about school? I have one last paper to turn in, take the BAR and then there's graduation."

"Where do you attend?" a bald man who looks familiar asks.

"Fletcher Law."

"And what is it that you study?" the same man asks.

"Criminal defense," I reply, running my hand up my arm. A cold breeze runs up my spine, my skin becoming goose-flesh.

"I will pull a few strings. You will still be able to do these things... after you pass the test," he pauses for a moment. "But you can only practice law to help your family. Once you are done and pass your credentials, you will be the family lawyer. All in favor of keeping Ms. O'Malley, soon to be Ms. Benedetti, on staff?" All members raise their hand except for Giovanni; I'm not sure if he can vote. "It has been voted on. Anything else?"

Great, so now not only am I going to be married to a killer, I'll have to protect all the other criminals. Giovanni said that I could choose if I wanted to have a job, but this one was just bestowed upon me. Just like our marriage.

"When will this," I raise my hand to put quotation marks around my next word, "'test' happen?" I place my hands on the back of one of the tall brown leather chairs.

Lorenzo says, "The test will take place in four days' time, but I will tell you, my dear, we haven't had anyone of your," he looks me up and down, lingering on my hair, "genetics join our family. If you somehow do pass, you better make your skin tough for the abuse of it." Lorenzo goes to stand but stops as if he remembers something. "And Giovanni, it was you who brought her into this mess. If she fails, it will be you that cleans up your mess." He leaves the room followed by the other men, leaving only myself and Giovanni standing.

I turn to face Giovanni with all that was said racing through my head. "What did he mean by 'you would have to 'clean it up' Giovanni? Does he really expect you to kill me?" My eyes start to water. Giovanni must have noticed before I did. Before I can wipe them away, his hands are cradling my face, his thumbs gentle across my skin to wipe away the tears.

For a brief moment, I think he leans in, and I take a small step back. I may have agreed to marry him, but not for love. I just simply don't want to die. It makes my stomach turn when I remember what Giovanni's job is. "Well, Fiore, I am his hit man, I carry out the jobs he needs done under the table, but he knows I couldn't do it myself. He would just make me watch." Chills run down my spine, and I can't hide it. I visibly shudder. Giovanni takes a step back as if he is scared of me. Why would he be scared of me? I'm not the one that kills people for a living. "Let's get you home; we will start studying for your test." He takes his overcoat off and wraps it around me. It's warm, and I'm not sure if it's from his body heat or if this is how suit jackets always are.

I don't remember the drive to Giovanni's. I only noticed we were there when I read the elevator floor. "Benedetti Tower." I look up and see my reflection in the silver doors. I don't look like myself; my red hair is a nest of mess and snarls. I don't think I could get a brush through it if I tried. Giovanni turns his doorknob and performs his normal ritual of taking his guns off and putting them away.

Taking off his button-up, Giovanni turns to me. "I know you probably don't want to sleep in the same bed with me. I have a spare room, much like my bathroom and all. I had it set up for you," he says, but instead of walking to another bedroom, we walk to the kitchen. "I ordered a pizza for us while we were on our way home. I know you don't feel like it, but you need to eat, Mio Fiore."

"STOP CALLING ME THAT. I AM NOT YOUR ANYTHING," I bark, louder than I meant to.

Giovanni just stares at me, putting his hands up. "Fine, what would you like me to call you then, if not flower?"

I turn to him and wrap my arms around my waist. "How about Iris? It is my name," I say, throwing his overcoat on the ground.

Giovanni looks almost hurt or disappointed. "If that is what you want, Fior... Iris."

Something in me breaks after he calls me Iris in such a sad tone. I'm not sure I liked it. "When is the pizza supposed to be here?"

Looking down at his phone, he replies, "It's coming up the elevator now." Just then, there is a knock at the door. Giovanni stalks to the door, stopping behind me as if he wants to say something but decides against it. I can smell his cologne from here; he smells of bourbon and wood. Why have I never noticed how amazing this man smells?

He dishes up the pizza and looks at me. "I should have asked, but are you allergic to anything?"

"No," I say, taking the plate that he has in his partly raised hand. We eat in silence and clean up our mess.

"I just want to shower and go to bed" I pause "In my own room" I say, standing taller than normal just so he knows I mean it when I say I want to sleep in a different room, even if I don't believe it. Why do I not want to sleep apart from this man who, all of two hours ago, admitted to being a killer? Am I sick in the head?

Giovanni starts down the hallway to his room but opens the door next to his. "Your bathroom and closet are over there," he points to a set of doors across from the bed. He doesn't enter the room; he just stands in the threshold and points to where things are. I open one of the doors he pointed to earlier, hoping to shower before I crash from the mental strain of my day and more of my life. I am surprised when I don't find a bathroom but instead a closet full of clothes that look like they could fit me.

I turn to Giovanni. "I had someone go shopping for you; they guessed your size from the dress you left here," he says, running his hand through his hair to his neck. "Well, I'll let you shower and crash for a while. I am down the hall if you need anything," he says, looking down and reaching for the doorknob. "Good night, Iris." He shuts the door.

I turn the shower on. That's when I see he also had someone stock the bathroom with my normal shampoo, conditioner, and body wash. I don't even ask how he knew, but I use them. If I had more energy, I would be sitting on the floor crying, but if I sat down, I don't think I could get up. I'll do that when I lay in bed.

I quickly finish my shower and rummage through the closet and dresser to find something I could wear to bed. I manage to find an oversized T-shirt and workout shorts. I crawl into bed and shoot Giovanni a quick text.

ME: *How did you know what shampoo, conditioner, and body wash I like?*

I place my head on the fluffiest pillow I had ever laid on and almost fall asleep immediately. My phone dings on the nightstand next to me.

Giovanni: *I made a mental note of it when we were in your shower together. Now go to bed; you need to sleep, Iris. I'll see you in the morning.*

Tears and a gasp escape my chest when my body relaxes enough to sink into the bed. When I fully let everything sink in, I can't hold back the waterworks that come forward and break the dam. I don't remember anything after that; I must have fallen asleep.

CHAPTER 9

GIOVANNI

I heard her, I heard Mia Fiore crying in the room right next to mine, and there was nothing I could do. Well, that's not entirely true; there was something I could do, but she made it clear she didn't want me. My chest felt like it was on fire, and I had no way to extinguish the burn. She cried for a solid twenty minutes before silence took over. She must have fallen asleep. I hate myself for bringing her into this. I should have listened to that little voice in the back of my head. Everyone in this family is a monster, including myself. We don't get nice things. And Iris isn't just a nice thing, she is the nicest thing.

I couldn't sleep, just lay in bed tossing and turning with questions swirling in my mind. "What will her test be?" "What do I need to have her study?" "Will she eventually forgive me?" "Could we ever be happily married, or is that just for normal people?" I needed to figure these things out quickly, not only for me but for her too. If I have to "take care" of her, I will lose the last thing that makes me feel anything, and not only will I be the cause of it, I will be the weapon of choice.

The last time someone had to test to get in was 22 years ago. I was too young to remember what it was, and the board can choose anything they like. The only thing I do know is what comes after that. We will be married, and she will be safe. I didn't tell her she would have to get the same tattoo we all have. I rub my knuckles where 'FAAE' is forever engraved into my skin. The women get to choose where they get theirs. If she is smart, she will choose somewhere she can hide it.

46

Fuck, I'll be a husband soon. I know how to be a mafia member and a mafia heir. I learned those roles from my father. That also means I learned how to be a husband from him, and he wasn't exactly husband of the year. What if I turn out like him? A shit father and husband, then what do I do? I refuse to give Iris the same life my father gave my mother.

My father broke one of the biggest rules in our family. Rule #3: A member shall never kill one of our own. Yet he killed my mother right in front of me, and nothing happened to him. Could he do it again, but this time to my wife? The only way I can fully protect her is for my father to die. I'll have to kill my father for the sake of Iris. She was still in danger, and I need her to be safe.

I opened my door and placed a chair just inside my door frame facing the hallway. I grabbed my gun from the cabinet in the entryway, cracked Iris' door open, and sat watching while my soon-to-be wife slept safely. Iris slept through the night. When she would turn or move in her sleep, I would slightly panic, thinking something was wrong, but she just moves when she sleeps. I learned that from our first night together. Occasionally, I would walk to the side of her bed and watch her sleep, just making sure she was breathing.

When the morning light began to shine through the windows, Iris stirred awake. She sat up in bed with her puffy eyes, and I knew then she had been crying. "Gio, what are you doing? Why are you in the hallway? Why is my door open? I know I closed that door," she said to me, stretching and grunting. "I told you I wanted space."

I couldn't take my eyes off hers. It hurt knowing she was crying because of me. "I was just keeping watch to make sure that you felt safe in a new place. I hope that was okay," I explained.

"Why do you have your gun?" she asked, looking down at my right hand where I was gripping the gun my father gave me on the day I turned 18 and joined him at his side as heir.

We both stood up. I slid the gun into the waistband at my back. "Just in case the monsters from your nightmares come to life." I moved the chair back into my room, just past the door. "I'm going to go make breakfast. Would you like some?"

"Yes, please" she said, walking towards her bedroom door where I was standing. "Plus, I need to keep my energy up if we are going to be training for my test." Iris did a cute little boxing kick and punch. This woman, just told she would be married to a monster, is already in a good mood. How?

"It's not that kind of test, Iris. They're going to quiz you on our rules, which I'll tell you about. After that, I don't know." She looks at me as if she thinks I'm lying, unwilling to reveal more. "It changes every time; it's up to the boss. And since you're the first for my father, we'll see." I glance at the pan with scrambled eggs in it.

"Wait, so it could kill me then? We don't know that, right?" she asks, pacing back and forth in the living room behind the large gray sectional that separates it from the kitchen.

"No, Fio..." I pause as I see her shoulders tense. "Sorry, Iris—it's a habit. No, it can't kill you. That goes against the point of the test. Why kill someone who could possibly pass it and risk a possible member dying?" I say, pointing the spatula at her.

"Okay, so we can't do anything to prepare for the second part of the test, but what about the first part? What is it?" She takes a seat at the island, looking at me, waiting for an answer.

I sigh. "It's something we all go through. You recite the 10 rules of the family and then the family motto before the board. There's a third part, more of an initiation. After your first two tests, you get this." I show her my knuckles where 'FAAE' sits inked into the skin. "But you can get it anywhere—most wives get it on their ankles so it's not visible." I serve breakfast as she stares at me, thinking about the tattoo.

"Does it hurt? Your tattoos?" she asks, rubbing her own arm as if feeling for the puffiness that a new tattoo leaves behind.

"Certain places do, but you're tough enough. I promise you, just pick a place to get it. It doesn't even have to be big," I say as I take a seat beside her and brush a piece of her hair behind her ear. I begin eating, and she interrupts the silence. "What are the rules that I have to remember? You said you were going to tell me."

I laugh. "Let's eat first, then we'll get a pen and paper to write it down so you can study on your own too."

She looks over at me. "Oh yeah, that's pretty smart. I didn't think of that." She looks away really fast and bites her lip.

"Hey, what is it?" I put my hand on her back.

She takes a deep breath and says, "How fast are we expected to have a baby? You said that was the only thing I have to do. I am not ready for a baby right now" She trembles, waiting for my answer.

I place my hand on the back of her neck, drawing a small circle, but she pulls away. I retreat my hand and rest it on the counter. "Just before I take power would be best."

We finish our breakfast and clean up. I get Iris a pen and notebook to write down anything she needs. We sit on my couch—soon it will be our couch—and start the lesson. It's been a while since I went over these rules myself, but I make the people I 'take care of' repeat the rule they broke over and over again while I 'talk to them.'

CHAPTER 10

IRIS

I know I should be mad or scared of Giovanni, but I'm not. Instead, I find him more attractive. He seems to understand that most men become monsters in the dark and angels in the light. Not Giovanni; his monstrous side is merely a show for others. I haven't been with him long, but when it's just the two of us, he is an angel. My thoughts are interrupted when Gio asks, "Do you know what FAAE means?" I shake my head.

"It means Family Above All Else, referring to this family, not your old one," he explains. I look up at him, confused—he had mentioned I could still talk to them. "Some husbands completely cut their wives off from their families. I won't do that to you, but you must understand that Benedetti family holidays and traditions must be followed."

"Okay, I can do that," I reply. It doesn't sound too difficult. It's just like how I live now; I talk to my mom but don't follow any of her traditions. I start to focus more. I missed the first half of the first rule.

"Remember, there are ten of these. You are expected to know all ten, okay?" he says, emphasizing the importance. I nod, "Yes, Gio, I know. Continue—I'll stop you if I have a question," I say, tapping the pen to my mouth. His gaze lingers on my lips; he lets out an audible breath, then licks the corner of his upper lip and shakes his head.

"Okay, next. Rule two: Outsiders are to be kept in the dark unless it is a situation like this, by marriage. What are the outcomes for finding out, Iris?" he asks, sliding his hands into his front pockets.

"Marriage or death, right?" He takes a seat next to me.

"You cannot sound like you're questioning it; you have to know for sure," he instructs, taking my hand and drawing circles on my palm with his finger. "Okay, I can do that. It's either marriage or death. Either you pass the test and marry into the Family, or they decide death." "Good, say it with that confidence, even with me," he encourages, looking into my eyes. At this close distance, I notice a freckle right by his iris.

"Rule four—," I interrupt him.

"Wait, you skipped Rule 3," I say, realizing it was a test when he smiles.

"Good job, you're paying attention," he winks. "Rule 3: Never kill one of our own. Any questions on that?"

I'm confused because he is a hitman. "Wait, but don't you sometimes have to kill your own when it's ordered for breaking one of the rules?"

He takes another deep breath. "The people I kill or injure are decided and voted on by the board, not just by one person. You can't kill one of our own for personal vendettas," he explains. I note it, and he moves on.

"Now, rule 4: The truth must always be the answer," Giovanni begins, rolling up his sleeves. Oh my god, his muscles are so hot. Snap out of it, girl, damn. "When asked a question by anybody, you must always tell the truth and not lie about anything. So," his gaze locks on mine, "do you really hate it when I call you Mia Fiore?"

My face turns red and gets hot. "No, I actually like it. I was just stressed. I'm sorry," I confess.

A smile wraps around his face. "Good, I like calling you mine!" His gaze traces me up and down as he crosses his arms over his chest. I hear an audible growl escape his throat, turning my core into lava.

His deep voice breaks up my arousal, "Rule 5: You must always be available for Eredi Nascosti." His eyebrow lifts; mine do the opposite. "It's our mafia name. It means Hidden Heirs." I take note of both the Italian and English names, so I can use both if needed. "Wait, will I have to learn Italian too? I'm not good at learning new languages." He lets out a low laugh, "No, you won't have to learn Italian. Most of us don't. We just know the words we use in the mansion, and it's very little. My great-great-grandfather was the bastard son of King Victor Emmanuel II," he adds, answering questions I hadn't yet asked. "So really, you're marrying a prince," he laughs out loud.

He reaches his hands up and stretches, which pulls the hem of his shirt up, letting me see the tattoos that cover his abs in full view of the daylight. "Shall we continue with the rules or something else?" I snap out of my daze. "No, the rules, please." He may be sexy as hell, but I am keeping my word and promise that this is just for convenience. Until I decide otherwise.

"I like when you say please," he says without leaving space for me to reply. "Rule 6: No Narcotics. We do deal in them, but we don't use them. If they suspect that you are using, they test you and..." I cut him off, "And what, kill you?" He gets up and walks to the kitchen. When he comes back, he has two cans of soda. "No, Mia Fiore, they help and send them to rehab, surprisingly."

Curiosity wins. "Why is that? Not that I use, I'm just curious."

"It's a rule my dad put into place when he became the head of the family. Fun fact: my dad was never supposed to be the head of the Benedettis. He had an older brother who died of a drug overdose at 20," he says so matter-of-factly, without emotion. "I am so sorry, Gio."

"It's okay, I never knew him," he says as he pushes a stray hair behind my ear. His thumb brushes my cheek and then my neck, and I can feel my face turning red. He removes his hand. "Rule 7," he says while taking a sip of soda. "We are businessmen; all appointments are to be respected and will start on time, with or without you there." I shrug my shoulders. "I mean, that makes sense," I write it down anyway. "Okay, got it."

Giovanni lets out another little laugh. "Time for my favorite rule," he stands right in front of my seated body. "Is this where I have to do what you do, so no matter what," he looks down on me and kneels on the ground where I sit. "No," he huffs as he takes my foot in his hands. "Rule 8: Wives are to be treated with respect. I like showing people, especially you, that I respect you and want to pamper you." Giovanni intensely stares at me as if hoping to see a part of my soul. "But then I also get to find out all your secrets, like where you are ticklish at the most."

"No, don't, Gio! I won't talk to you for the rest of the day," I laugh out, like I would actually do that. Even when he told me he was a killer, I couldn't not talk to him. Giovanni puts his hands up in surrender. "Fine, I won't tickle you... today."

"It means something different to each person." He interlocks his fingers "for me it means I am yours and "No one else can touch, and I won't let them," Giovanni says, rubbing his hands down his pant legs. "I won't step out on this marriage, even if it is just to keep you safe. I take my commitments seriously, especially marriage."

"Good, because so do I. I hope to come around someday to the idea of this," I gesture between us.

A wicked smile crosses Gio's face. "Rule 9: All the feuds within the business are to be brought before the board and voted on there. The board will vote on it and ensure the decision is held to the vote. It can be anything as simple as land disputes to something as complex as claims of treason for any of the rules." His eyes rise from the floor to meet mine. "That's when I get called into play. I take care of the complex punishments and questioning."

My body shakes at the thought of the sweet, well-hearted man I've come to know hurting or killing anyone. Giovanni takes the seat next to me on the couch, replacing my notebook with his hands. "I understand this is not what you wanted out of life; it's not what I wanted either. But I promise you, I will not let my monster out when it is not needed. Especially not to you, ever. You have my word."

A small smile works its way onto my face. "I don't think you'll hurt me. It's just... I don't know how to react to this. It's going to take time for me to feel comfortable with you again." I move my hands to bring my knees to my chest.

The thing is, I am comfortable around him—his personality, his smile, and the way he makes me feel. What I am not comfortable with is the touch of his hands; that's not even entirely true. How is it they bring me to life and awaken me but take the life of others so easily? Does he do it easily, or does it weigh on his soul? Does he hide it so well that maybe he doesn't even notice the scars on his heart?

"I understand, and I will give you all the time you need to get there on your own, without force," he stands as if to continue the lesson, "but that doesn't mean I am not going to stop trying every day." Giovanni turns to walk out of the living room towards his room.

"Wait," I stand, grabbing his arm. "You forgot rule 10."

He turns with shock on his face, as if he didn't expect me to stop him or maybe touch him. He takes a deep breath. "You have to be Italian or marry, which is what you're doing, I hope." His brows raise, questioning if my mind might be changing. Like I have a choice—it's this or death, not just for me but for my mom too. My head nods without me even noticing. I drop my grip on his arm and take a step back. He walks to his room, and I don't see him for the rest of the night.

On my way to my room later that night, I hear muffled hisses coming from Giovanni's room as I pass. He must be working off the tension of earlier with the help of one of his hands. I shut my door and quickly fall asleep.

I hadn't had a nightmare in years, but they came back with unusual intensity that night. I dreamt of someone doing Giovanni's job, but it wasn't him—it was me, and he was the one being "taken care of." I awake with sweat dripping down my forehead. I calm my mind and lay in bed, tossing and turning for the rest of the night, wondering what Giovanni was doing. Was he awake? Thinking of new ways to take care of people? Or was he thinking of new ways to take care of me in a completely different manner? I shake my head to clear those thoughts. I cannot think of this man that way, not again, not yet.

CHAPTER 11

GIOVANNI

The morning after our lesson on the family rules, I left my room not expecting to see Iris this early. My watch read 0643. To my surprise, I saw a familiar figure in my kitchen, lit just enough to confirm it wasn't an intruder. "What are you doing up this early? You should be sleeping," I said, causing her to jump.

"Jesus fucking Christ, Gio. You scared the shit out of me," she exclaimed, spilling a bit of the orange juice she had just poured.

"I'm sorry, Mia Fiore, I didn't mean to scare you. I just didn't expect you to be up yet. I'm used to being the only one up this early in the house. The staff doesn't even start showing up until 9. Do you want me to make you something for breakfast before I leave?" Her face twisted into a look of confusion.

"Leave? Where are you going?" she asked, getting closer. The scent of her apple shampoo filled my nostrils and unexpectedly, I erupted into an erection. Thank god my pants were dark and a little loose today.

"I have to go to the mansion today and take care of a few other things, but I have someone coming by later today for you." I pushed her hair away from her face. She looked nervous, as if I planned to have her hurt every time I moved. I grazed her cheek with my palm. Her cheeks felt warm, and at this distance, I could see she had dark circles under her eyes. She hadn't slept. "It's a personal shopper, so you can get some

56

clothes and things you need that are your style, without having to leave," I explained. She ripped away from my grip.

"Am I your prisoner now? I would like to know," she asked, her tone sharp.

"Mia Fiore, it's the one rule they put on you before the test. You aren't allowed to leave the penthouse unless you are going to the mansion. Once this is all over," I waved my hand, gesturing to the world, "you can come and go from this house as you please. You have my word, as long as you come back home at the end of the day." Looking around, a tightness hit my chest; this wasn't her home, she had nothing here to represent her, just me. "And yes, this is your home, change it as you see fit," I suggested. "Put a little splash of you in it." I ran my hand down her arm and placed a light kiss on her forehead. I realized that was the first time she didn't flinch at my touch since I told her.

When I turned and shrugged my jacket on, pain ran down my spine. It always hurts the first day after, but I push through. I cannot be seen as weak by anyone. Pain is not supposed to bother me, so I don't let it. I grabbed my gun from the cabinet, my keys from the bowl, and left for the day.

My father had called shortly after I went into my bedroom last night, requesting my presence in his office this morning at 0745. I pulled up to the mansion with a heavy breath. I don't normally conduct my line of work here; it gets too messy. So why was I summoned here today? My uncle was walking out of the house as I walked in. "Hey, kid, your dad call you in?" he asked, patting my shoulder.

"Yeah, last night. Seemed... upset," I replied, straightening my suit coat. The pain had now dulled to an ache rather than sharp pain.

"Yea, kid, he's pissed... not at you... anymore." He runs his hands through his hair. "Vinny's dumb ass knocked up some chick he just met, and to think we all thought it would be you who did that. Not my dumb-ass kid." He lets out a deep breath and relaxes his shoulders. "Luckily, he's young enough and hasn't had a job with the family yet, so he will be leaving… soon. You might want to say bye." He walks down the stairs and gets on his motorcycle. Sam only rides that thing when he really needs to clear his head.

Leave, what did he mean by leave? Was that really an option, or would my father just hunt him down later when he needed him back for something? Sam isn't dumb enough to take my father's word at face value. He must have a plan on how to hide him. Was that why I was here? Did he want me to take care Vinny?

I knock on my father's office door and wait. "Come in," he says. He doesn't sound mad. Maybe Sam was wrong. My thoughts change when I push his door open. My father sits at his desk with his feet up and a cigar in his mouth. My father didn't smoke unless he was trying to make it look like he wasn't mad. He was pissed.

I take my usual seat. I take a deep breath, calming myself. "Morning, you called for me?" I ask, clenching my fists.

"Yes, it's about your wedding. We need to set a date and find a place as soon as possible. We need to have it all planned before next week," he says, slumping in his chair and taking a drag of his cigar.

"Next week, why next week? Iris hasn't even passed the test yet, let alone taken it," I say, tilting my head to the side, unsure of his endgame.

"Yes, well, you see, when your little girlfriend—" I interrupt him, "Fiancée," he takes a longer inhale of his cigar, "whatever we are calling her," he exhales deeply, "when she told the board that I made you tell her, they were anything but happy. They called over to the Italy chapter," he pushes up from his desk, "and now your grandfather is coming into town for the wedding." I had never met my grandfather before, but I had heard stories about how he was the one who instructed my father to kill my mother and then tasked my father with the job he so 'lovingly' gave me. He was my mother's own father, and he had her killed.

"That doesn't answer the question of why the wedding has to be next week. Instead of allowing Iris to plan properly—" my anger slowly taking over, I stand, "it is not the wedding she chose. She should at least get to plan it the way she wants. I am not her groom of choice; at least let her have her wedding of choice." My voice is deep and unrecognizable, even to my own ears.

"You do as you are told, you do not ask questions," a small grin grows on his face, "We will hire her a wedding planner. She can get it done. It will be done by Thursday, and the wedding next Saturday," he walks behind his desk.

"That is not enough time. I can't convince her by then, and on top of it, her test is in 2 days. How—" he cuts me off as he sits, "Oh yes, that got moved as well," he laughs, "her test is today. She is already being brought here for it." He puffs another cigar, "now leave my office."

Panic sets in. We only went over the rules once, and I have no idea what else they are going to do to her for the rest of the test. I run out of my father's office, down the hall to the boardroom. I am alone and allow myself to sink into the actual panic that she may not live, and it is my fault. Would any of this have gone differently if I had just told my father we could have introduced her slowly instead of all at once? I am not the man she wished to marry, I know. Even though we do not know each other yet, and I cannot claim her without her saying so, she is mine, and I will keep her safe after she makes it through this... if she makes it through this.

CHAPTER 12

IRIS

After Giovanni left, I decided to take a shower, hoping it might clear my mind and allow me to nap before the personal shopper arrived. Giovanni mentioned she would be here at 11:30, giving me at most four hours of rest. I've survived on less sleep during law school. It hadn't fully hit me until now that I wouldn't be able to attend my college graduation. My mom was going to be so disappointed. She always believed I was destined for greatness beyond our little town of 3,500. Tears welled up in my eyes when I heard a noise from the living room; I assumed it was one of the staff Giovanni had mentioned.

Suddenly, my bedroom door was kicked in. A large man stood in the doorway. Panicking, I tried to run to the bathroom and lock myself in, but a sharp pain shot through my head as he grabbed my hair and yanked me back toward the bed. I flailed my arms and legs, managing to kick him as he tied my legs together, then my hands. I screamed, hoping someone would hear me. I was wrong. Before I could scream again, my mouth was taped shut, and a bag was thrown over my head. I refused to go down without a fight. As I attempted to sit up, something struck my head, and everything went black.

When I regained consciousness, a pounding headache throbbed through my skull. I heard a door shut. Trying to move my wrists, I found myself bound by ropes to a chair. I was still blindfolded when suddenly, the hood was ripped from my head. As my vision focused, I saw the man from my room, along with another man in a suit with blond hair and a scar on his left cheek. Oh, shit. The room had concrete walls and floors with a drain at my feet.

Drip. Drip. Drip. Crimson blood fell from my forehead to the floor. These bastards made me bleed.

"Hello, Iris," the man in the suit said, staring down at me with his arms crossed over his chest. Damn it.

"Do I know you?" I asked.

Play: Me and The Devil By Soap and Skin

"No, but we have mutual enemies—the Benedettis. I figured we could help each other," he replied, taking a knife out and flipping it from finger to finger. "I know for a fact that you're not one of them and you're being forced. We can help," he gestured to the man who had brought me here.

Even if I wanted to help him, I didn't know anything about the Benedettis or Giovanni himself. I was unsure how I could be of any assistance.

"I don't know who you're talking about. You have the wrong person. I'm just a law student. I go to class and come back to my dorm," I argued, tugging against the chair.

He pulled out a photo of me and Giovanni from his jacket. "Do you think I am stupid? You don't gain power by being stupid or playing ignorant," he said, dragging a chair closer. "I've done my research on you and Giovanni. I'm not dumb. You two have been together, and since you're definitely not Italian," he ran his hands through my hair. I jerked away, "either his family doesn't know, or they do, and you're being forced to marry him."

Taking his seat across from me, he crossed his ankle over his knee. "Listen, buddy, I don't know what you're talking about. That's not me in those photos. You can't even see the girl's face in them, so you couldn't identify her even if you tried," I said, leaning back with a smile on my face. "So no, sir, you might not be dumb, but you seem reckless. You pick up girls who have nothing to do with your enemy and drag them into this."

"Look, we won't hurt you if you tell us what we want to know," he said, though I knew better than to believe him.

"Dude, first of all, I don't even know that guy, and second of all, that's not true. If you weren't planning to kill me, you all would be wearing masks so I couldn't identify you. I watch enough shows," I say, a smile creeping across my face. As I speak, my hand gets loose from one side of the rope, then the other. "I can't tell you things I don't know. What else do you want me to do?"

His head cocks to the side. "Fine, but if you don't know anything, why are you so calm? Are you not scared?" he challenges, standing and getting an inch away from my face. I wait for the perfect moment for my plan, which I'm still kind of working on.

"Maybe I can help you understand how this will end if you don't help me," he says. He takes his knife, places the sharp edge against my hip right where the waistband of my shorts fall, and starts to swipe against my skin. I scream as pain sears through my skin with each swipe. This might be the day I die, but if it is, I won't make it easy for him. Crimson blood slides down my leg to my ankle.

The man from my room walks past us, and I notice he doesn't have a gun. My eyes drift to the man in my face; his suit jacket is gone and his sleeves rolled up—I'm not sure when that happened, but he doesn't have a gun either. Now is my chance to at least try and help myself.

"You know what's funny?" I laugh through tears searing my cheeks. "For being a bad man, I would think you'd be better at doing your job." I make quick work of standing up and grabbing the chair in one swift motion. Swinging the chair over my head, the man doesn't notice fast enough before it comes crashing down on him. As I push his body to the floor, I grab the knife from his hand and run towards the door in front of me. Pain heats up my head again, pins pulling at the nape of my neck as the man from my room grabs my hair. He spins me to face him, but I turn with the knife raised in my hand. The knife slices through the meaty part of his hand on my way down. I force the knife into the middle of his palm. He releases a scream as blood flows from his hand to mine. Freed from his grasp, I dash to the door.

Twisting the doorknob, I find Giovanni and his father standing on the other side in the hallway.

"I knew you would come for me," I exclaim, throwing my arms around Giovanni's neck. I have never been so relieved to see anyone in my life. He wraps his arms around my waist and pulls me into the tightest hug. "It's okay, Mia Fiore, I have you," he murmurs, inhaling deeply as he smells my hair. His body seems to relax with the exhale. In that moment, I feel at home. My knees buckle, nearly collapsing at Giovanni's feet. His hands steady my elbows to ensure I don't appear weak to the onlookers who await us.

As we turned the corner of the hallway, I saw all the board members from the first and only time I had been called in front of them. "What the hell is this? Why are they all here?" I looked up at Giovanni, my eyes nearly closing from the fatigue of the adrenaline surge and the stress of my day.

"You just passed the test, and you did amazing," Giovanni said, giving me a questioning look. "How did you know how to do all that? I didn't train you in hand-to-hand combat."

"I'll tell you tonight at dinner," I murmured, tucking my head into his chest as we walked out of what seemed to be a warehouse. As we got into the car, pain flared up from my leg where the man had made his mark.

"We'll clean that up at the penthouse," Giovanni said, glancing down at my hip, his voice tender as he tried to stifle tears of pain and sorrow.

"You mean our home?" I asked, a smile breaking across my face for the first time I called it our home.

"Yes, at our home," he replied, a serious tone reclaiming his voice. "We do need to talk about something too."

My eyebrows raised as Giovanni slid his hand into mine and smiled. This man could be angry one moment and then tender the next, just as our skin touched. Despite the worst day of my life, I couldn't help but feel comforted with his hand in mine. Giovanni lifted my hand to his lips, placing the sweetest kiss on my crimson-covered knuckles.

CHAPTER 13

GIOVANNI

I help Iris into the house. We are met by Cassio, our family doctor. My father and the board paid for his medical school since he was born into the family. His brother is the state's attorney, and he is our doctor. Cassio doesn't say anything; he knows what happened, as he was there, but I didn't want her to be treated around everybody. "I can't believe my father allowed this to happen to you."

"We know your father is an ass; he probably gave that guy the idea. Ouch, fuck," she mutters, biting into the throw pillow with her eyes closed.

Cassio looks up at me, holding out a small tracker, asking for permission to insert it into her wound before closing it. I nod to him. "This is going to hurt just a bit, Iris. I need to make sure nothing is in the wound, okay?" She nods, her head still pressed into the pillow. A loud hiss escapes her mouth. My heart breaks even more for the pain she must be feeling.

Cassio finishes her stitches and puts us under very strict orders to do nothing but lay on the couch. I walk him out and return to the couch with rubbing alcohol to clean up the blood around her cut. I dab a little on a cotton ball, rubbing it around her cut. She hisses from the sting of the liquid.

"Shit, I'm sorry, I didn't mean to hurt you. Are you okay? Other than just being stabbed, I mean."

"Yeah, I'm just tired. I didn't sleep last night," she looks at me. "I never sleep well alone."

I reach up and drag my thumb across her bottom lip. "So why did you? You could have come to our bed. I hated it too."

"I thought you would be okay with it from all the noises coming from your room last night. I thought maybe you preferred it as your special time and liked it."

Oh, shit. She heard me. I cocked my head. She may have heard but she didn't know what I was doing. She wouldn't think I liked it if she knew why I did it and how it started—whipping myself. It started the same day my mother died… was killed. My father gave me a lashing when he turned and found his 12-year-old son crying after his mother was shot in front of him. He gave me four lashes with his special whip that had thorns on the end to really make his point.

I shake my head, trying to move the memory to the back of my mind. "What are you talking about?"

"I thought maybe you had a girl over or were trying to work off some steam."

"You thought I was enjoying myself there? And i told you I told you i wouldn't step out on you"

"I heard hissing coming from your room when I walked by. I just assumed it was you enjoying yourself. I've heard those noises coming from you before, Gio." She places her hand on my cheek. "I don't care; we aren't married and we are anything but normal."

"No, that's not what I was doing, Iris." I look at her with heat in my eyes, trying to prove to her I want her and no one else. "I would never do that to you. We may not be married, but those vows started the first day I took you to my bed."

"Then what were you doing?" Her eyebrows rise.

I look down, afraid to see her expression when I tell her the truth. "I was punishing myself for the monstrous deeds I do." I feel my face get hot and tears come to the edge of my eyes. I have never told anyone this part of me. Nobody other than my father has seen my back. I always make sure to hid it.

She places her hand under my chin, pushing up to make sure we are eye to eye. "What do you mean by punishing yourself? What did you do?"

I shake her hand out of my grip, stand up from the couch, and take my shirt off.

"Now is not the time for sex, Giovanni," she says, rolling her eyes, standing to meet me.

Play: Pain is my only home By Zevia

I slowly turn my back to her so she can see the markings up close, including the new ones. I tremble with fear of how she will react. She gasps. Her hands run up my back, tracing all the other scars I've inflicted on myself. When she reaches the new one, her long fingers delicately trace the space where my skin is split open, revealing the newly exposed flesh underneath. It doesn't deter her or scare her away. She grasps my shoulders and walks around to face me, her hands still on my body. Our mouths come so close that our lips graze each other.

"Who did this to you? Who hurt you, and why do you continue to do this to yourself?" she asks.

I take a deep breath; tears well up and slide down my cheeks. Her hands are quick to wipe them away. "It started the night my father had my mother killed in front of me," I continue, telling her the story. Just when I think her facial expressions couldn't get any graver, I add, "When he saw me crying, instead of comforting his child, he tied me to his desk and whipped me to teach me that men don't cry over stupid things." I gasp to catch my breath while Iris keeps wiping the tears away. "The first job I ever did for him, I felt guilty about taking a man's life. He again tied me to his desk and whipped me until I no longer felt guilty. So, every time I start to feel guilty," I sigh, "I do as he taught me. I punish myself for feeling bad about the things I have done."

Her hand reaches to my face, and she thumbs my bottom lip. "Look at me," she commands, pulling my face towards hers until our foreheads rest against each other. "You are allowed to feel; you are human, and it is normal. Do not let anyone force their feelings on you or make you think you are any less because of the things you do." She places a light kiss on my forehead. "Monsters are made, not born, Giovanni. You were made to be like this; you were not destined for this. Your father turned you into what you are. I don't blame you," she murmurs, her gaze dropping to our feet then back to my eyes. "You are Mio Monstro," she whispers.

Iris called me hers just as I call her mine. She accepts me as I am. She cares for me, even with all the things I have done that she knows about. She doesn't see them as flaws but understands me. For once in my life, I think I have found my salvation in this woman. She is my light in this world of darkness.

I wrap her hair around my hand and gently tilt her head towards my mouth. Our lips crash together in a desperate need for each other. Her lips part, allowing my tongue the space it needs to explore her mouth. My core turns into an inferno, traveling to the length of my cock as it swells to full stature. Small moans get sucked into each other's mouths, and moans of pleasure escape when our lips part. "Is this what you want, Iris?" I ask as she looks up at me, biting her bottom lip. She doesn't answer verbally but jumps up, wrapping her legs around my waist. I slide my hands to grip the round of her ass, my length sliding along her opening. I lift her arms to wrap around my neck as I carry her to my room—no, this is our room. I place her on the bed, being careful not to hurt her leg or head. She has had a hard day, and I don't want to make it worse.

I force her back onto her elbows so she can watch me as I explore her body. "If you need to stop, can you just tell me, so I understand?" I growl from down by her knees. Iris nods her head. "I want to hear you say it, Mia Fiore. Use your words," my deep voice insists against her leg.

"Yes, I understand. If I need to stop, I will tell you," she whispers.

I move up her legs, leaving kisses on her smooth, glorious porcelain skin. She gladly spreads her legs to invite me deeper. I pull her shorts down and notice she's wearing nothing underneath. "Mhm... no panties, Fiore? You were ready, weren't you?" I dive my head between her thighs and circle her clit with my nose, taking in the scent of pure desire. One long lick up her center until my tongue meets her clit. "Fuck, Gio," she moans. Slowly sucking it between my lips, I murmur, "You smell marvelous, Fiore." Iris' hips buck up with the reverberation of the words on her clit. I slide one finger inside, feeling the tightness that's built up after only three days apart. My other hand snakes its way up her body to find her nipples at full peak, just as my thumb and index finger pinch one, eliciting the loveliest moan.

"Giovanni... please, I need... need you... in me," she whimpers out.

God, I love the way my name sounds coming from her lips. I need to hear it every minute of every day. Who am I to deny this beautiful woman what she asks for? But first, I am going to make her come with just my fingers. "Not yet, Fiore," I hiss, just as I push a second finger into her opening. My mouth leaves her clit to find her nipples. I take one between my teeth.

"Oh God... Please, I need to come," she gasps through broken words.

"Are you going to come for me, baby?" I ask deviously against her nipple.

"Oh my God, yes," the moan slips between her lips.

I find the spongy part of her inner walls and rub vigorously, finding her clit once again. She throws her head back. I stop. "No, I want you to look at me. I want you to see everything I do to you, and everything you do to me." Her gaze readjusts to meet my eyes. Iris' eyes are like the stars; no matter how many times you look at them, you can never grow tired of seeing them. I go back to working her clit and the spongy wall. Her thighs tighten around my ears. "Fuck. Don't you stop; I'm gonna come for you, Gio," she screams as her body tightens around my fingers, gushing her juices all over my digits. I pull my fingers out from her opening and lick up the mess I made around her pussy. Iris grabs my wrist, bringing my fingers up to her lips. She shoves my fingers into her mouth and sucks until her juices are gone. "I wanted to taste what you taste."

My mouth searches for hers with a need for connection. When I find her lips, her tongue greets mine, licking them clean of her arousal.

CHAPTER 14

IRIS

I had never done these things with another man before. I've had sex but not like this. Before Giovanni, it was never an amazing experience, but now it's like I am an addict and he is my drug. I had never said I wanted to taste myself. It sounded so wrong coming out of my mouth... but it all felt so right.

Giovanni positions himself above my head, his elbows on each side with his hands meeting at my crown. His lips crash into mine as our tongues find each other. I remember his new kink is biting. On the next kiss, I pull his bottom lip between my teeth and bite, not hard enough to draw blood. He pulls back, initially shocked, but his gray eyes turn dark. His head dips to my neck, placing sweet kisses. Pain sears my shoulder when I feel his teeth sink into my arm. My core is on fire, and I am ready to come again. He trails kisses from one shoulder to the other. He bites down again, this time on my collarbone, as he shoves his full length into me without warning. My head falls back as a loud gasp leaves my body, arching off the mattress.

"Fuck, baby, you are so tight, I'll take it slow," Giovanni growls into my ear. I look up at him with water at my eye line. "take it" I lightly kiss his chest and grab hold of his arm, waiting for the next thrust. But that's not what came.

Giovanni gathers both of my wrists into one hand and pulls them above my head, forcing them into the mattress. He takes my nipple into his mouth and starts licking it repeatedly. My hips start to buck in anticipation when Giovanni bites my rib cage on my side as he forces in and out again. I cry out, moaning and panting in pleasure. To my surprise, so does Giovanni, "Oh fuck, baby, stop fucking me back or I'm not going to last long."

"I want to ride you then," I cry out.

He pulls his head back, "Fuck yes, baby"

He flips us so fast it has my head spinning. I lower myself down onto his full length, ending in a hiss from both of us. I start to rock my hips in a slow circular motion to help adjust to his size this way. I swear I can feel him all the way in me, deeper than anyone has ever gone. Giovanni slides a palm up my stomach, cupping a breast in each hand, kneading them. His hands work their way from my breasts to the sides of my body, sliding down to my hips. "You're so fucking beautiful, Iris. I can't take my eyes off of you," Giovanni moans out between his gritted teeth. Just his words turn my inferno into a wildfire that can't be tamed.

His fingers grip into my hips and force them back and forth instead of in a circle. His cock hits my spot every time, making me almost come apart on him too quickly. Being with Giovanni makes me feel as if no woman can compare to me in any way. I lean forward to grab the headboard as he changes the direction of my hips. I rise and fall onto his cock as he directs me. I can feel him coming apart slowly when he moves his hands from my hips to the headboard, his hand white-knuckling the top of the headboard next to mine. I grab his hand, interlocking our fingers. Giovanni starts to buck his hips up at the same time that I come slamming down on him as he is rising to meet me. He inclines enough to take my breast in his mouth while I continue to ride his full length about to come apart. "Baby, I'm going to cum and I need to cum at the same time. Are you going to cum for me?" he says, sitting up fully. I simply nod my head. Giovanni takes my arms, draping them over his shoulders, and forces me out of bed, not leaving his cock.

He presses my back against the wall closest to the bed, pushing my head into his shoulder as he thrusts into me repeatedly. We both grunt and moan as my pussy tightens around his cock, and I hit euphoria. I feel my juices coating my insides while his cock pulses within me. As he finally releases, he lets me collapse on the bed, both of us trying to catch our breath. Giovanni then takes his place next to me in our bed. I lay on my stomach, one knee slightly bent, facing where Mio Monstro lays—this man is mine, and I am his.

"Is it always like this with you?" I ask breathlessly.

"Non come quello," he replies, placing a kiss on my forehead.

"What?" I ask, confused.

"Not like that it isn't," he answers in English this time.

"I thought you didn't speak Italian," I question.

"I said I don't speak much Mia Fiore" he responds.

Giovanni slides his arm under my leg, around my center, up to my stomach, pulling me into his arms. I lay comfortably with my head on his shoulder and my leg sprawled across his torso.

Giovanni had been so open about his upbringing with his father. If I told him my secret, he would understand. We had never actually discussed how I was able to pass my test; there was no time like now. I take in a deep breath, "Something was wrong with my dad," I start. "He was a good dad for a long time, and then, like someone flipped a switch, he woke up and decided the government was after him. He began stocking up on food and first aid, at one point buying a gun and ammunition. My mom didn't know at first; I would catch him sneaking things into the house and hiding them in the attic. I never really knew what my dad did for work, only that he worked at a military base in Alaska."

I feel his fingertips tracing the length of my spine, leaving goosebumps in their trail. The feel of his skin on mine calms every nerve ending I have. "When I was 7, he woke me in a frantic state, screaming for my mother and I to grab the bags he had packed. He even reached into the back of his pants, pointing his gun at us when we weren't moving fast enough," my hands tighten into fists, recalling how terrified I was of my father as a child. "I got even more scared of him as I got older. He eventually dragged us to the middle of the woods in Alaska. That's when he found a new group of friends, people who believed the same things he did. They started their own group called 'Army of the People.'"

I start to feel my chest tremble with the memories running through my mind, the horrors about to spill from my mouth. "There were other kids there, but they were just like my father. The other men could tell I wasn't like them. They would throw sacks over my head and tie me to beds or chairs," I feel his hands clench at my back. Placing my chin on his chest to look into the gray of his eyes, I continue, "They put me through interrogation simulations. I would be waterboarded, cut, and even electrocuted. If I survived without saying anything, I was 'good to go.' Until the next time. If I failed," water gathers at the rim of my eyelashes, "my father would zip-tie my hands behind my back and throw me into a wooden box." I sniffle, trying to hold back tears, "Sometimes they would bury me, sometimes just leave it in the middle of the woods. It was like that for six years until my mother got sick. He wouldn't take her to the hospital. She got so bad one night that I could hear her bones rattling as she tried her best to suck in air. I used everything they taught me to try and run. My father caught me trying to get my mother out. He pulled a knife and threw it at my head, barely missing me," I sniffle again, closing my eyes and breathing in Giovanni's scent.

"I grabbed his knife from the ground, keeping it at my side, but he ran at me." I can hear him trying to settle his own breathing "and before I knew what I was doing my hands were up and the knife was just there. I didn't know I was just the right height for it to end up in his chest." I let the tears fall free from my eyes. "My mother and I ran when he fell. I turned around but didn't see him moving. I killed him. I killed my own father." His arms wrap me into the hardest embrace my bones could handle.

"You did nothing wrong. You did what you need to, to survive" he places a kiss to the top of my head.My eyes close and my body's too tired to stay awake from the euphoria it experienced not even 20 minutes ago. I hear Giovanni whisper, "My grandfather is coming for our wedding next week." My eyes are closed, and I am gone, lost in dreamland.

CHAPTER 15

GIOVANNI

Now that Iris is asleep, I have a minute to just lay here and think. Yesterday, I was scared shitless as I watched her undergo her test unprepared. My father seems scared that my grandfather is coming for our wedding. My guess is that it has something to do with the fact that Iris is definitely Irish. There's no hiding that fact. From what I've heard, my grandfather isn't one who likes to mix ethnicities. He believes it "messes up" the bloodline.

In the morning, I need to tell Iris about how our wedding got pushed up. I don't know how she will react. All girls dream about their wedding; why would Iris be any different? I can't expect her to be. Maybe we could have one wedding to satisfy my family here and then have another that she can plan properly. It might work.

She won't be happy, but at least she will have help planning it. She seems to understand that I don't have choices in these matters either. Just like her, I am a pawn in the game my father plays. I may be his heir, but I'm still a pawn. My mind finally drifts off with the scent of apples invading my mind.

When I wake from the early morning light shining into the room, I reach for the spot where she should be lying, but she is gone. I sit up in a panic and rush to the kitchen—no sign of her there. I run back to our room to grab my phone, just as the shower turns off. I hadn't even noticed it was running. I breathe a sigh of relief and run my hands through my hair. I need a haircut.

Iris walks into the room with just a towel around her, stopping when she sees me sitting at the edge of the bed. "Hey, are you okay?" she asks, following the same path through my hair. I look up at the marvelous woman standing in front of me and pull her closer. "I'm fine, it's just when I woke up and you were gone, I thought you were taken again." She cups my face. "No, I'm right here," she says, placing a light kiss on my lips.

"We should make breakfast; we need to talk," I say, thoughts running through my head trying to play out the conversation before it happens. She nods and heads to her old room to get dressed. We still need to move her things into our room.

Thirty minutes later, we have our breakfast sitting in front of us: eggs, bacon, hash browns, and toast. This woman puts ketchup on everything—hash browns, yes, but eggs too? "Did you just put ketchup on your eggs?"

She shrinks in her chair. "Yeah, it's a North Dakota thing," she says with a laugh.

"Tell me more about North Dakota."

"There's not much to tell, really," she replies, placing her hand on top of mine. "You're the one that said we need to talk, what is it?" I take a deep breath, bracing for her reaction.

"My dad told me the only reason your test got moved up is that my grandfather is coming into town next week for our wedding," I explain, waiting for her to question me, but she doesn't. "Our wedding will be next Saturday," I say, flinching slightly. After seeing what she did to the man from her test, she can be intimidating.

"Wait, I have to plan a wedding in a week? That's impossible," she stands, beginning to pace. "Well, my father said he has someone to help you plan. Some kind of wedding planner," I say, crossing my arms.

"Okay, when will I meet with them?" she turns to me.

"I'll call my father later today when it's a decent hour and get details," I reply. She licks her lips. "But hold on, I didn't go through the family rules with them, don't I still have to do that?"

"I'll ask about that too," I assure her.

Until I call my father, we lay on the couch reviewing the family rules just in case. Her head is perched on my lap, so close to my restless arousal. I want her to turn her head and take me in her mouth until I explode, but she leaves to get a drink. When she returns, she positions her feet where her head used to be. I glance at my phone; it reads 08:37. I shoot off a text to my father.

ME: *I told her about the wedding. When will the planner be here? ME: Are her tests done as well?*

Twenty minutes of practicing rules and rubbing Iris' feet go by. I turn the news on as background noise. My phone dings.

DAD: *She will be there at 09:45. Yes, all tests are done. Congratulate her for me.*

Relief settles on both Iris and me as I tell her about her tests being over. Just as I thought we could relax, Iris jumps up. "Oh no, how am I going to get my mom out here this quickly for a wedding? I need a dress." She starts scrolling through her phone. I place my hand on hers. "I hate to say it, but I think we are going to have to have two weddings, Mia Fiore." Tears start to gather in her eyes. I cup her face. "And for the dress, I'm sure the planner has someone who can bring a bunch for you to try on."

"You're right," she looks at me. "My mom can never know, by the way," I wipe her tears away, "what you do."

"Believe me, I don't plan on telling her." I huff out. "Now, I'm going to go shower and get ready for the planner. I'm sure I'll have things I'll need to do too. I do need a tux—I am the groom after all." I release her face and proceed to the bathroom.

I work off the tension from this morning in the shower. It may not feel like it does when she does it for me, but it will have to do. I grab her shampoo and press it to my nose as my hand makes work of my length. Smelling her shampoo helps me trick my mind into thinking my hand is hers. I squeeze a dollop of her soap into my palm, making it sudsy. It feels like her mouth now. I inhale her shampoo, the scent penetrating my soul. Just then, I envision Iris on her knees at my feet, sucking and licking my cock, and I explode. My hot seed drops to the shower floor, and a hiss leaves my lips, "FUCK."

CHAPTER 16

IRIS

How did I get myself into this mess? Not just having to marry a mafia murderer, but the whole thing—planning a wedding in a week, being a chess piece on someone else's board. Talking to Giovanni about my parents was not easy. I haven't even opened up to Lexi or Avery about them. Oh shit, Lexi and Avery! I haven't seen or talked to them since my dorm room almost a week ago. They must be going crazy wondering where I am or if I'm okay. I need to talk to Giovanni about seeing them.

I walked into our room—that's the first time I thought of it as "our room." Gio must have been in the shower; the room is steamy. I see him sitting on the bed in just his towel, his chiseled chest and back catching my attention. He runs his hand through his water-soaked curly hair. I want to use his hair and direct him to my...

"Yes, Mia Fiore, did you need something?" he turns his head to me, water dripping down his nose rolling to the ridges on his chest. I lick my lips. I can't afford to be turned on right now. I have too much to do. I swallow hard.

"Umm yea, Lexi and Avery, my friends from the club. They are probably worried about me. I haven't talked to them since all this happened," he shifts his body to face me still seated on the bed. "I was wondering two things."

"What is it?"

80

"Can I still be friends with them?" I don't give him a chance to answer before I blurt out, "And if I can, can they come over for dinner?" The speed of my words increases. "I promise I won't tell them anything. I just miss them."

He runs his hands up from his chiseled chin over his cheeks to his temples before answering. "Yes, you can, but very discreetly. They will have to use the staff door." One of my eyebrows arches up. "I already got you into this mess; I don't want your friends to be in a similar situation. I don't want my father to know. He will think they are my staff."

My face relaxes. "Oh, that actually makes sense." I cross the room to the edge of the bed. "So then I think I already know the answer to my next question. But can they come to the wedding or be part of it?"

His eyes shoot to mine. "I don't know, Mia Fiore. How are you going to explain all of this to them? We just met and are already getting married." His tone has a certain sense of concern weaved into it, not for me though—I'm already a part of his "family business." He's worried about Lexi and Avery this time. He was right; the girls know we just met and started sleeping together. The wheels in my head start to turn. I look at him as if a light bulb went off above my head.

"What if we lied to them?" Now he has a confused look on his face. I round the bed and take the seat next to him. The smell of my body wash fills my nostril. He must have run out. "Listen, what if we tell them that we have been friends for a while and it turned into something more really quick, and we just knew. I think it would work; they would believe me."

Giovanni crosses the room to his closet, and when he emerges, he is wearing nothing but a pair of sweatpants that show off the V his hips leave in trail to his cock.

"Let's test the waters at dinner tonight, and if they fall for it," he lets out a deep, regretting breath—wait, did he just say tonight? "Then yes, they can come to the wedding." I jump off the bed excited, running out of the room. "But we have to make sure we don't let anything slip. Dinner at 8," Gio yells after me as I am already shooting off a text to our group chat.

ME: *Hey girlies, sorry I haven't messaged you, I lost my phone at the club just got a new one today. Dinner tonight? I have some news, not sure how you'll react. I'll text you the address.*

It takes them not even a minute for the texting bubbles to pop up.

LEXI: *OMFG where have you been bitch? We went to your dorm and you weren't there. I tried to call you and text you.*

Not even two seconds later, Avery's text pops up. I cringe just a bit. Avery was the mom of our group, and her anger showed through when she was mad, not hiding it.

AVERY: *YA, WE ALMOST FILED A MISSING PERSONS REPORT. WE THOUGHT THE GUY KILLED YOU!!!!!!!!!!!!!!*

They have every right to be mad, I know, but they will eventually forgive me, I hope. I take a seat at the kitchen island.

ME: I know, like I said though, I lost my phone and had to get another one. I will explain over dinner tonight at Giovanni's house, bu*t I have some news.*

Their texts come in at the same time.

LEXI: OMG, no, you're knocked up. You just met the guy.

AVERY: *You better not be pregnant, IZZY!!!!!*

First of all, why would they both think that? Second, I wouldn't even know if I was—it would be too early. It does get me thinking that maybe I need to get on the pill. Kyle and I used condoms, so I wasn't on a daily contraceptive. We had one scare when a condom broke, but thank God

I was not and still am not ready for a baby. If I am being honest, Gio and I have been having sex all the time without a condom. I honestly don't know if we have ever used one. I didn't think of the consequences until just now when the girls said something.

ME: *WHAT? NO, OMG. Stop being dramatic. I have known Gio for a while, just not in a romantic aspect until recently. Again, I'll explain at dinner tonight.*

ME: *109 Burgundy St. PH 2. Go to the lobby!*

LEXI: *Fine.*

AVERY: You better explain everything, or I›m kicking your ass.

LEXI : *I thought you just met? Explain!*

ME: *I will explain…. Tonight*

I am interrupted by a knock on the front door. I look at my phone, and the time reads 09:40. Wow, the planner is early. I open the door and am greeted by a middle-aged woman with long brown hair that falls to her hips in waves, dark green eyes, and a button nose. She isn't much taller than myself.

"Hi, can I help you?" I already know why she is here.

"Hi, I think I have the right place. I am looking for Iris and Giovanni," she pauses. "I'm the wedding planner," she says, brushing her hair behind her shoulders, holding out a hand waiting for me to shake it. "I'm McKayla."

"Oh, of course, hi, I am Iris. I'll go get Giovanni. Come in and have a seat."

McKayla walks to the island, taking a seat and pulling three big binders out of her ginormous tote bag she brought with her. I walk down the hall to Giovanni's office. I knock on the door as I crack it open a tiny sliver. "You can come in, I'm not doing anything," Gio calls from his chair. I have never seen his office before now. It's a navy blue room with a large white desk and black chairs. The flooring is different here; it's carpet, not hardwood. My eyes lock with his. The man sitting in front of me is a work of art. The cool lighting in the room only enhances his chiseled chin and the raw beauty of him. He leans back in his chair, raising his arms above his head in a stretch. His voice is raspy. "Did you need something, Mio Fiore?" I walk from the door to the edge of the desk, where I take a seat, crossing my legs one over the other just next to his hand. Gio reaches up to rest his hand on my knee. He slides his glasses off and places them on the desk.

"We have a guest. Our wedding planner is here. Her name is McKayla," I say, looking down at Gio. He stands, grabbing my hand to help me off his desk.

"Alright," he says, placing his hand on my lower back. He turns me to his chest. "Remember, this is your wedding. If she can make it happen in the few days, I want you to have it." Tilting my head up with his finger on my chin, he places a sweet soft kiss on my lips. "Anything you want."

"Really? I feel like it's gonna be expensive," I say with my nose scrunched.

"Money is no object, I only plan on having one wife. Happy wife, happy life, right?" he says briskly, tilting his head down and placing another kiss on my lips.

"Okay." We start to turn to leave the room with his arm around my waist resting on my hip. "Oh, by the way," I stop and look up at him, "I texted the girls and they said they'll be here tonight at 8. Is there any way we can have Julius bring them up the staff way?" I let out a small smile.

"Yeah, I'll call down later or stop by his desk," he wraps his other arm around my waist and interlocks his hands behind my back. "I'll have you tell the chef what to cook. He comes in at 10:30," he says, placing a kiss on my forehead.

CHAPTER 17

GIOVANNI

Iris and McKayla discuss wedding venues. Iris dreams of a beach ceremony but wants the reception in a ballroom. McKayla suggests a hotel in Cape Cod or Nantucket on the beach. I interject, "The family has a big house in Nantucket if you want to use it. My father will let us." Iris turns to me, surprised, "You have a house in Nantucket?" "Well, not me, Mia Fiore, the family does. I can give you the address if you want to look it up online, and then you can drive out there tomorrow with McKayla to plan it on-site." Iris' eyes light up, giving me a fluttery feeling in my stomach. When she looks at me like that, the butterflies don't just stay in my stomach; they warm my entire chest from the inside out. I jot down the address for them: 2659 Burnt Cherry Ave, Nantucket.

McKayla turns to me, "So, Mr. Benedetti, what budget are we working with here? We need to discuss that before diving into food, flowers, and decorations." I glance at Iris. "Whatever my fiancée wants; we don't have a budget. You only get married once, right?" Iris mouths a 'thank you' to me, and I nod, signaling 'you're welcome.'

"Well, this is going to be easy then," McKayla says, clapping her hands together. "Do you have a tux already, or will you be buying one?" she points at me. "I'll be buying one. I just need to make an appointment with my tailor." McKayla waves dismissively. "Oh, God no, I'll call a high-end tailor I work with a lot. He can have it done in three days, and seeing how your wedding is in seven" she breathes out, "I'll stick

85

with reliable." She turns back to Iris. "You, my dear, need a dress. I'll call my dress lady and have her bring all her dresses in size," she leans back, eyeing Iris, "14 to the penthouse later today."

Iris blinks, her eyelashes fluttering just below her waterline, looking both confused then relieved. "How did you guess my size right?"

"I've been doing this for a while. You get good at guessing," McKayla steps away to make her calls to her on-call tailor and dress lady.

"This is all so crazy; she's good," Iris murmurs, watching our planner sweet-talk her contacts. I touch Iris' back, and she turns to me.

"I know this is a lot, how are you holding up?" I whisper.

"I haven't had to do anything, it's all her," she gestures to the pacing planner in the living room.

McKayla strides back, pointing at Iris. "Alright, the dressmaker will be here in an hour," turning to me and taking a deep breath, "my tailor can't make it here today, but he can see you at his shop if you can get there in 45 minutes."

"Yes, that's fine. What color are we doing, black, or something else?" the girls exchange a look.

"I've always dreamed of a navy blue and maroon color scheme," Iris suggests.

"I can do that with a deep navy blue suit and a white or gray shirt?" I propose, nodding.

Both ladies appraise me and say in unison, "Sounds good."

"You should get going. Here's his address," McKayla says, rummaging through her purse and pulling out his business card.

I grab my keys and slide on my tennis shoes. I leave my gun at home today—it might be weird to get fitted with a gun strapped to me at a tailor's shop. My tailor usually visits here but takes about eight days to tailor my suits. I walk over to Iris, placing a kiss on the top of her head. "Don't forget to tell the chef about dinner tonight, Mia Fiore," I say at the door.

"Oh, don't forget to ask Julius about walking the girls up later," she calls after me.

"I wouldn't dream of it. Love you." I shut the front door to the penthouse. It isn't until the elevator door shuts that I notice what I said. It was an accident, I think. No, it for sure was an accident—I didn't mean to say it. I may not have meant to say it, but was it true? I definitely desire the woman and like her, but I don't know if I love her. I have never been in love with someone; I don't know what it feels like. I know that even just seeing her makes my day ten times better. I feel like a blubbering fool around her. I never know what to say. Has Iris ever been in love?

The elevator door opens to the lobby. I head to the concierge desk.

"Hello, Mr. Benedetti, what can I do for you?" Julius asks.

"Hi, Julius. My fiancée"—his face twinkles at the word—"will be having two friends over for dinner tonight. Would you mind sending them up the back way?"

"Well, of course, sir. Also, congratulations! I was unaware you were engaged."

"Thank you, Julius. It's still new."

I walk to my car slower than I should in the parking garage. I can't stand leaving that question etched in my brain: Had Iris ever been in love, and with whom? Did she still love that person? I decide I'll make it my personal mission to make sure she never thinks of him again.

I remember putting the address for the tailor's in my GPS, but I don't remember anything after that. I pull up to his shop in downtown Boston. I fucking hate driving in this city—most of the roads are one-way with hardly any parking. Iris and McKayla are driving to the beach house tomorrow. Does Iris even have a car? I'll have to find out; if not, she'll need one.

I get measured for my new wedding suit. We land on a navy blue so dark it looks almost black. I also grab a white shirt and a gray shirt, not sure which one Iris will have me wear. It's all pulled together with a maroon tie that has a subtle design. I bring home everything except the actual suit. I'm told it will be delivered to the house in three days. The man wasn't my usual tailor, but he'll make do.

On my ride up the elevator, I wonder how the conversation will go about the two words that slipped out before I left three hours ago. When I walk in the front door, I find Iris and McKayla still trying on dresses.

"Hey, get out! You can't see me in the dress!" Iris screams at me as she runs to the hallway.

"Sorry." I cover my eyes with my hand. "I was just asking if you needed your car from campus to do wedding things this coming week," I yell back at her.

"No, I don't have a car. Now leave!"

I was right; she doesn't have a car. I guess that means I need to go shopping. She needs a car, not just for wedding things but in life, too.

"Do you even have your license?"

I hear her scoff. "Of course I have my license, Gio. Now please leave; you can't see me!"

"Okay, sorry, I'm leaving. Just shoot me a text when you ladies are done. I'll go find something to do." I walk out, shutting the door behind me.

Just down the street from my building is a Mercedes dealership. An old friend of mine, Ryan, owns the place. I knock on his office door.

"Yeah, come on in," he yells from behind his oak door."Holy shit, Gio," he says, standing up and shaking my hand. "Where have you been? I haven't seen you since you bought that Bentley off me a year ago. Are you in the market for another one already?"

I let out a laugh. Ryan may own a Mercedes dealership, but he's a Bentley man at heart.

"Yes, but not for me. My fiancée needs a car."

He takes a step back, blinking a few times.

"I'm sorry, what? I think I heard that wrong. Did you just say you, Giovanni Benedetti, were getting married—of all people?"

That stings a little bit. "Yeah, it's crazy, isn't it?" Ryan knew about the family business. He's our car dealer; we all go to him.

"My dad found out about her—you know how he is."

Ryan scrunches his face. "Oh yeah, good old Lorenzo. So what are you looking at getting her?"

"I was thinking about the new EQS. She's going to need an SUV."

Ryan lets out a small laugh. "Oh, popping out heirs already?" he says, hitting my shoulder.

I don't even know if Iris wants kids. Hell, I don't know if I can be a good father. I'm a murderer. What would happen if I got caught? I'm not ready to be a father. "No, she just shouts 'SUV girl' to me," I say with a deep, angry voice I barely recognize. It doesn't sit right with me, having another man refer to Iris like that.

"My bad, dude. I didn't mean anything by it," Ryan says, backing away. "Look, I've got three here right now—one black, one silver, one blue," he adds, pointing to them from his office window.

I normally go for black—that's just my preference. "Not black. I was thinking silver. Is it fully loaded?" I reach into my coat pocket to grab my checkbook.

"I only sell fully loaded vehicles, Gio. Come on now. You know it is."

I take a seat, laughing at the look on Ryan's face. "Yeah, man, just wanted to fuck with you. What do I owe you?"

Ryan taps away on his computer and calculator. His eyes widen at the final number. "Listen, Gio, are you sure you want to get this car for her? You only spent 140K on yours."

I slowly look up at Ryan, squinting my eyes. "Just tell me the price, Ryan."

"180K," he says in a hiss.

I bark a laugh. "Dude, that's nothing. I'll take it." My job allows me to charge what I want. I charge 150 grand for a normal, low-tier hit. The judge from the seminar won me 2.4 million. I write the check and tear it from the book. "It will be delivered today at the tower, correct?" I say, placing the check in his hand.

"Yes, Gio. Does tonight at 6:30 work?" he asks, taking my check.

"Yes." I stand. I don't stay to do the paperwork—Ryan knows me better than that. He'll fill it out, and I'll sign when it's delivered.

My phone pings:

Mia Fiore: *Hey, you can come back now. I'm done with the dresses.*

I just have a few more errands to run and then i'll be on my way back to her.

CHAPTER 18

IRIS

"I wouldn't dream of it. Love you."

Did Gio just say what I think he did? It makes my chest grow tight, as if someone has my heart in their palm, squeezing. I push the thought to the back of my head. He only said it to play it off like we're a real couple to McKayla. We are a real couple. We may be new, but we're a couple all the same.

"Awe, he looks at you with such love in his eyes. You two are by far my favorite couple," McKayla says to my back, putting a hand on my shoulder. I think she says that to all her couples.

"Thank you, it feels like a fairytale," I reply, a smile crossing my lips.

"So how many people are we thinking for a guest count?" the planner asks.

"I'm not sure. I can get the list to you tomorrow when we go to Nantucket, to see how much space we have to work with first," I say, lifting my shoulders.

"Oh yes, did you get the address from the groom?" she asks, lacing her hands together and shaking them by her chin.

"Oh yeah, let me grab the laptop."

I walk to Gio's office to grab the laptop he left sitting open on top of his desk. I move my thumb along the mouse pad to wake up the screen. My eyes nearly pop out of my head when I see what Gio had pulled up. There's a number the size of a phone number on the screen—his bank account. First of all, he needs to not leave that up. Second, how does he have that much money? I read the number on the screen: **$28,556,325.25**. I exit out of the tab Gio left open as I walk back into the kitchen, where McKayla and I have set up a wedding-planning station.

"I found the laptop. Let me just type in the address." Grabbing the paper off the counter, I type it in as he wrote it: **2659 Burnt Cherry Ave., Nantucket**. An old listing pops up, and my mouth drops open. I look at the address he wrote down versus what I typed in—no mistakes.

It's a ginormous, light-gray, old Colonial-style home with a wraparound porch held up by columns, backed by the ocean shore. The listing from ten years ago says it has 15 bedrooms and 12 bathrooms. There's a gazebo in the backyard, almost on the sand. Going through the photos, I can see it's plenty of room for Gio and me to get ready on the morning of our wedding. I keep scrolling to find where we can have the reception. The last 12 photos show a plot of land just off from the main house, looking like it can be turned into something beautiful for a party.

Small breaths warm my shoulder. "Okay, so is it just me, or is this place made to be a fairy tale?" McKayla huffs out. "Good for you, girl. Lock down the rich ones," she says, walking around the kitchen island to take her seat.

"Umm, thank you." My face twists at the odd, slightly demeaning comment.

"So I am just going to plan for that place to be the venue for both," she says, writing it down. "What are you thinking of for food?" she asks, tapping her pen on her notebook and touching her finger to her lips.

"Umm, I don't know. Where I'm from, we do taco in a bag or brisket," I say, shrinking into myself where I stand.

"Oh God, no, sweety. Rich people do a salad, steak and chicken with some type of vegetable and potato, then dessert." She places her hand on mine.

"Okay, that sounds good. Let's just do that." I smile back at her.

We're interrupted by a knock on the door. I'm secretly hoping it's Gio coming home. When I look through the small hole—placed just high enough that I have to stand on my tiptoes to see clearly—I see a woman with short blonde hair, almost silver, surrounded by four garment carts covered in white tulle and satin. A big smile spreads across my face. I turn to McKayla.

"The dresses are here!" I yell as I yank the front door open.

McKayla walks to the door to stand beside me. "Adriana, so nice to see you." They kiss each other on both cheeks. "This is Iris—she's the bride," McKayla introduces me. Adriana takes in a deep, audible breath.

"Oh lord, you are stunning. I have not had a bride with two different eye colors. Are you ready to find your gown?"

"Um, yes," I say with a little yelp and jump. With all these dresses, I'm bound to find one.

"Now, are we doing one gown for both ceremony and reception, or are we switching after the ceremony?" she asks me.

"Oh, I never thought about it. Let's see what I find first."

Adriana starts pulling dresses from her rolling carts, having me strip down and try on dress after dress. They're all so different—tulle, satin, and lace fill our living room, draping across the couch and hanging off any window frame we can reach. McKayla goes to the kitchen and grabs the bottle of champagne Gio opened two nights ago without me. Rummaging through the cabinets, she finds three flutes and pours a glass for each of us.

"So, are we finding *the* dress, or at least learning what you do and don't like?" Adriana says, taking a sip.

"I love the sweetheart neckline and the lace, but I also like tulle and fluff. I just don't know," I say, looking at myself in the mirror.

I'm in a long-sleeve lace mermaid gown with a keyhole cutout in the back, showing off the top of my spine to my mid-back. I glance at Adriana in the mirror, her fingers tapping against her glass.

"And the sleeves?" she asks.

"I'm okay with or without them," I say, sipping my champagne carefully so I don't spill on this amazing dress.

I spot the front door opening slowly behind me in the mirror. Giovanni walks through the door with his keys and a bag in his hands. Oh no—he can't see me in a wedding dress before we walk down the aisle. It's bad luck. We may not have met in the most traditional way, but I still want this wedding and this marriage to be as real as anybody else's.

"Hey! Get out! You can't see me in the dress!" I yell as I run down the hallway to our bedroom, hoping he didn't see me. This isn't *my* dress, but it's *a* wedding dress.

"Sorry. I was just asking if you needed your car from campus to do wedding things this coming week," he yells from the entryway.

I don't have a car here. I drove to Boston but sold it a few months after starting school; I needed the cash, and the city buses run everywhere anyway. "No, I don't have a car. Now leave!"

"Do you even have your license?"

I roll my eyes. Of course I have my license. "Yes," I say quietly, then raise my voice. "Of *course* I have my license, Gio. Now please go—you can't see me."

"Okay, sorry. I'm leaving. Just shoot me a text when you ladies are done. I'll find something to do."

I hear the door shut.

"You can come out now; he's gone!" McKayla yells out. That was close. I can't choose *this* dress now, just in case he saw it.

"Well, I can't wear *this* one anymore." I let out a sigh and step back in front of the mirror.

"That's okay. I think I have the dress for you," Adriana says, clapping her hands. "Take that one off."

McKayla helps me unbutton the dress and shimmy it off my body. Adriana holds up a stunning lace gown with multiple layers at different lengths. I try it on and instantly know *this* is my dress: It has a sweetheart neckline with a see-through corset covered in floral lace, plus detachable sleeves. McKayla and Adriana top it off with a tulle veil and a short, sparkly tiara. A tear rolls down my cheek and onto my chin. Adriana brushes it away.

"Well damn, I think you found the dress, girl," Adriana says.

McKayla lets out a whistle like a man catcalling women on the street. Movement catches my eye from the kitchen. I turn to see the chef preparing dinner. "I think you're right—this is the one." We all clink our glasses together in a toast of pure happiness.

McKayla and I help Adriana pack up all the gowns except for the one I'll wear on my wedding day. I run it to my old room and hang it in the closet. When I come back from my old room, I stop in the kitchen, where a man in a white shirt and black pants stands at the counter.

"Hello—Giovanni told me to let you know we're having two guests for dinner tonight."

The man nods his head. "Yes, ma'am. I will set two more places."

"Thank you."

When I return to help, the dresses are already put away and hung on their carts. Adriana is waiting by the door, ready to leave.

"I am so happy I could help you find your wedding gown. We also do regular gowns. I just started a maternity line," she says, winking at me as she hugs me from the side. "I'll see you later." She exits the penthouse.

Does everybody think I'm knocked up? Is that why they think we're getting married? I turn to McKayla with my mouth in a frown.

"So, for flowers, I was thinking we could do a white and light pink flower wall. It's a great photo op for the couple and other guests," she says, tucking her hair behind her ear.

"Yeah, I like that idea. It sounds beautiful." I shoot a text off to Gio.

CHAPTER 19

GIOVANNI

When I get home two hours later, Iris is standing in the living room, looking at the TV mounted above the fireplace and watching a not-so-real reality show—one woman yelling at another, plates being thrown at someone's head. She turns to me with her sea-and-olive-colored eyes, brighter than I've seen them since she found out about me. She stalks toward me, arms wide open.

"Oh, hi. You're home."

I accept any kind of touch this woman wants to give me. Her presence is intoxicating—a pull that my body and heart can't resist. The mixture of apple and passion fruit invades my nostrils and fills my soul. I may not have meant to say it before, but I know it's true now: I love the woman standing in front of me.

"You sent me a text. Of course I came home." I take a look around. "Did the planner leave already?"

I slide my hands down her back to rest on the shelf above her ass.

"They both left a little bit ago. McKayla and I can't do much until we're at the venue. It's beautiful, you know—the house." She looks up at me, her chin propped on my chest where I want her presence most. "Are you sure your dad is gonna be okay with us using the house for our wedding?"

I didn't ask him, but he told me to get it done quickly. He won't stop it; he needs this wedding to happen no matter where we have it.

"Mia Fiore, he told me to get it done. I don't think he's gonna say no."

She leans back with her hands still draped around my neck. "Wait, you didn't ask him? You need to call him right now so we know if that's where it'll be or if I need to find a new place." She releases my neck, throwing a small hand against my chest.

Reluctantly, I slide my phone out of my pocket and dial my father. One ring, two rings, and on the third he answers. "You never call. what do you need Gio?" he barks out.

"How lovely to hear from you, Father," I bark back. Iris and I exchange looks of annoyance.

"Get to the point, Gio. I'm busy." A light laugh from a woman filters through the phone on my father's end. OF course he is with one of his whores.

"We want to use the Nantucket house for the wedding." I wait for an answer, but he doesn't speak. "I assume that'll be okay?"

I hear the flick of a lighter and groan. Is my father really hooking up with someone while on the phone with his son? What the actual fuck.

"Yes, I don't care. Just get it done," he says, then hangs up before I can say another word.

"He said he doesn't care what we do as long as the vows are said," I paraphrase. Iris gets the message either way.

Iris and I get ready for the dinner party she requested. She helps me pick out a gray suit, white shirt, and a dark-blue tie. Iris walks out from the bathroom with her hair in loose curls, cheeks rosy, wearing a smooth satin lilac dress that hugs her beautiful curves. I can't wait to get that dress on the floor. I lick my lips as she struts over to me.

98

"Are we being too formal for this? It's just Lexi and Avery."

We turn to the mirror. We do make an amazing-looking couple, but I think she might be right. Our eyes meet in the reflection, and we both let out a laugh. After five minutes, we decide to go for a more comfortable approach. I change into a pair of loose-fitting jeans and a simple black T-shirt. My breath is taken away again when my fiancée emerges from the bathroom. She looks even better in black leggings and a white hoodie than she did in that dress. I love her in both, but something about her not even trying—yet still being this gorgeous—sends my heart into an uneven beat.

I've almost forgotten about the delivery that's due any minute for Iris. Just then, my phone pings.

RYAN: *Hey, the car is parked right next to yours. I even put a bow on it—free of charge, of course. Hahaha.*

I laugh. It had better be free of charge. He may be a friend, but not a close one.

I grab Iris's hand. She turns to me. "I have a surprise for you. Want to see it?" She looks at her watch—6:48. Eighteen minutes later than I wanted it delivered. Ryan will hear about that another time.

"Right now? The girls are gonna be here in half an hour. You're good in bed, but not *that* good," she laughs out. My head moves back, my face contorting in mock pain.

"First of all, I *am* that good. And second, that isn't the surprise."

She flicks her hair over her shoulder, closing her eyes. I take the maroon tie I once used to tie her to my bed and wrap it around her eyes. "No peeking," I whisper in her ear, my lips brushing the sensitive skin there. I feel a shudder run through her body. Leading her down to the parking garage is a task in itself. I've never been the type of man who wants to surprise a woman just to see the raw joy in her eyes. But I'm not the man I was before I met this woman—the one whose hand is in mine, drawing small circles on the top of it.

When I remove the tie, the silk slips slowly from her long eyelashes, revealing her enchanting gaze dropping to the silver car with a flashy red bow.

"I didn't take you for an SUV kind of guy," she chimes.

My hand moves from her shoulders to her elbows. "That's because it's not for me," I say, nudging her toward the car. She digs in her heels, planting them against the concrete.

"I can't accept a car from you, especially not one this nice. You didn't need to spend your own money on it," she stutters out.

"Well, I'm *not* returning it, and my money is your money too."

She opens her mouth, but I cut her off. "Oh, that reminds me..." I reach into my pocket and pull out a deep blue card. Grabbing her arm and lifting her hand, I place the card in her palm. "This is your card. I added you to my bank account."

Iris looks up at me with tears brimming in her eyes. "Gio, you didn't have to do that—or any of this." She wraps her arms around my chest, snuggling her head into my shirt.

Placing a kiss on her head, I say, "Oh, I have something else for you, too." I pull out an emerald velvet box from my pocket. Opening the lid, light glints off a dainty silver band topped by a pear-cut clear diamond surrounded by moonstones.

"I figured if we're engaged, you should have a ring. I picked it up today."

Her hand flies to her mouth. "Oh my God, Gio, it's amazing. I love it—thank you!" She takes the ring and slides it to the base of her ring finger. She doesn't notice the words inscribed on the inside: *Always Mia Fiore.*

100

CHAPTER 20

IRIS

I have never been given so many gifts on the same day by anyone. "I really don't need the car, though. I like walking or riding the bus, Gio. You should save your money," I say, turning to face him.

"I will not have my wife walking the streets or riding the bus," he says, grabbing the nape of my neck, his eyes burning a hole into my soul. I lick my lips, hoping to catch my breath before it leaves my mouth dry. He presses a kiss to my lips. With minds of their own, they part as his tongue invades my mouth. My hands fly to his chest, clutching his shirt. We've kissed and done much more, but with every unplanned kiss, I feel like I fall deeper into a pit where Gio is the only thing I need to survive.

Gio pulls away, cupping my face with his hands. "We can't do this right now," he says, raising an eyebrow, "unless you want to cancel dinner with your friends. If we continue," he adds, pointing from his lips to mine, "your friends will be in the penthouse while I fuck your tight little ass." He taps my ass gently as he turns around, walking to the elevator.

A knock rattles the front door as Gio and I start cooking dinner. I jog to the door, so excited to see my best friends for the first time in almost two weeks. I swing it open with such force—but it isn't just Lexi and Avery. Tears trail down their cheeks, and behind them stands a man who isn't Julius: he's a pale man with dark tattoos curling up his throat and onto his face. He pulls a gun from behind Avery, pointing it at me.

I raise my hands and slowly step back, saying nothing as I retreat from the doorway.

I move until Gio can see me. I turn my head toward where he should be cooking, but he's not there. Tears begin to fall down my cheeks. The man starts to yell, "WHERE THE FUCK IS HE?" He grabs Lexi's hair, and she screams in pain. Trying to answer, I yell back, "I don't know who you're looking for! You have the wrong house!"

My eyes catch movement in the corner of the hallway. I exhale in relief when I see it's Gio with a kitchen knife. He moves quietly behind the man, ready to pounce like a cat playing with its toy. Gio grabs the man's arm and pulls it to his hip, locking it into place as he presses the knife to his throat. Lexi and Avery break free and run behind me. Gio yells orders at me, "Take them to our room. Don't let them out of your sight. Wait with them until I come and get you."

I do as I'm told.

Lexi and Avery are a sobbing mess. I go to the connected bathroom to grab warm, damp washcloths, hoping to soothe them somehow. I sit and wait—wait for anything—but they do nothing. They don't look at me, they don't say anything; they just stare at the floor.

The sound of screams from somewhere in the house shatters the silence. They both start sobbing again, but there's nothing I can do to calm them down. I begin to see spots, and my breathing quickens. I try to take a deep breath, but everything goes dark as my body goes limp, and I collapse onto the floor.

Some time later, I wake up with a cold washcloth on my forehead, Avery and Lexi kneeling over me. I don't know how long I was out, but tears are still falling from their eyes.

"What the fuck is going on, Iris?" Lexi demands.

"I don't know. I need to talk with Gio." I turn onto my side, facing the wall as tears start rolling down my cheeks, accompanied by quiet sobs I'm trying to hold in. My hands fly to my ears, blocking out the screams coming from inside my home.

Rolling over, I crawl to the bath, turning the handle as far as it could. Lowering my body into the water not caring at the sting the hot water leaves on my body. The water creeping up my bottom half.

CHAPTER 21

GIOVANNI

As soon as I see that the girls are locked away in our room and safe, I knock out the stranger who came into my—our—home uninvited.

I cuff the nameless man's hands and tie his legs to the chair. If it weren't for the small breaths I can hear, I'd think I hit him too hard and killed him. But I didn't. I know what I'm doing.

Grabbing a few things from the kitchen, I set them in a perfect line like a meticulous surgeon, in the exact order I'm going to use them:

1. Grill fork
2. Metal skewers
3. Butcher knife
4. Metal salad spoon
5. My gun

Tapping the metal salad spoon against his head, I taunt, "Wakey, wakey, motherfucker." He starts to stir in the chair, his eyes locking onto mine.

"What's your name?" I ask in the same tone. He just stares up at me.

Leaning over, I grab the shiny grill fork, twirling it in my hand. I ask one more time, "What is your name?" sliding the fork across his chest down to his dick. His eyes widen slightly. He hisses, "Kallum Mackenzie." The fucking Irish. I knew this was going to be a problem at some point.

"What do you want? Why are you here?" I press the fork into his thigh now. Is it because of Iris? What does she have to do with this? Has she lied to me? Is she with them? Slowly guiding the fork into the meaty part of his thigh, screams erupt from him.

"You're marrying one of us. I was told to get rid of you so it wouldn't happen," he answers, anger and tears ripping through him as I push even harder on his thigh.

"What do you mean by 'one of you'? Is she part of your little group?" I raise my hands, adding air quotes around *little group*. My heart is pounding, thinking Iris lied to me. Thinking the worst, I recall the story of her father she told me. Was any of it true? Is anything about us true, or was I just part of some assignment her family gave her? What the actual fuck!

"What? No. But you're supposed to stick to your own kind. You aren't supposed to marry *ours*, and we can't marry any of *yours*. That was the agreement 20 years ago, and here you are fucking it up."

Oh, thank God. I inhale a breath. She didn't lie to me. Of course she didn't. Why would she lie? She's seen the worst of me and my lifestyle and chose to stay—she wouldn't lie. Would she?

"Okay, so why do you care if she isn't one of you?" I ask, grabbing the metal skewers from the counter. As I turn, I see him trying to wiggle his arm free. Walking around him, I position one skewer at the traps near his neck.

"It doesn't matter—you're still mixing the blood." He lets out a scream as I push one into the muscle. When I feel resistance, I push just a bit harder until it pops through. My lips curl into a grin. Most of the time, it's a gun to the head for me, but I must admit, pushing a person to pain has a certain pleasure to it. His screams ring out through the apartment.

Leaning close to his ear, I say, "Why does your boss care if she isn't one of you?" I flick the skewer. He just stares at the trash bag covering the floor beneath him. Pulling out the other skewer, I move to his other side, where his shoulder blade meets his back; I press it against his skin. Adding a bit more pressure, the tip dips below his skin. Bright red blood runs down, matching the other side as though it was always meant to be there. Another blood curdling scream leaves his lips soon muffled by the knife I pull from the counter.

"Look, I don't know. I just do what I'm told," he cries out as I place the knife against his pinky, which has a gold ring bearing their crest. Ronan McCarthy was the son of the old boss of the Irish family, but the old man died three months ago. Some say Ronan offed his own father to take power—apparently, he didn't want to wait until the old man croaked. Some even say *we* killed him, but that isn't true. I'd have been given that assignment if so. Honestly, I would have thought this was about that until he said her name.

"Look," he says as I apply pressure to his pinky, "you let me go, and I'll give my boss whatever message you want me to… okay?" he pleads. breathlessly between sobs.

"As good as that might sound to you, it doesn't work for me. Sorry," I say, pushing down. His pinky falls to the floor, rolling between his feet. The sound of his scream deafens me. There's no way the girls down the hall don't hear this. Leaning into his ear once more, I whisper, "Actually, I'm not sorry." My voice grows darker and louder the more I speak, fueling my anger as I think about what would have happened if I wasn't here—what he would have done if Iris was home alone.

"This is what you get for coming into my home and trying to kill my wife," I scream, cutting off his other pinky. His scream matches mine. "I wasn't going to kill her," he promises, tears and snot dripping onto the trash bag, mixing with his blood.

"Really? What was the plan then, Kallum? Were you going to kidnap her? Scare her? Or maybe even rape her? Either way, you fucked with the wrong person, and now you'll pay the consequences." Pulling the spoon from the counter, I continue, "Not Ronan, but you. You see,

Kallum, not only did you break into the next Don's house"—I laugh, stepping around to his side—"you came into the monster's den."

Grabbing the hair at the back of his head, I force him to look at the ceiling. "Speak!" I yell. "What was the plan?"

He cries out upon seeing the spoon approach his eye. "I was just supposed to take her to Ronan. I don't know what he had planned for her." He's cut off by his own screams as I scoop out his eyeball. You'd think it would be harder to scoop out an eye, but it's like scooping ice cream that's been in the freezer a little too long, pressure and pop out they come.

His screams suddenly stop. Is he dead already? No—I can feel the thump-thump under my fingertips; he's just passed out from the pain. I finish the other eye without caring if he's conscious or not.

I wake him with smelling salts. "Kallum, we aren't done with our conversation." He jerks awake.

"Why can't I see?" he screams.

"Oh, that. Yeah, I took both your eyes," I say, laughing out the last word. "Now, I know you don't know what he's gonna do, but I can't let you live. What kind of boss would that make me?" I ask, rhetorically. "I can't allow a man who came into my home and tried to kidnap my wife—"

I'm interrupted by Kallum spitting out, "She's not your wife yet, and if Ronan has anything to say about it, she won't be your fucking—" He's cut off by a bullet. My bullet, right between where his eyes used to be. I don't even remember pulling the gun from the counter.

Pulling my phone from my pocket, I call Luka, our cleaner. Luka isn't really family, but he's been with us since he was eighteen and has worked his way up to Capo. He has his own crew under him. His daughter, Cecilia, is even associated. She doesn't actually do anything hands-on, but she does all of our tattoos.

Luka answers on the second ring. "Gio, what can I do for you?" he asks, like I call him for anything else. He may be one of us, but he's much older than me.

"I need cleanup at the penthouse. It's a fucking Irish work bitch," I hiss back at him.

"Oh, I'll have two men on the way in five minutes. Will two do it, or is it gonna require more?" he spits out.

"No, two will be perfect. I also need them to send the fingers to their meeting house. Can they do that?" I bark my order.

"Yeah, you know they can," he says, then clicks off the call.

Ten minutes later, two men—whose names I don't know but whose faces I've seen—stand at my door with everything they need to dispose of any evidence of what happened here. Luka's guys are quick, but I made it easy for them. They place his fingers in a small gift box wrapped with a red bow the Italians' color for an extra 'fuck you' and send it off with a boy who looks maybe eighteen. The two men take the body, wrapped in the trash bag, down the hall and vanish with it.

I walk to our room where the girls are hiding. When I walk in, I see my fiancé's friends cowering on the floor by the window. I scan the rest of the room but don't see Iris anywhere. The two look up at me with tears running down their faces.

"What the fuck just happened?" the black-haired one asks between her sobs.

"Where is she?" My tone darkens almost to a growl. They fall silent, and that's when I hear water running.

Heading to the bathroom connected to our room, I see Iris's lower body submerged in bubbles, steam rising and fogging the mirror. Taking a seat on the ledge of the bathtub, I say, "Fiore, are you okay?" while rubbing her cheek. She is paler than I've ever seen her—her face blank, her arms limp and red. Reaching into the water for the drain, I recoil; this water is *fucking hot*, way too hot for her body.

Whispering in her ear, "I need to get you out of that water, baby. You're gonna burn yourself," I watch her turn her head, and take it as my invitation to help. Lifting her by the arms, I let her stand and then grab a towel. Wrapping it around her, I can feel her trembling. Pulling her close, I place a kiss on her forehead, pressing it to my chest, whispering, "I'm sorry you had to see me act like that. I never wanted to show you that side of me. I understand you're scared or in shock because of me, but—"

She pulls away, looking up at me. "I'm not scared or in shock *because of you*," she emphasizes. "I'm in shock because a man I don't know came into our home and held a gun to my friends' heads." Her hand flies to my chest. "I already told you, I'm not scared of you. You won't hurt me," she says, starting to laugh. "I mean, you haven't yet."

Running my thumb across her bottom lip, I say, "I don't ever plan on hurting you." I move closer to her face. *"Ever."* Then I place a kiss on her forehead.

CHAPTER 22

IRIS

Wrapped in Gio's arms is where I feel safest, and I know it's probably crazy, but I meant it when I said I know he won't hurt me, not now not ever. Looking up at the man who's going to be my husband in a week, I whisper, "Maybe we shouldn't tell them." I nod toward the door that I know Lexi and Avery are on the other side of. Confusion spreads across his face.

"Maybe we tell them that..." I start, looking around the bathroom as I think, "my phone broke, so I couldn't text them, or"—I pat his chest—"we tell them we just fell in love really quickly and we're gonna do a very small wedding at city hall."

"Mia Fiore, I know you, and I know that's not what you want. You want your friends to be there," he says in a commanding tone. "Why don't we tell them the story we tell most people—you know, the one that pops up when you google me?" he says, staring into my soul.

Shrugging, I admit, "I didn't google you. I don't know that story."

He leans in close to my ear. "You're telling me my little lawyer didn't even do her research on her newest client?" He peppers kisses down my neck.

"To be fair, I'm not a lawyer yet. I haven't taken on any clients, *Mr. Benedetti*," I say in a joking manner, kissing his lips.

"We just tell the world we own a personal security company. That's how I got my money, that's why that guy wanted in the house. It explains a lot—and it's not really a lie," he says, holding me tight to his chest like he's scared I'm going to leave.

"I guess that makes more sense than my lies, but what happens when they start noticing other things about our life?" I ask, looking at the floor.

He lifts my chin with his finger. "We'll cross that bridge when we get to it."

A plan forms in my head: We will tell them Gio owns a personal security company, but after the wedding, I'll start to cut them out—saying I'm too busy, that I have things to do with Gio's family. Eventually, they'll move on and forget me as a friend. A tear slips from my eye. These girls are my best friends, the only people besides Gio who will ever really know me. That's not even true, only Gio really knows me.

Silently, we agree on the personal security company story with an embrace. When we leave the bathroom, we find Lexi and Avery standing by the bed, still breathing heavily.

"You need to tell us what the fuck just happened!" Avery's voice slices through the silence of the room. Gio rests his hand on my back, guiding me to tell them the story. If *he* started explaining, they wouldn't believe him. But if I do, they just might.

Taking a breath, I say, "Okay, but you need to let me finish the whole story with no questions until the end. Then, if you have any, I'll answer them. Deal?" The air escapes my lungs; it feels like I can't breathe until they respond.

Lexi speaks first. "No wonder you went into law. You're so bossy."

I'd take them into the living room, but I'm almost certain of what happened there, and I don't want them to see it without an explanation first.

"You both know how Giovanni and I met, but that's not the end of it," I say, looking at Gio as his face shifts in confusion. A small smile curves my lips. "Gio and his family own a personal security company," I continue, jumping into the lie and embellishing it. "Gio was in the military, and when he got out, his dad helped him start the business. Like any company, they have ups and downs. That guy was from a job gone wrong."

Gio takes a seat on the bed, giving me an impressed look and a slight smile.

"That man lost his wife in an assignment where he didn't disclose all the information to Gio and his team." I pause, realizing how easy it is to make up this lie—but it's already begun, and I can't stop it now, for their protection.

Gio cuts in, continuing the lie.

"Since then, he's always claimed it was my fault and that I would pay for what I've 'done,'" Gio says, putting air quotes around the last word. "He still has mutual contacts"—he sucks in a breath through his teeth—"so when word got out that I had a person I cared about, he thought he'd try to take his revenge." He looks to me to finish.

"When Gio and I met, we knew how we felt—it's quick, but when you know, you know. And as for not texting you guys back, I've been really busy with planning the wedding, and on top of that, my phone broke. I just managed to get a new one." I look at the floor. "I'm sorry I didn't tell you sooner, or really at all."

I feel their eyes on me, like holes burning into my skin. My body starts to shake as I hope they believe all of that. What if they don't? Would

Gio be forced to kill them? Or would they be given an option like I was? Avery is the first to speak, just as I expected.

"Okay, I mean, it makes sense, but if that's the case, why didn't Gio just call the cops on him instead of beating him up? I heard the screams coming from out there." She points to the door. I heard the screams too, but I don't actually know what Gio did to the man. I can only guess it ended in death.

Gio stalks toward the door. "I did call the cops. I showed them the footage, and they took him away. The screams you heard were me fighting to get the gun out of his hand. I broke his arm, that's all I did. The cops did everything else. You can go out and see for yourself." He says holding an arm up to the open door.

I know that's a lie. Gio would never call the cops for anything—he would handle the problem himself. I walk out first to make sure the girls won't see anything they shouldn't. Honestly, I don't know what they are or aren't allowed to see. I'm not even sure what *I'm* allowed to see. But everything's in its place; not a hair out of place, no mess inside. I turn to Gio, and he nods as if telling me to keep going.

We take seats in the living room on the couch. Neither of the girls asks another question. Silence settles in until I break it. "Do you guys still want dinner? It'll only take thirty minutes to cook. It's just steamed—" I'm cut off by Avery.

"No offense, but I'm not really in the mood for food, you know, after the whole gun-to-head thing." She gestures to her temple with her finger.

A sigh slips from my mouth. I'm partly relieved they don't want to stay any longer. Glancing between Lexi and Avery, I say, "No, I totally get it. Maybe another time—or even at the wedding." I pause, hoping they don't want to cut Gio and me out of their lives now. "Unless you guys don't want to come."

Lexi speaks first, finally pulling her gaze away from Gio. "No, we'll be there. We wouldn't let you do this without us. Are you crazy?" She grabs my hands.

"Look, I know this is fast, but thank you for respecting our decision. And on that note, I was hoping you girls would be my bridesmaids?" I glance at Gio apologetically. "We would pay for the dresses. We just need you to show up to get fitted, and we'll handle everything else." I pause, studying my friends, trying to gauge their reaction.

"Of course we'll be there and be your bridesmaids—just tell us when and where," Avery says, followed by Lexi's "We love you, girl!"

We walk the girls down to the garage, Gio right behind us, and give his driver their college address to take them home and make sure they get into their rooms safely. Avery seems to be doing better, but Lexi hasn't said much. I only hope they both bought our story.

As the car turns the corner, Gio walks with me back to our home. Once the door is shut and I know there's no one around to see me, I fall to the floor, tears streaking down my face. I can barely catch my breath. Gio sinks down beside me, repeating "Baby, are you okay?" over and over, his frantic voice echoing in my head.

I finally cough out a response: "I made up my mind." Wiping tears from my eyes, I feel his hands replace mine. Still struggling to breathe, I continue, "I am going to slowly cut them off so they forget about me and never find out about"—I start flapping my arms—"any of this."

Gio lifts me from the floor, carrying me to our room. Pulling the blankets down, he tucks me in. I turn onto my side, trying to silence the screams threatening to leave my lips. I hear him walk out of the bedroom. I think I'm alone when I feel big hands resting on my back. Leaning down, he places a kiss on my cheek.

"I brought you some tea, honey."

"Honey" sounds so odd coming from his mouth as a pet name. Through the tears filling my eyes, I can just make out his shape. Leaning closer, he whispers, "Baby, you don't need to cut them off. This lie has worked for years; we can keep it going."

I curl into his side, closing my eyes. Exhaustion slams into me like a truck. Yawning, I feel him roll onto his side, holding me tighter against his chest. Before I know it, I give in to the fatigue and fall asleep.

When I open my eyes, Gio's side of the bed is empty. Stretching, I reach for my phone on the nightstand—he must have plugged it in for me. Blinded by the screen's glare, I see it's 2:30 in the morning. Where the fuck *is* he?

Sliding out of bed, I walk down the hall until I reach his office door. I hear the distinctive crack of his whip. My heart fractures a bit more as I piece together what's happening. He's punishing himself; he didn't hand that man over to the cops—he got rid of him. If he's using the whip, it means he feels guilty about the killing. But why? That guy broke into our home. I don't feel bad about it—*it was him or us.*

I respect Gio's privacy and go back to bed. I'll ask him about it in the morning. Just then, the bedroom door opens. He heads to the bathroom, and I can see fresh cuts on his back. The air in my lungs disappears like I've been sucker punched.

The water starts running, and I can tell it's trickling over his body by the way it splashes in a sporadic rhythm. My body makes the decision before my mind does.

Play: Addicted by Jon Vinyl

I'm standing by the bed with the sheet puddled at my feet. I force myself to steady my breathing. Entering the bathroom, I see the silhouette of a god standing under the waterfall shower. My breath catches in my throat. This man—*my* man—is a damn god, but I'm not here for that. I want to know why he marked himself. I need to understand why.

Walking into the shower, I can make out eight new marks on his back. These aren't like the others. They're deeper, as if he struck the same spot twice on purpose. Gio's broad body turns to face me.

"What are you doing up, Fiore? You're supposed to be sleeping."

He slides his hands around my waist, meeting at my lower back, twisting us so my hair now absorbs the spray of the shower, goosebumps rising up my back to the nape of my neck under his hand. Gripping my hair, he forces my face into the water. "Answer me, Iris."

"I couldn't find you when I woke up earlier," I moan as our lips meet. "Then I heard you, and the evidence is here," I say, running my hand up his back, over the grooves of fresh and healed scars. "I just want to know why. I know you got rid of him, but why do you feel bad for it? It was him or us."

His head tilts to the side. Running his hand from the back of my neck to the front, he takes hold of my throat.

Leaning into my ear, he says, "I don't feel sorry for killing him." Pulling back to look into my eyes, he continues, "I'm sorry that *you* almost got killed. I'm sorry that another man almost touched what's mine." His voice grows deeper, his gaze shifting between my eyes and my lips. "I'm mad at myself for almost losing the thing I love most in this fucked-up world, and it would've been my fault."

I can't breathe; I'm panting. Did he mean that? He was pushed into this marriage as much as I was. I break eye contact, looking at the walls and floor. "Gio, you don't mean that. You were forced to marry me. You don't have to love me. I know that you—"

I'm cut off when his lips crash into mine, his hands tangling in my hair. My lips part, inviting him to invade my mouth. I *want* him, not just *need* him. He pushes me against the wall.

116

"You're mine. I chose you. Why wouldn't I love you? I get you and only you for the rest of my life," he huffs into my neck, peppering it with kisses. "You never judge me, even though I'm a monster. You *are* scared of me."

My hands glide over his back, making sure to avoid his fresh cuts. Taking his face in my hands, I look right into his silver eyes. "Gio, I love you too, and I think I have since we first met." I pull him in for a kiss, wrapping my arms around his neck. He lifts me, and my legs instinctively wrap around his hips. He backs us into the wall, his cock poised at my entrance. He looks at me, almost asking for permission.

"I need you, Gio," I breathe out.

"Fuck yes, baby," he hisses, pushing inside. "I need you and only you, Iris."

He starts thrusting with a rhythm that makes me cry out. Gripping his shoulders, I move with him, matching his rhythm. I cry out, "Fuck, baby, you fill me so good!" just as he hits that spot inside me, nudging me closer to my release.

Gio brings my leg up to his shoulder, forcing me to grab the top of the shower's glass wall. Thrusting even deeper, he takes my throat in his hand and my peaked nipple in his warm mouth. The sensation is more than I expected.

He pushes me to my limits every time we have sex. I need more of him—I want to feel only him. I place my hand over his on my throat. He continues to thrust into me hungrily. Lessening the pressure on my own neck, my eyes snap to his, seeing him glance at my neck.

"No—tighter," I cry out. His hand returns to its place, gripping harder. I buck my hips just as Gio sinks deeper into me. My body starts to jerk from lack of airflow. I try to breathe through my nose, but little air reaches my lungs, and they start to burn. My vision goes black as I focus on Gio's face, now looking at me.

"Are you going to cum for me?" he asks, slamming into me. I try to nod my head, but his hand keeps it from moving. Without warning, my body starts to tighten, my legs begin to shake, and my vision is just spots. One last thrust, and Gio is spilling into me.

"That's my girl," he whispers, replacing his hand with kisses on my throat. "My wife likes to be choked, don't you, baby?" he asks, running his hand along my leg and releasing it from his shoulder.

"I guess I do," I say as I gasp. My lungs burn, desperate for air. The first breath feels like water quenching a fire—I swear I hear the sizzle of the flames being put out.

Gio grabs my body wash, lathering it into my purple sponge. He starts washing me, from my neck—where I assume his hand will leave a bruise—down to my toes. I laugh when he reaches the spot on my thigh where I know his seed is dripping down.

Looking up at me, he says, "What are you laughing at?" and slaps my ass.

"It tickles. I'm a little sensitive there right now," I say, holding back laughter as he rubs my clit. "Gio, stop— I can't do it again," I pant.

His face twists into a serious look. "Oh yes, you can." Sliding his finger into me, jerking and rubbing my G-spot, and his thumb circling my clit, he dips a second finger in. My hands fly to his hair, twisting it through my fingers, while the other hand covers my mouth to stifle my sobs. I feel a sting on my right hip. Glancing down, my eyes meet Gio's as his teeth sink into my flesh, marking me.

"Don't you dare quiet those cries," he demands. And I come undone— my body tightening and shaking as he frantically rubs my clit. It pours out of me again, just like it did that time in the dorm room shower.

I collapse to the floor, heaving from exhaustion. Sex with him takes so much out of me. After a minute or two, my body stops trembling.

Gio washes my body again, this time without making me cum. When it's my turn to wash him, he stops me at his back. "Baby, I can do it," he says, grabbing the sponge from my hand.

"I know you can, but I *want* to," I say, placing my hand over his. He releases the sponge. As I pass it gently over his cuts, he hisses. "I'm sorry—does it hurt?" I ask, immediately thinking *What a stupid question, Iris. Of course it hurts.*

His head hangs. "Yeah, it always does," he says, shoulders rising and falling. "I don't normally use soap on them, just water." His hands fall to his sides in fists.

Dropping the sponge, I grab the showerhead and run water across his shoulders, letting it trickle down his back. With my free hand, I take his, tangling our fingers together. I let the water run over his back until there's no more tint of red pooling at our feet. Kissing each one of his scars, I count fifty-eight, though most have clearly been hit more than once.

Grabbing the towels that hang by the shower, I wrap myself up and hand Gio his. "Go sit on the bed. I'll be right there," I tell him. Surprisingly, he actually listens.

Rummaging through our bathroom cabinets, I find a tube of triple antibiotic cream. Gathering some Q-tips, I walk into the bedroom, where I find a very tired Gio sitting on the edge of the mattress, gazing out the window.

"Hi, baby," I say, sneaking up behind him on the bed. Leaning over his shoulder, I see his eyes half-closed. "I'm going to put some cream on these, and then we'll go to bed," I whisper, kissing his cheek. He says nothing—he's so tired.

I apply the cream gently, trying not to hurt him any more than he's already hurting. Then I help him lie down. This time, I'm the one to tuck him in. I crawl into bed beside him, turning on my side. He drapes an arm around me, pulling me closer to his chest.

He kisses the back of my head. "Thank you for that. Nobody's taken care of me since my mom died." Tears slip from my eyes. He breathes heavily, his voice thick in my ear. "I love you, Iris."

A smile forms on my face. "I love you too, Giovanni." And just like that, we both give in to sleep.

CHAPTER 23

GIOVANNI

I'm woken by the buzzing of my phone against the nightstand. Blinded by the light when I open it, I let out a soft, deep "Fuck." Why would my father be calling me at seven in the morning? I've never known this man to be awake before nine. Reluctantly, I answer.

"What?" Except it isn't my father who speaks to me.

"Is that any way to talk to your grandfather?" he coughs out.

My grandfather Niccolo—my mother's father—hasn't had anything to do with me since my mother died. He said I reminded him too much of her, yet he was the one who told my father to get rid of her. I assume that he felt so guilty that he went back to the old country because he couldn't sit idly by watching my father live his life after her. Acting like nothing happened.

"Grandpa… where is Dad?" I say, sitting up. Iris is still asleep on her side of the bed, twitching when I get out. Not wanting to wake her, I walk from our room to the kitchen.

"He's in the kitchen. I don't have your number, so he let me use his phone," he pauses, like I'm supposed to say something. Grabbing a cup from the cupboard, I make myself some coffee. "Anyway, he just had Angelo pick me up from the airport. Thought you'd want to know I'm in town for your wedding. And by the way Angelo will be in your wedding"

The wedding is three days away now, and as far as Iris has told me, everything is done. I was told I have to plan our honeymoon somewhere warm—*that's* all I've been told. The coffee maker beeps, bringing me back to our conversation.

"Okay… sounds good. I guess I'll see you at the house at some point today. Iris and I will be around." Without another word, I hang up. We'll be stopping by on the way to the beach house. The only thing I was able to keep of my mother's was a watch her mother had given her to pass on to her son. I managed to steal it before my father had Sam remove everything of hers from the house.

Bringing my flower a cup of coffee, I see she's already sitting up. She really is a vision of beauty—long curls falling down her mid-back, bright eyes still half-closed, rubbing and stretching her arms up to the ceiling so the hem of her shirt slides up, revealing smooth skin at her stomach. Just the thought of this woman being mine for the rest of my life eases my chest. I'll never have to wonder what life would be like without her. We may not have met or done this whole relationship in the "normal" way, but neither of us is normal. If *she* were, she'd have left the minute I told her my family was dangerous and had bodyguards following her. But she chose me—and this life—together.

A little yawn brings me back to reality. "Good morning. I made you coffee." I place the cup in her hands and press my lips to her forehead. Sitting on the bed, I add, "I got a call from my grandfather today—he just arrived this morning." I fold my hands together. I haven't seen this man since I was a child. I'm not even sure I'd recognize him, or if he'd recognize me.

"We're three days away, Gio; we knew he was coming. Now, is this your dad's dad or your mom's dad?" she says, placing a hand on my back and running it along my spine.

"Fiore, my father's dad is dead. My father couldn't have come to power if he was still alive." I mutter. In our line of work, my father will have to die before I take power, and I'll have to be dead before *our* son can take power.

"I was wondering about that. I wasn't sure how it worked." Pulling my face so I have to look at her, she adds, "Hey, why do you look nervous? He's your grandfather. When was the last time you saw him?" Her hands slide down my arms to mine.

"Since my mother's funeral. He left after realizing he couldn't do anything about my father." A shaky breath leaves my lips. "He moved back home to Rome so he could forget everything. He even forgot *me*. He didn't show up for anything after that—not even my inking ceremony." My hands tighten. "The ceremony that shows your father you belong and want to be one of us… he couldn't even come to that. Those are bigger than birthdays."

"Maybe he wasn't ready. You said yourself you look like your mother—maybe he didn't want to see how he failed her by bringing her into it," she says, playing with my curls.

Pulling her onto my lap, pressing my head against her chest to hear the beat of her heart, I rasp, "How did I get so lucky, finding such a smart and beautiful woman to put up with my shit?" My hold around her waist tightens.

She chuckles. "Well, you see—you trapped her," she jokes, poking my nose. Laughing with her, I plant a kiss on her chest.

"Gio, stop. We have to get ready to go," she says, standing up to her full height. I grab her chin, needing her lips on mine. She obeys, kissing me back. Parting her lips, I invade her mouth, claiming every inch of space she allows. She pushes me away. "I *mean* it—no sex until our wedding night. Now go," she says, slapping my ass as I walk to the closet. My eyes dart to her. I've never had a woman touch my ass before. She'll pay for that later.

Standing in our entryway, I hear my soon-to-be wife murmuring something over and over. She turns to me. "Do you have everything?" Her eyes are wide and focused on me. Her hair is in a messy bun on top of her head, and her black leggings hug every curve of her body, a slight green crop top showing a sliver of her toned stomach. She looks beautiful with no effort.

"Yes, I have everything—take a breath," I say, pulling her to my chest. Glancing down at her, our eyes meet.

"Tux?" she questions.

"Check," I reply.

"Our rings?" she asks, looking around.

"I'll be right back," I say, releasing her and running down the hallway, hearing her mutter, "Goddamn it, Gio."

I fish the rings out of our safe in the closet. Rummaging around, I also find the only photo I have of my mother, tucking it into the inside pocket of my suit jacket. If she can't be here in person, I want her near me. I grab the rings and head back to the entryway. Iris is waiting with her arms crossed, a death stare locked on me.

"Check," I say like a smartass, holding out a black velvet box containing our matching wedding bands.

"Give me that," she snaps, snatching it from my hand.

We both chuckle as she puts the box in her duffel bag. "You would lose your head if it wasn't for me."

Opening the door for her, I reply, "I would lose my mind, that's for sure."

Her car is packed with everything we might need for the weekend: her dress, my tux, her shoes, my shoes, our suitcases for the honeymoon, and our rings tucked safely in her duffel bag. We're ready to go—just one last stop. Iris doesn't like driving in the city; traffic in Boston is a bitch, and most people don't know how to drive. I don't blame her, so I drive.

Iris sits in the passenger seat with her feet on the dashboard, knees pulled to her chest, singing along to "Don't Stop Believin'" by Journey. I know she shouldn't sit like that in case we get in an accident, but I can't tell her to move—she looks so comfortable. Plus, I've never heard her sing before. She's good, and she's not even trying, just mindlessly scrolling through her phone and singing. Her Pandora is hooked up to the car, playing all her music. She doesn't stick to one genre; she serenades me with everything from Whitney Houston to Nicki Minaj to Celine Dion to Paramore. She loves music. I should have realized it sooner—whenever she showers, cooks, or even sits on the couch, she's got headphones in. How did I not piece that together before?

Pulling into the meeting house, I see my uncle and Angelo standing by the front door. I help Iris out of the car, and we walk to the steps.

"Do you two just hang out here all day?" I say to Angelo and Sam.

Sam, being the smartass he thinks he is, answers, "Well, someone has to be close to your father when he needs us."

Angelo just rolls his eyes, not sure if it's at me or his father's answer. Sam walks past Iris and me, and Angelo straightens his posture. "Don't worry about him. He was just chewed out by your dad."

Putting Iris in front of me, I say, "Why don't you go in and wait for me by the stairs?" and place a kiss on her cheek. She does as I ask—she learned quickly how things go around here. I look at Angelo, who's staring at my fiancée's ass. My hands ball into fists.

"Wanna keep your teeth? I suggest you stop looking."

Angelo turns to face me quickly. "Sorry, Gio," he coughs out.

125

He may be bigger than most underground fighters, but he knows I could ruin everything for him with one call.

"Why did your dad get chewed out?" I ask as I walk up the front steps.

"He forgot to pick up Niccolo this morning," he mutters as I disappear into the house.

Inside, I find Iris in the entryway, talking to a short girl with long black hair reaching past her ass and tattoos covering her arms—Cecilia, Luka's daughter. She's twenty-six and has been doing all our tattoos since she was nineteen. Some of mine are her work, and so will be Iris's. I catch Iris's eye, and she wraps up her conversation, coming to my side.

"Sorry. We were talking about ideas for my inking ceremony. I didn't know I got one, too," she says, leaning her back against my chest.

"Yours will be different, but yes—there's a big party the night after you get your tattoo. They watch us get ours done," I say into her hair, breathing in the mix of green apple and passion fruit that always gets me hard, stirring memories of what we did in our shower.

"Well, then I need to make an appointment with her. She's probably busy enough with you boys alone." She glances down the hallway where Cecilia went, then brings her eyes back to me.

Resting my hands on her hips, I warn, "Go, but be careful. You're still an outsider until Saturday."

Walking away from me, she holds her head high and proud. Watching her sway her hips—adding a little more swing than usual—I head upstairs and nearly run into my grandfather.

"Oh, damn, slow down, kid." My breath hitches in my throat. "Sorry, I didn't see you there. I was watching something else."

He looks me up and down, and I do the same. He's eighty-two, and every bit of his body shows it. His face is lined with deep wrinkles, his hands so pale they're almost transparent, veins clearly visible. He's wearing a dark-blue suit, white shirt, and red tie, adorned with gold chains and rings on each pinky—an old-style Mafia type. My generation prefers to keep it more under the radar.

"Gio, it's me, your grandpa," he says, opening his arms for a hug.

Turning my body slightly, I mutter, "Yes, Grandpa, I know who you are." Reluctantly, I go in for the hug. He pats my back, and I follow his lead, careful not to hurt the fragile man.

"Iris and I are heading to the beach house now," I say, releasing him. "I just had to stop by and grab something from my old room."

He pivots on his heels. "Oh, yes. The bride—is she here?" He cranes his head side to side.

Placing a hand on his shoulder, I answer, "Yes. Give me a second, and I'll introduce you. I just need a moment."

Walking away, I head down the hall and open the third door on the right, slipping inside and closing it behind me. Looking around this room, I start to feel sick. All the memories flood back: the sound of my mother's screams, the gunshot, the feel of my father's hand gripping the back of my neck, forcing me to watch. My back even starts to burn the way it did that first time he whipped me. It's not just my mind; it's like my body hates this room.

I pull back the area rug that covers most of the floor. It doesn't seem like anyone's been in here since I moved out—under the rug, the wood is a much darker brown, almost black, compared to the worn, distressed floor. Pacing around, I find the loose floorboard. I pry it up with a pen I found, reaching into the gap. I feel around for the small box I dropped there seventeen years ago. Finally, my hand hits it. Pulling it free from the cobwebs that kept it in place, I blow away the dust and see the small letters carved into the wood: **I.G.B.** My mother's initials—Isabella Grace Benedetti.

My thumb traces over the letters, trying to recall the details of her laugh, her smile, the sound of her voice. My mind has long since forgotten them. I feel a tear threatening to slip if I don't hurry.

The creaking hinges of the box are loud as I open it. Inside is the gold watch, sitting on a blue velvet pillow, still shining like the day I hid it all those years ago. Tucking the watch into my pocket, I return the box to the floor and replace the board. It remained hidden for seventeen years, so it must be well concealed. I smooth the rug back into place. The memories burn in my mind, but I tuck them away.

I find my fiancée in the kitchen, at the island, talking to none other than Niccolo and my father. **Fuck.** Matching my steps to my heartbeat, I keep my eyes on both men. I cut their conversation short.

"Are you ready to go?" I say, looking at my father and grandfather. "We have to meet with the planner at the beach house."

Iris looks between my father and me. I grip her hand, tightening my hold to signal her. Clearing her throat, she says, "Yes, we were just talking about my inking ceremony. Cecilia's going to meet us at the house later tonight to start." She glances at me, then walks away from the island. "See you all on Saturday," she manages, giving a small wave as we exit.

I let her hand go so I can open the car door. "Are you mad at me?" she asks.

"No, just get in the car, please," I snap. Doing as I say, she slides into the seat and fastens her seatbelt. Once I hear the click of the buckle, I shut the door. Climbing into the driver's seat, I bring the engine to life.

"Are you okay?" I demand, anger swelling in my chest. My hands are white-knuckling the steering wheel.

She pries my hands free from it. "Yes, I'm fine. Look at me." Out of the corner of my eye, I see she's intact—just how I left her. Bringing her hand to my lips, I can breathe again, my heartbeat slowing.

"I don't want to leave you alone with them again. I should've kept you by my side," I breathe out. In a matter of minutes, they could have said or done anything to her.

She catches my attention. "Hey, as of Saturday, I'm gonna be part of this family. You need to trust that I can hold my own," she proclaims.

Pulling out of the driveway, I say, "I trust that you can, but I don't want you to *have* to." I focus on the road, and she stays quiet. Glancing over, I notice her raised eyebrows and wide eyes. "What?"

She lets out a small, cute laugh. "Well, that won't work. We're gonna be married, and you can't be by my side *all* the time." She laughs again.

"I can damn well try," I say, more sharply than I intend. If I had my way, she'd never leave our house after our wedding, but that's not possible— she needs a life, too. "Is Cecilia really meeting us at the house?" I ask, my voice reflecting remorse as I try to change the subject. I didn't mean to sound so angry.

She keeps sitting up straight, staring at her feet. "To start my tattoo. I figured we can use our wedding reception as my inking ceremony, too," she says, turning her head toward me. "You know, kill two birds with one stone." Then she looks back at her feet.

"Wait, *start*? How big is this thing? It's just four letters," I say, surprised.

"Yes, I know, but I have a different idea for it, so she's gonna help me," she snaps back.

Taking her hand in mine, I soften my tone. "Baby, I didn't mean to snap at you. You just know how I get around my dad, and my grandfather isn't much better. I'm sorry." This woman on my right is the only person who will ever get an apology from me.

She shifts in her seat. "Thank you. But you need to understand that I *can* handle myself. And when the day comes that you come to power, I'll be there and I'll have to deal with it on my own." She places her hand on my cheek, forcing me to look at her. "I can do this."

Trying to refocus on the road so we don't crash, I find I can't be the one to break eye contact first. "I need to look at the road, baby. I don't want to crash."

Like it's a challenge, she keeps her gaze locked on mine. "Then look at the road, *baby*. Nobody's stopping you," she says, challenging me. This will be the only time I let her win. My wife knows how to pick her battles, that's for sure, and it turns me on—she knows that, too.

CHAPTER 24

IRIS

I can see the buldge in his pants grow. I said no sex until the night of our wedding but nothing about blowjobs. Getting on my knees in my seat Gio looks at me "what are you doing Mio Fiore" Crawling the top half of my body over the center counsel. "Nothing what are you doing Mio Monstro" reaching my hands i unzip his pants freeing his cock. "Fiore I'm trying to drive" he hissed out; Thumbing the bead of precum across his head "again nobody is stopping you, im just entertaining you" i say sucking the head of his cock into my lips. "Jesus fuck" he breaths out.

Play: Belong to you By Sabrina Claudio

I begin bobbing my head up and down on his shaft. Spit comes to the front of my mouth, letting my body lead the way. Hearing the hissing and sounds that come from his mouth makes me want to keep going. I get wetter with every pass my mouth makes on his length. The deeper I push him down my throat, the more he moans. He fills my mouth and throat. Even as he's driving, he applies just the right amount of pressure on the back of my head, forcing my mouth to the base of him before letting me go to breathe.

"Fuck, Iris, your mouth feels so good wrapped around me," he hums. The warmth in my core ignites into an inferno. With my mouth still wrapped around his length, I slip my hand under the band of my leggings, between my thighs, and down to the apex of my legs. One of Gio's hands leaves the steering wheel, sliding down my back and slapping my hand out of the way. He inserts one finger into me.

"Goddamn, baby, you are soaking for me, aren't you?" he growls. I hum back in agreement.

Pushing myself further and further down his shaft, I hear him taking deep breaths, followed by, "FUCK." He inserts another finger inside me, rubbing against the spongy part of my wall. I start to buck on his hand.

"Fiore, you better cum for me, my dirty little whore," he demands. I buck my hips even more.

Gio calling me his dirty little whore sends me over the edge. I force his entire length down my throat. He's so big that I have to force air through my nose, tears streaming down my face. Gio's other hand tangles in my hair, pressing me farther onto him.

"Don't fucking swallow yet," he orders. I gag in response. The walls of my pussy begin to clench, and I let my juices fill his fingers, dripping down my thighs. Gio bucks his hips, pushing his cock deeper into my throat. With a gag, I feel him throb, shooting hot liquid into my mouth. Freeing him with a pop as he exits my mouth, I gasp for air.

Gio's hand wraps around my throat, and I know it's the same hand that was just inside me, still wet. "Let me see," he demands. Opening my mouth, I watch him spit into it. "Now fucking swallow all of it." I do as I'm told. His hand tightens slightly, feeling the lump slide down my throat.

Grabbing his hand from my neck, I suck his fingers clean. "Do you like how you taste?" he asks. I nod in response. "Do you like tasting what I do to you?"

Looking through my lashes, I lower my voice. "Do you like what I do to you?"

He fists my hair, pulling me to his mouth. "You are the only one who's ever been able to make me cum this much," he murmurs, kissing the spot just under my ear. "Do you hear me?"

I growl back, "Good—it better stay that fucking way."

Pulling into the big stone house, we're greeted by Cecilia and Angelo. I glance at Gio. "Are they together?" I ask.

"I'm sure they've slept together. Angelo's been with half, if not all, of Boston," he says, opening his door.

Angelo is good-looking; don't get me wrong, they even look like cousins. Gio and Angelo are both muscular, but Angelo's body is a different type. You can tell he's a fighter; he has the marks to prove it—scars and tattoos all over. Gio has tattoos, too, but mostly on his arms, legs, chest, and stomach. When he wears a suit, you can't see them. Angelo has tattoos on his neck and face, so no matter what he wears, they're visible.

Opening my door, I see Gio already has my suitcase out of the trunk. I spot Cecilia walking toward me. "Wow, y'all got here fast," I shout over to her.

"Yeah, apparently Angelo doesn't know what a goddamn speed limit is," she says, walking over to us and glancing back at her car, where Angelo stands.

I nod at Angelo. "Are y'all together?" I ask, grabbing my dress from the car.

"Oh God, no." She looks at me, while Gio walks over to Angelo. "The idiot lost his car in a bet on a fight, and I needed to draw up your tattoo, so I asked him to drive," she explains, holding out her sketchbook to show me what she drew on the ride.

When we were at the meeting house earlier, Gio ran off to get something while I sat down to talk with Cecilia—or "Cece," as she told me to call her—and we went over in a lot of detail what I wanted. I told her I wanted it on my right ribs, going down to my hip. Even though she warned me it was going to hurt, I still wanted it. I wanted something to show everybody, including Gio, that I chose this and I'm ready. We came up with the idea of **FAAE** engraved on a dagger with bright red flowers twisting around the blade and trailing down my ribs.

"Oh my God, that is gorgeous. You should think about being an artist—like, selling your work," I compliment her.

She laughs. "I do! You've seen my work on your husband, Angelo, and most every other guy you've seen with the family. I tried the whole 'poor artist' thing, and let's just say I am *not* cut out to be broke." She laughs again.

I remember Gio telling me she does *all* the family's tattoos. I just didn't know he had any done by her—she's only been tattooing for seven years, so I assumed he got all his before then.

Entering through the front door, I'm hit with the scent of vanilla, apples, and a hint of the sea. The entryway is open to ceilings at least thirty feet high, with a staircase on each side leading to an open landing and banister walkway. It looks like something out of a fairytale.

Angelo walks in behind Cecilia and me. "I'll take you to your room," he says, looking at her, then turning to me. "Yours and Gio's room is up—"

I cut him off. "Gio and I aren't sharing."

From behind me, I hear his deep voice. "Ugh, you were being serious," Gio huffs.

I see him standing at the top of the stairs, leaning against the banister with his fingers interlaced. "Yes, I was. Can you help me with my bags, please?" I ask, using my sweetest voice. Angelo and Cecilia are already gone down the hallway to my left.

"Leave it," he demands, walking down the stairs. "I'll get it later. I'm going to show you around first." His hand reaches for mine at the same moment his foot touches the white tile. Placing my hand in his, he pulls me closer and whispers in my ear, "This will be *ours* someday."

That leaves a sour taste in my mouth. I know Gio will take over for his dad when he dies, but I never really thought about it in actual terms. All the houses, all the problems, and all the...everything will be his—and he's adamant that it'll be both of ours. Does he mean *all* as in just the houses, or is he really going to make the businesses mine too? I know he said I'll finish school and then be the family lawyer, but what if I don't want to? I'm not sure I want to know the workings of anything that's done.

He walks with me, hand in hand, showing me the kitchen, the living room, and, as he calls it, "his favorite place"—the pool. Who has a pool when the ocean is only three hundred feet away? Rich people, that's who.

The house is beautiful, but it needs color—it's all white. It's like no one truly lives here. Homes are meant to reflect the people who inhabit them; his has nothing. Making a mental note of what I'd change if I ever had the chance, I'm shaken back to reality by his voice.

"This is going to be your room, because I guess you don't want to share with me," he says with a laugh and a half-smile.

"Hey, we didn't do *this*"—I point between the two of us—"the traditional way. I want at least *something* to be traditional for our wedding." I step into his chest, looking up. "So, different rooms it is," I say with a smile.

Slamming his lips to mine, he huffs, "Fine. I guess I'll just be by myself in that big bed." Rolling his eyes, he points to the door across the hall. "If you change your mind, *that's* my room. Door'll be unlocked," he adds with a wink.

I close the door behind me before I break my own rule. The room is like the rest of the house: plain, no color, no patterns—just a blank canvas waiting to be turned into something beautiful. The bed frame is gold with a white fabric headboard. There's no dresser; I'm guessing one of the three doors in the room is a closet. The nightstands are distressed white. It feels very much like a hospital.

Strolling across the white tile floor to the wall with two doors, I open them and find not one, but two walk-in closets, both identical in size and layout.

"Holy fuck," I whisper.

They're still white, with an island in the middle and built-in shoe storage at the base. Built-in drawers rise past my waist on the bottom, and a clothing rack at the top covers two walls in each closet. A full-length mirror shares one wall with yet another built-in area for shoes. Now I'm curious: if *this* is the closet, what does the bathroom look like?

My mouth drops when I push the next door open. Marble floors climb up the walls, and the shower is so big the tub is actually *in* it. Not just that it *could* fit in there—no, it really *is* in the shower. The large soaking tub, which could easily fit both me and Gio at the same time, occupies a corner of this enormous shower. The vanity is white with gold handles. The sinks seem to be cut from the same stone as the walls and floor. There's a door open in one corner of the bathroom—it's a separate room for the toilet. I've never seen a bathroom this nice. The one at our house is all black, which fits Gio's aesthetic.

Pulling myself from *my* room, I head off to find Cecilia's on the first floor. I fail a few times by opening the wrong doors. Finally, I find Cecilia sitting on a bed that matches mine.

"Hey," I say, knocking.

Looking up at me, she puts her phone down. "When did you want to start? I know it's gonna take a long time. I did some research about the pain."

She stops me. "Don't worry about the pain." Leaning over, she grabs a large jar that looks like lotion from her bag. "I have numbing cream."

"Wait, so I don't have to feel *anything* at all?" My eyes widen.

I'm cut off by her laughter. "Oh, lord no," she continues laughing. "You'll still *feel* it, but without this"—she taps her nails against the jar, the clicking imprinting in my brain—"it would feel more like your side is on fire. This will make it more of a quick poke."

My eyes widen even more. "Okay, so when did you need—or want—to start?" I stutter.

"Give me half an hour to get set up. Then I'll need maybe ten hours," she says, looking around and grabbing her bag, moving it to the side of the bed.

Checking my phone, I see it's three in the afternoon; we'll be done by 1 a.m. Biting my lip, I nod.

"Okay, sounds good. I'll go get into some comfortable shorts and a sports bra."

Turning to leave, she speaks up again. "Grab a ton of water and snacks, too. We'll both need it." She looks up from her bag, tucking her hair behind her ear.

CHAPTER 25

GIOVANNI

"Yo, fucker, you in there?" I hear Angelo rattling his knuckles against my door. I'm hoping if I stay quiet, he'll just go away.

Angelo and I were close when we were younger, but when my father became the boss, his dad just kind of kept us separate. Uncle Sam stopped bringing them around unless it was "family business." I even remember overhearing a fight between my dad and uncle; my uncle was mad at my dad for giving him orders. Of course, my father, being who he is, yelled right back, "Get used to it, Sam. I'm your boss. You will do what I say when I say. Your kids will learn to listen to—" followed by the sound of my father's palm slapping my skin. The sound was all too well known for me to ever forget it. It was never the same between Angelo and me after that. Angelo got into fighting, and he was damn good at it. As it stood, he was undefeated in his underground ring. They even call him *The King of the Ring*. If he wasn't part of this little family where it was already decided what he would do with the rest of his life, he would be a pro fighter.

With my luck gone, he opens the door, peeking his head in. "Hey, you asleep?" he whispers.

"No, just laying here. I was forbidden to try and go looking for Iris," I respond, getting to a sitting position. "What's up?"

Fully entering my room, he says, "The girls are busy. Want me to order dinner? I was thinking we could do Chinese or pizza and watch a movie in the hot tub?" He asks as if he were a shy kid scared of being yelled at.

If he was trying to patch things up or form a 'friendship,' I wasn't going to stop it. Every time we tried to be friends without doing something for the 'family,' Sam would freak out. I remember when we were fifteen, just before our inking ceremony, we wanted to go bowling—one last thing to do together before we became working machines. We knew what was going to happen to our social lives after we were inked. Sam found out about it and grounded Angelo, locking him in his room with a padlock so he couldn't leave.

"Yeah, man, that sounds pretty cool actually. Let me text Iris and see what the girls want." Shooting off a quick text, I wait for the three little dots to pop up, letting me know she's responding. Bing Bing. "The girls said pepperoni pizza," I see, closing the message screen. Bing Bing. "They also want cheesy bread." I chuckle, a smile forming on my face.

"It looks good on you. Just so you know," he says, leaning against the wall and thumbing through his phone without even looking up.

"What does?" I bark out, coming out angrier than I intended.

Shooting me a glance from his phone, he replies, "Chill, I'm talking about married life."

"I'm not married yet," I laugh.

"Oh please, you too have acted married since you first brought her around," he says, stepping away from the wall. "You know it's not a bad thing—to find someone who knows the true you and still wants to spend the rest of their life with you," he says, looking to the ground.

I stand from the bed. "Dude, are you okay?" I ask, closing the distance between us. Between the two of us, he was always worse at hiding his emotions.

After my mom's funeral, my father's friends came up to me, telling me I was a strong man. It wasn't because I was a twelve-year-old boy who just buried his mother—no, of course not—it was because I didn't cry. What they probably didn't know was my father threatened to whip my back if I cried or acted like a "bitch."

Angelo's mom died when he was fourteen in a car accident. She was hit by a drunk driver. He cried at her funeral, and his father embraced him with a comforting hug. When my father talked to his friends that night, they would discuss how Angelo would grow up to be a weak man because he cried. The boy cried at his fucking mother's funeral—why does that make him weak?

"No, and I really don't want to talk about it." He chokes out, turning and heading out of the room. Following him, he looks like the shell of a defeated man—shoulders lowered and head hung low.

Placing my hand on his shoulder, he stops. "I know we aren't close anymore, but you can tell me. I won't say anything. I'll just listen."

Pausing, he just turns to face me. "Nah man, I'll get over it. It's all good." To my surprise, he wraps his arms around me. It catches me off guard. The only person to hug me in a very long time was Iris. This feels foreign.

Pulling away, I say, "Sorry, I miss not being us. We used to be inseparable. Why didn't you want to hang out anymore?"

Stepping back, he responds, "Me? Dude, no, your dad wouldn't let us hang out. Remember? He would lock you in your room or just not let you go out."

I can see him shutting down like a real shutter. "You knew about it?" he asks softly, looking around.

Shaking my head, I reply, "You told me he locked your room when we were going to go out before our inking. Remember?" I question.

140

Raising his shoulders, he admits, "Oh, I guess I did."

Walking backward, I say, "We are grown. They can't stop us now," turning my palms to the ceiling.

Thirty minutes later, the pizza is here. The girls asked me to place theirs on the floor outside Cecilia's room. Like little shut-ins, as soon as I walked away, the door opens and the boxes are snatched inside. Angelo and I enjoy catching up on life. Yeah, we see each other often at the house, but that's in passing. Sometimes we pass each other on a job. He is a finder, and well, I'm the disposer. He tells me he has a fight coming up two days after we get back from our honeymoon.

I planned our honeymoon so that we can be truly alone with no one to bother us. I'm not even bringing our phones. Unfortunately, we will have to bring Iris' laptop; she has to sign up for her BAR exam two weeks after we get back. One week of just us. I chartered a yacht to take us to the Florida Keys and back to this very house.

"You guys should come cheer me on. I'll get tickets for you," he says, taking a bite of his pizza.

"Underground fights don't have tickets, dumb ass," I laugh at him. The beer that we had to wash down the pizza is starting to take effect. "Hey, did you wanna watch that movie still?" I point to the hot tub outside. We used to watch a movie every night in the hot tub when we were little and we came up with our parents. It's like a tradition that we should bring back.

"Dude, fuck yea! How do you feel about the Avengers?" he asks, tilting his head.

Looking around, I want to make sure the coast is clear. "I love the damn stupid movies. Nobody watches them with me," I whisper out.

"Bro, same," he stands with his hands on his hips. "Avengers assemble!" he yells out and walks out the door carrying the pizza. I grab the beer and follow him out.

We decide on just sitting on the ledge and putting our feet in the hot tub. Booze and hot water don't mix well. I don't remember what happened after finishing the pizza and beers. Laying down with my hands interlaced behind my head, I look up to the sky and smile, remembering that in just two days I will have the most beautiful woman, and we can do this whenever we want. Just come out on the porch to see the stars at night. Only one problem with that: no stars in the city. I guess we will have to buy a new house. The stories of people growing old and sitting on the front porch in rocking chairs, watching their own kids parent their grandchildren, falling more in love every day. I want that, and I want that to be with Iris. I want her more than anything. No, I need her at this point. And then nothing. Sleep overtakes me with the sound of waves crashing on the sand that sounds just feet away.

CHAPTER 26

IRIS

Pushing the door open to Cece's room, I see her hunched over her nightstand drawing. "Are you always drawing?" she does and says nothing. Her head starts to bob up and down. I really hope she is listening to music. Reaching for her shoulder, I see what she was drawing. It looks like the tattoo she drew for me but much bigger, with a pocket watch wrapped around the flowers.

Whipping her head around, she says, "Oh, shit, you scared me," grabbing her chest and taking deep breaths.

"Sorry, I didn't mean to make you jump," I respond, peering around her on my tiptoes. "Who is that for?" I point at the paper in front of her.

"Oh, nobody. Just an idea I had. I'll finish it later." She grabs the paper and puts it in her bag. "Anyway, I have your stencil ready if you wanna take off your shirt and lay on the bed," she adds, pointing to the bed. She used one nightstand to set up her supplies.

Pulling my shirt over my head, my hair falls to my back. I decide to tie it up into a messy bun so it's out of the way. "Is it okay if I put my headphones in? I have a feeling I'm gonna need to chill out," I ask, pointing to the AirPods in my hand.

"Yeah, of course. I encourage it. I actually have Angelo put them in too." I feel my eyebrows shoot up. "That boy doesn't shut up unless there is music going," she says, looking around. She sits forward. "He

143

doesn't do needles well." She lets out a little laugh, then, as if the mood changed just that quickly, she looks to the floor, blinking and taking a breath to steady herself. "Alright, let's get this started." She grabs the large stencil from the counter of the bathroom. I take that as my cue to lay on the bed.

After we have decided on the best placement and Cece is setting the tattoo gun up, I interrupt. "So, did you have an inking ceremony?"

Not missing a beat and still laser-focused on the task at hand, she replies, "Yeah, I was born into it, so it's a little different. I got mine at 18 instead of 16 like the boys. Ours already decide where they go, just like the boys," she proclaims. "Same thing FAAE, but ours go behind the right ear instead of on our knuckles. There's a stupid meaning to it that the first generation made up." She pours black and red ink into little cups lined up on the nightstand.

"What is it?" I ask, doing one last adjustment of my body.

Dipping the gun into the ink, she says, "Boys will always fight for the family," she pauses, turning it on and looking at me, "but we girls will always listen to our men because they know what's good for the family. We do what we are told."

Leaning over me, she places her hand on my side. We put the numbing cream on before I change. Taking a deep breath in, I hit play on my phone. Music comes through my headphones just as the needle hits my skin.

There is a deep stinging on my side, much like being stung over and over by a bee. Grabbing the blanket, I squeeze my eyes closed as I try to breathe through the first minute, letting the needle break my skin to the raw extent. The stinging turns more into burning. I change the song on my phone to something a little darker, something that matches with the emotion just a bit better, trying to distract myself.

Evanescence's "Bring Me To Life" rings in my ears as the burning of my skin being ripped open turns into nothing. I have always tied things in my life to music—dances, graduations, parties, and now I guess tattoos. Removing one earbud, I listen to the harmony that the song and the buzzing of the tattoo gun make. "Hey, so I don't know if this is normal, but I don't really feel it much anymore. Is that the numbing cream?" I ask over the buzz.

"So, women have a higher pain tolerance than men. I didn't use that much on you, actually. Plus you're distracted with music. It helps," she says, running the ink down my side and wiping away the extra. Just then, the song in my ear changes. "What are you listening to anyways? I love to be surprised by people's music choices."

"Well, right now it's 'Heaven Knows' by The Pretty Reckless," I hiss out as unexpected pain hits me from my side once again.

Stopping the buzz, she says, "Really? I didn't take you for a rock kind of girl," and starts the buzz again.

"I listen to a bit of everything," I say, hearing a door close somewhere in the house. The song pauses for a brief second, letting me know I got a text. "Hey, the boys want to know if we want pizza. I guess they are ordering dinner." Cece is locked in on my side, her face only a few inches away from my skin. "Of course, and cheesy bread. Whatever topping is fine with me," I shoot the text back. I hear the boys laughing from the kitchen. I didn't think Gio and Angelo were that close.

Thirty minutes later, we hear feet shuffle to the door. I told Gio to leave it on the floor outside the door. I didn't want him to see the tattoo before it was finished; it is his wedding gift from me. We decide on a quick break, and Cece steals the pizza as soon as we hear the feet retreat from the door.

Eight hours later, wrapping up the tattoo with the red of the flowers, I finally get to stand and see the full picture of the art on my side. I am stunned at how it turned out. "It looks amazing, Cece. Thank you."

Turning to see her stretching her neck, she says, "I love it." I can't stop staring at it. I start to think. "If you could have decided where yours went, where would you have put it?"

Looking at me, she opens her mouth and closes it again as if to take back her first thought. "Nobody has ever asked me that. I don't get to make decisions, really." Thinking again, she says, "I would get it in the same space as the boys," pausing, "I also wouldn't be the tattooist. I would be an enforcer." Taken back by her answer, I know not to ask her about it any further.

I help her clean up her makeshift tattoo shop so she can get to bed. She has a busy day tomorrow. She agreed to help McKayla decorate the reception space, and she's even picking up a few things I'm going to need for the inking ceremony. She says I will need to show off my tattoo and will need a different dress. She's going to find that while I do the wedding rehearsal.

Going to leave her room, I say, "Well, you know who to call when you need a lawyer. Just give it a month; I have to finish the BAR," I laugh, walking to the door.

"Wait, you're a lawyer?" she asks. "How did you get them to agree to let you go to college when you and Gio were dating?"

It almost slips my mind that most people think Gio and I have been together for awhile. "Oh, I was already in school when Gio and I met, and when I found out the truth about the family business, I made my case on how I would help the family in some way. I am now. Well, give it two weeks, and I will represent the family in lawsuits or criminal cases," I explain giving a half lie half truth.

Nodding her head, she says, "Well, I'm sure the idiots will make you a busy woman," she huffs, putting her things away. "By the way, that was a good lie but I know everything. I tatted Gio the night he told you"

I leave, pulling my shirt over my head, hiding the new art that's stamped into my fresh skin. Padding through the kitchen, I find the back door open. Going to lock it, I see the boys lying on the ground by the hot tub watching one of The Avengers movies. Gio is lying with his hands under his head, looking at the screen. Neither of them are asleep; they are laughing at something someone said in the movie.

The boys are getting along like normal cousins. I never had any cousins, not that I know of. Thinking about it, Gio doesn't have any siblings. Will our kids have cousins? I guess maybe Angelo's kids. My hand runs to my stomach with a mind of its own. Even though I'm not on birth control anymore, why haven't I gotten pregnant? It's been a month and a half but yet nothing. What if I can't get pregnant? Will Gio still hold his place if we can't have kids because of me? I'm overthinking this. We haven't really had a lot of sex—well, he has—but we certainly weren't trying by any means.

Walking back to my room, I see that Gio's door is open. I sneak in and grab the black t-shirt he had lying on his floor. Replacing my shirt with his, I can still smell him on it. His warm scent of bourbon and leather envelops me with comfort and peace.

Returning to my room, I want to shower, but Cece told me that I can't shower until the morning. I lay on my left side, bringing my knees to my chest, falling asleep in what I imagine are his arms. Closing my eyes, I feel at peace.

I know I shouldn't feel at peace. I am going to be marrying a man I only met a month ago. I have seen this man basically kill someone in our house, I was kidnapped, and forced to marry him. But I feel like I'm doing the right thing either way. I love this man even though I should be scared of him. It sounds crazy to say he's different with me. I truly believe that he is different. He doesn't let me see his monster side unless it is absolutely necessary. Even the few times I have seen that side of him, I know I have nothing to fear. I'm not scared of him. I realize I never was. Even when he told me everything in his father's office.

KNOCK

KNOCK

KNOCK

I stir in the bed, not wanting to wake up yet, when my door starts to creak open. A very cheerful Cece walks in. "Good morning, bride. Let's get you up and get you showered."

Rubbing my eyes, I ask, "What fucking time is it?" trying to sit up in bed. I have a stiffness in my side almost stopping me from moving.

"It is 9:30. I have a special soap for you to use on that. I can help you in the shower if you want," she mentions, pointing at my side.

Then I remember the large tattoo on my side dedicated to my soon-to-be husband. "Oh, um, yeah, if you don't mind. Will it hurt to wash?" I question.

"Not as bad as getting the thing." She takes a tube out of her pocket, goes to the bathroom, and runs the water. Grabbing a fluffy towel for the cabinet, the steam rises around me.

The water running down my side burns at first but then soothes the irritated, raised skin. Running my hand across the colors that brighten my skin, I feel the raised bumps of the lines and letters that are now a part of my body just as he is a part of my soul.

She lathers the soap between her hands, running them across the color. I can tell just how delicate her hands can be, but I also remember our conversation from yesterday: they can be delicate but also coarse and durable. The water washes the soap down my legs, leaving only the new color on my skin. I saw it last night, but the color seems more vibrant today. The dagger looks like a real dagger—the color of the walls, the handle as black as night. The FAAE on the blade is the color I can only describe as ash left behind from still-warm embers. The roses look like blood from the vein leaves, the color of grass on a fresh spring morning. Altogether, it's the colors to represent the Italian flag.

"Are you ready?" Cece asks, wrapping the towel around me.

"Ready for?" I ask, squeezing the water from my hair.

"Your inking ceremony today," she laughs.

I'm trying to catch my breath, coughing. "Today? I thought that was tomorrow after the wedding," I yell out to her as she walks out of the bathroom to the closet.

"It was," she yells from the closet, "but you have far too much to do tomorrow. So I talked to Lorenzo this morning and he said that it was okay if we did it tonight. He said he will be able to get the board here tonight by 7," she says, carrying out a garment bag that I did not put in there. My wedding dress is in there, but that bag is not big enough to hold my dress. My brows arch as I watch her carry the bag. "Your inking ceremony will be at 7 tonight, Mrs. Benedetti," she says.

"Wait, what about Avery and Lexi? They are supposed to be coming up today for the wedding. They will definitely notice something is up."

"Don't worry, I have everything planned out. For now, you'll just wear leggings and a sweater or T-shirt, and I'll take care of everything else." Leaving my room, she leaves the door open. I look to see she hung the dress in the closet now, out of the bag. It is a white dress with long sleeves; it looks normal... then I turn it to the side, and my mouth drops open. The sides are nothing but two strings: one set tied at my breast and one set tied just below my hips. It will show off my entire tattoo, which I assume is the point of it.

CHAPTER 27

GIOVANNI

Bright lights hit my eyes, burning for them to open. Groaning as I sit up, I realize I'm still outside. Oh god, my head. I can't drink like I used to. Angelo and I went through a 30-pack of beer, and I'm pretty sure I only had ten. I need coffee, and like, now. Angelo is nowhere around; he was lying next to me on the ground. He must have gotten up in the middle of the night. My feet were in the hot tub all night, and they are pruned and pale.

Leaving footprints on the cement, I wander into the house. To my surprise, Iris is standing at the counter, her hair wrapped in a towel, my shirt on her like a dress. She is facing away from me; I can't see her face, but I can tell the difference between Iris and Cece. For one, Iris reaches the spot on my chest just above my breastbone.

Sauntering over to the counter where my soon-to-be wife stands, I wrap my arms around her core. Tilting her head, she invites my mouth to the crook of her neck, where I smell her sweet body wash. "Good morning," I say in a rich, velvety morning tone. A deep breath rises in her chest. My hand snakes a path up her torso, enveloping her breast as her breath picks up pace. Tightening my grip on her breast, a small whimper leaves her lips, my mouth peppering kisses on her neck. "How baby you sleep, baby?" My hand leaves her breast, tracing her cleavage to her throat, flexing before settling into place. "Mmhm," falls out from her lips, tongue swiping across her plump cherry lips. "Better than you did, I'm sure the ground sucked," she chuckles the last two words. Holding the coffee to my nose, I release her throat, taking the hot drink to my lips.

150

Iris goes around the island to the stove. "Do you want me to make you breakfast before we start our crazy day and an even crazier night?"

Sending my ears into a peak, I say, "Crazy night—I like how that sounds," smirking at her.

Facing me, she responds, "Yeah, well, you might not after you hear what I'm gonna say. It's my inking ceremony tonight," flipping the skillet in her hand. "And I don't know what I'm doing."

Standing to refill my coffee cup, I ask, "One, we aren't married yet. Why is it tonight?" Pausing, I wait for her reply.

Cracking an egg into the pan, she says, "Oh yeah, Cece convinced your father that it's gonna be too busy tomorrow and do it tonight," she beats the egg like I would beat a target.

"Okay, well then Cece has been to a few of them. Why don't you ask her for help?" I say, placing a hand on her lower back.

Breathing for her chest to rise again, she says, "Why can't you tell me what to do?" Her gaze goes from the eggs to my eyes, then my lips. I know when my girl begs for a kiss.

"I haven't been to an inking ceremony for someone married in before," I give her what she hungers for and lean into her lips. It was a sweet kiss, not a claiming one; I don't need to claim what we both already know is mine.

"Fine, I'll ask her. Apparently, your father is gonna have the board here tonight at seven, so be ready by then for it, please," she tells me, placing a plate of eggs, sausage, and toast in front of me.

"Yes ma'am," I joke out. "When does everything start? I should probably get a haircut before the wedding. I have to look my best," I joke out, running my fingers through my curls.

Waking back to me, she takes my chin in her hand. "Don't you get rid of my curls," she taps her hand to my cheek. "Rehearsal is at 4," she smacks her lips to mine and saunters away.

"It's crazy they were able to get us in at the last minute," Angelo says from the chair next to me. I found him after talking to Iris. He was sprawled out on the couch in the living room.

"Yeah, man," I say, lifting my hand, rubbing my pointer and index fingers against my thumb. "I paid these two guys five thousand dollars each to do our hair and beards. That's gotta be double, if not triple, what they make in a week."

"Yeah, dude," Angelo says, sitting up and looking in the mirror, checking out his new hair and beard lines. "If only I could look this good all the time."

I roll my eyes. "Never heard of a barber; they are in Boston, you know," catching his eyes in the mirror.

"Wait, you're not gonna cut your hair?" I ask, his eyes staying on mine.

"Oh no, Iris would kill me," a smile falls to my lips. "She likes her fingers in my hair," I snicker at him.

"Dude, TMI," a suspicious look falls on his face with an eyebrow arching up. "Well, actually, continue."

"Do you like your teeth, Angelo?" I bark at him, turning my head to look at him. He simply raises his hands in defeat, bellowing a guttural laugh.

On the car ride back, Angelo sits silently, scrolling through his phone. From time to time, he huffs while reading what I assume to be text messages and then angrily types a response. Last night, he told me he didn't want to talk about it, and I'm cool with it. We just started patching our relationship; I don't want to push it. I told him he can talk to me about anything, and I hope he knows I mean that.

I don't have siblings, so growing up, I thought of Angelo as my brother most of the time. Then the fight between our dads happened, and that was the end of that. I wouldn't mind getting back to that. Hell, I wish our kids would be close, kind of like a do-over for us.

Pulling into the driveway, I feel my eyes widen at the number of people I see. People I don't know wandering around the outside of the house. It is complete chaos. People yelling out orders on where to put things, a group of men yelling at each other from the backyard, throwing up a clear event tent.

Tearing myself from the car, I am hit with the aroma of flowers. I see Iris leaning against a delivery van, pointing a man to the house. Three men pop out of the truck, carrying our large wedding cake into the house. Her hair looks freshly curled, and her makeup is freshly painted on. Even though she isn't dressed in her gown for the night, she still looks flawless. A smile creeps across my face, knowing I get to call this beautiful woman mine for the rest of my life. Catching my attention, her lips uplift to a smile, waving at me. "This is crazy," she yells over the noise of chaos.

Striding to her side, I can tell she is flustered—her cheeks pink, obsessively licking her lips. "Why don't you go in and relax? Let McKayla worry about all this," I say, waving one hand to the row of cars and bustling people, the other on her hip. "It's what we are paying her for." Placing a kiss on the top of her head, I lead her into the house.

Twenty minutes later, a knock is rattling the front door. Iris' screams make my chest tighten, air leaving my lungs. Running from the kitchen, I meet Angelo halfway to the door. My brain runs a million miles an hour. I swear to god if another fucker is trying to get into this house, I will burn this place down. Air fills my lungs, and my mind calms when I see Iris, Avery, and Lexi hugging each other, hopping in a circle. Angelo and I shoot each other a glance. It eases my mind knowing Angelo would run to protect Iris just as much as I will, for the rest of my life.

Cecilia runs out from the hallway with a knife, fisted in her hand, wearing shorts and an oversized T-shirt. "What the fuck is happening?" she huffs out, catching her breath. Apparently, it's not just Angelo and me willing to protect. Cecilia was always different from the rest of the girls raised in the family. She never cared for clothes or makeup. She was with us boys more than anything. Hell, she was responsible for most of our first fights, and I don't mean arguments—I mean straight-up fist fights. She said she always wanted to be a button hitter like me, but the men would never allow that.

Finding three pairs of eyes staring at me, Iris says, "Sorry, I didn't mean to scare you." She pauses a quick moment, looking at us three individually. "Any of you," looking at me, her eyes narrow to where my hand is placed behind my back. I didn't even realize I was reaching for my gun.

Angelo is the one to break the silence. "No, it's ok. We just heard what happened at the Penthouse and wanted to make sure nothing was going on."

"Again," Cecilia shrugs her shoulders.

Looking at the girls, I notice Lexi's eyes are narrowed on mine. Taking the girls down the hallway to her room, she can't help but look back at me. I give her a small smile, letting her know everything is fine. Everything isn't fine, though. I didn't know anything about what was going on, and I was going to pull my gun. I was going to go against all my training with even the slimiest chance that she was going to be hurt.

I hear the door of her room click closed. "Dude, something is wrong with me," I huff out, looking to Angelo and Cecilia.

"What do you mean?" Angelo questions, looking over me, just like we are taught—looking for flowing blood.

"Did you not just see that I almost pulled my gun on my wife?" I yell out.

"Yeah, but you thought she was in trouble," Angelo rolls his eyes.

"I was going to pull it without even seeing around me. I had tunnel vision," I say, running my hands back and forth through my hair.

Play: Turning page By Sydney Rose

"Both of you are stupid," Cecilia chuckles out. "That's called being in love," swaying from foot to foot, she continues. "You would do anything for the person you love, forget everything you think you know. Real love changes all of it. That person becomes the reason for your air. They are the first and last thing you think of. They are your literal light in darkness. They challenge you to be better, to do better for both of your sakes." She says, her voice trembling. "You would kill anybody to make sure that the person you love most is safe," looking to her bare legs, sniffing. "Even if the thing you have to kill is your true self and feelings. As long as they are happy. That's all that matters. You would protect them over yourself any day." Tears fall to her cheek as she turns and walks to her room. Angelo is gone from behind me before her door even clicks closed.

I was infatuated with Iris before when I found her on the job, but now... Now it's different. Cecilia put it in a way that only someone who has lost everything they cared about could. If anything happened to her, I would die—not physically but emotionally. yes my body would be there but i wouldn't care about anything or anyone.. When she's not near me, I find it harder to breathe, only catching my breath when I see her again. Not only would I kill for her, but I would die for this woman. I would give up my dreams to see her dreams come true. I surrender every piece of my being for hers. I would jump in front of a bullet for her, fix every piece of her with the pieces I have left of my broken soul. Now that I know what it feels like to be loved by her, I couldn't imagine my life without her—a bare wasteland of nothing.

CHAPTER 28

IRIS

"What the fuck was that, Iris?" Lexi barks out as soon as the door closes.

Looking from her to Avery, my eyebrows shoot together. "You were both there at our house," I say, "when a man broke in and had us all at gunpoint. Gio is still worried. That's all."

"No, I mean the other two?" she barks back. Avery says nothing, her shoulders slumped, eyes open.

Do they really think we just went back to normal after someone broke in? Normal people wouldn't, but again, Gio and I are anything but normal. I can't let them know that. Remembering the story we told them, trying to tie Angelo and Cecilia to it. "Those are his cousins; they work for him," I blurt out. It's a quarter lie. They both do kind of work for him, but only Angelo is Gio's cousin. "He told them about the house, and now they work more as my bodyguards. I scared them by screaming, I'm sure," I cough out, hoping they believe the story.

"It makes sense," Avery finally butts into the conversation. Surprisingly, she's the one who is okay with all of this. Out of the two, I thought Lexi would be the one that was chill. Avery was always the mother of the group. Hell, when I found Kyle cheating on me and she wanted to cut his balls off, Lexi was the one who told me to get over it—you have to get under.

I did my hair and makeup earlier this morning, but Lexi and Avery helped me get dressed for the party. I chose a white knee-length puffy dress with snow-white sleeves and sparkly heeled boots just so I'm not so short next to Gio. I was told not to wear any jewelry. I'm guessing my 'husband' will be giving me some.

I'm still nervous; I don't know what I am supposed to be doing at the inking ceremony. I didn't have a chance to talk to Cecilia between when Gio left and McKayla showed up with her hoard of people and tasks to do. Shooting off a quick text, hoping I can get the answer over text before it's too late and I don't look at my phone for the rest of the day.

ME: *Hey Gio said I need to talk to you. What am I supposed to do at this ceremony? We didn't go over any of it.*

I sat on my bed waiting for her quick response, but it never came. My heart rate picks up, and I find it hard to breathe. Running to the connected bathroom, I kneel in front of the toilet, my hand wrapping around my hair to secure it out of the way. I begin to shake, my nerves getting the best of me. I stay on the floor, trying to control my breath. Everything from the past month hits me like a ton of bricks. I feel the pleasure and the pain all at once. Sitting on the floor, I look down to my leg where a small scar is raised against my skin from one of my fathers test.

I'm ripped from my thoughts when I hear a knock on the door. Quickly brushing my teeth, I walk out to find Gio standing at my door. He is in a full black suit, slicked-back hair, and no facial hair. I can even see a gold chain sticking out from under the collar of his pitch-black shirt. Sauntering over, taking me in his arm, he says, "You look absolutely gorgeous, Mia Fiore." He says to the top of my head. As he holds me to his chest, I can smell that he is wearing the same cologne he wore the first night we met. My mind races back to that night, my core ignites.

A small moan slips from my mouth. Putting my arms around his neck, I pull his ear close to my lips. "Don't worry, you can make me unpretty later," I say, pulling his ear into my teeth.

157

"I feel something cold around my neck. My legs weaken, thinking it's his hand. Flipping me around to face the mirror we pulled from the closet, he runs his hand across my throat, showing the gold chain he placed there. His fingers trace from the back of my neck to my jaw, tilting my head to the side. Peppering kisses on my skin, he whispers, "No sex until tomorrow night, Mia Fiore." The nape of my neck begins to burn. My hands fly to find Gio's hair. I make eye contact with him in the mirror. My eyes burn a hole in his as he bites down harder, marking his territory. "It matches mine," he says, running his hands to the flat on my stomach. His hand flies to my neck. "Think of it as your collar," he says, tightening his hold on me.

My pussy is slick with juices, dripping down my leg. My breath is caught in my throat, my lungs burning for the relief of air, but my mind and body want him—his lips, his hands, his cock. I want the weight of him on top of me, pushing into me. I want....no need for my dress to be ripped off and him to be inside of me. Still looking into his reflection, I see he wants the same. He runs his thumb across my bottom lip. I part, sucking it into my mouth. My head falls back to his chest. I start to grind my hips against him. A groan slips from his mouth. Inch by inch closer to my mouth, a knock interrupts us.

"Gio, your guests are here. Come and greet them," a man yells.

"Sorry, Mia Fiore," he says, unable to leave them waiting. He slaps my ass and walks to the door, holding it open for me to leave. Taking a deep breath in, I fix my hair and wipe under my eyes, in case my mascara smeared.

I don't leave Gio's side all night. He keeps introducing me to people he said I'll need to know. I meet a governor and his wife, the police chief and her husband. These are nice people; they don't seem to know about the family, but again, in order to run a city, you gotta have some important people in your pocket.

Gio pulls me to a man in a blue suit. I have watched this man argue in a room full of juries. Dax Russo, the state's attorney in the Boston area. Gio goes to introduce me, but I cut him off before he can get a word out.

"Mr. Russo, I have seen you in court. You do good work." I say, reaching my hand out. I had many assignments in school to try and break his arguments, and I must say there was no way it was going to happen. Dax graduated top of his class from Harvard Law. If only I could learn under this man, it would be a dream of mine.

Shaking my hand, he says, "Have I had any cases against you? If I have, please forgive me. I don't remember every attorney I have won against," letting out a chuckle.

"Oh no, I'm not an attorney," Gio cuts in. "Not yet," looking into his grey eyes, his hand falls from my shoulder to my lower back, pushing me slightly forward. "One of my professors had me study your arguments in court. I watched a few of your cases."

Angelo approaches us, nodding his head at Gio. With that, his hand vanishes. The pressure that kept my nerves at bay is gone. My stomach twists, and my train of thought derails.

Dax saying my name brings me out of the daze. "So, Iris, when are you going to be done with school?" he asks, keeping my eyes and attention on him.

"I take the BAR two weeks after we get back from our honeymoon," I answer, moving my head up to look over his shoulder, where I see the back of Gio's head disappear into a door.

"Do you have anything lined up for after that?" Dax asks, tilting his head to the left, slapping a small smile to his lips. It just hits me how handsome this man is. When my curiosity gets the best of me, I look to his Rolex and see the small scars that make out an FAAE on his hand. Is he one of them? Of course he is.

"No, nothing set in stone yet," I chuckle back when he sees my eyes locked on his hand. He begins pulling down the sleeves of his jacket. Twisting his watch, the gold catches my eye, and I'm almost sure I see FAAE engraved on the band.

My attention is drawn away when Cecilia taps my shoulder. Pulling me into her body, she whispers in my ear, "We need to get you dressed." I excuse myself from Dax. Following her to my room, a familiar voice stops us. "Where are you guys going?" Avery and Lexi stand behind me. I didn't prepare a lie for this. Cecilia said she had everything figured out. Cecilia steps forward. "Gio needs her to meet with him and the board." Realizing what she said, my eyes grow larger, my stomach twinges, and my breath halts. "You know, to be part of the business, she now owns half of it," she recovers. "They will only have her for 20 minutes. Do you think you could go help the planner? She is making last-minute changes." I stand through the whole interaction saying nothing, moving not a single muscle.

Walking into my room, my old dress is shredded from my body, pooling at my feet. "Okay, you need to tell me what to do." I scurry out, swiping the dress from the closet. Trying to take in all the information being thrown at me, I do what I can to help Cecilia get me into the dress. Feeling her cold hands on my skin, I meet her bright blue eyes. The dress is tied into place. "Who will all be there?" Not sure what faces I am going to see.

"It will be Gio, his father, Angelo, his father, his grandfather, and two other board members. I don't remember their names, though..." Looking to the side at her, I'm nervous. I have to do this in a room full of men. "Oh, and me." Oh yeah, that makes me feel better. So not only do I have to perform for Giovanni, I have to perform for other men.

Cecilia walks me down the hallway, mindlessly telling me, 0what I need to do. I Haar but don't take anything in. coming to a stop in front of the door Gio vanished into with Angelo. The door is dark, almost black wood with swirls covering the frame. Was this door here before? I do not remember from my tour. Cecilia takes my hand. "Just remember to breathe, you'll be fine," she says, giving my hand a quick squeeze. Vanishing into the door, I'm left standing by myself. I still hear the distant noise of chattering coming from the party just feet away. Doing one last final look over myself, I catch a glimpse of the fresh color that now uses my skin as its canvas. What if they don't like it?

Play : Paint it black By Ciara

Rubbing my hands together, I try to stop my nerves from overcoming me. The door flies open, and my mind races as I look into the room—it's filled with smoke. My nostrils are assaulted with the smell of burning wood and leather. Rolling my shoulders back, lifting my head, and fixing my posture, my right hand meets my left at my lower back, showing off the tattoo. My first step quiets the room; all eyes burn on me. My eyes meet Gio's thunder grays. He sits in a high-back chair, his shirt's top three buttons undone, showing the entirety of his gold chain and the upper part of the black ink scribbled into his skin. Passing the men, I hear small quiet whispers and gasps escaping their lips. My eyes never leave his. I stop when I reach his father, looking to my right and catching his eyes on my skin. He gives me a slight, reluctant nod. He stands, placing his hand on my back, guiding me to Gio. The chair is on a raised platform, slightly higher than the flat floor. Gio looks to his father, giving him a slight, quick nod. Bending my knees, I lower my head just as I was told to do. Once my knee hits the floor, Gio grabs my hand, pulling me to his right knee. Not sure what he is doing, I follow his lead, making sure my tattoo shows at all times. Tossing my hair over my shoulder to my back, I feel Gio's hand in it. His warm breath hits my ear.

"I will not have my wife bow to me. You will always be at my side, never below me," he whispers.

When I go to sit at my full height, he pulls my hair, pulling me closer again. "Good job on the tattoo, Mia0 Fiore. I'm proud of you," he says, placing a kiss on my shoulder.

Gio's father is the first to move. Looking at Gio and me, he claps his hands once, raising his palms to the ceiling and shouts, "Mia Figlia." I don't know any Italian, so I have no idea what he said. The room erupts into cheer.

"My daughter," Gio says into my shoulder. The cheers turn into chants—"Eredi." (Heirs.)

CHAPTER 29

GIOVANNI

Introducing my soon-to-be wife to all the people in the home that will be ours one day., I already know she won't remember any of their names. There is one person I personally invited that I know Iris will be very excited about meeting.

I walk over to Iris with a glass of champagne for each of us. I find her talking to Avery and Lexi. I place her glass in her hand. Resting my hand on her back, I feel her muscles relax under my touch, tracing the line of her underwear that only my hand can feel. I start to tease her just a bit, running my fingertips under the band. She squirms, moving ever so slightly. Her breath picks up, and her hand slides around her side to her back, meeting mine, stopping it from roaming her body.

She wears the matching gold chain to mine. If only she looked at the inside of the chain, she would see the engraving: "Only Mine." I want her to know she is mine and mine only. She will be the only person who can get me to my knees, whether it be to apologize or to worship her body. The world will know I claimed her. I am a king in the Mafia, and she will be their queen. Me staying by her side and introducing her to people shows she will hold power in this family.

Spotting the state's attorney Dax Russo. Russo was one of us; still, there is no leaving unless your voted out like Vinny. He came to my father about 15 years ago and asked to get the tattoo removed to become a lawyer and later a state's attorney with the final goal of being a judge.

My father saw the advantage of having a state's attorney and a judge as one of us. It was one of my first jobs. I tied him to a chair and gave him something for the pain. Once he was basically knocked out, I spent the next 10 hours sanding off the skin of his knuckles and burning the flesh underneath to leave as little scarring as possible.

Grabbing her hand, I pull her to stand in front of Dax. I go to open my mouth, but Iris cuts me off, already knowing the man. How the fuck does she know him? If I find out they screwed, I'll kill him. A shake racks my body; just the thought of her with anybody else makes me sick. My mind and body come to a calm when she says he was homework from her teacher. What was I thinking? Of course, she didn't sleep with him.

Angelo walks up to us, nodding his head. Normally I would think it's normal until his hand taps my back. Turning to see him, he tilts his head toward the entryway. Reluctantly, I leave Iris with Dax, knowing he won't do anything to get himself killed.

Following behind Angelo, I see my father, my uncle Sam, and two board members, Leonardo and Francesco, who also happen to be the recorders. Whatever they see is written down into a 'history book.' If it isn't in there, it didn't happen. They have been at every wedding, every birth, and every death.

"What's going on?" I ask, looking at each of the men individually. Did the board change their mind on the wedding? It has happened before. The board says yes but then decides not to let it happen. They would hold the groom hostage while a contract was fulfilled with her name, most likely by me. I've only had to do it once.

My father pours an amber-colored drink into a glass, extending it to me. I hold my hand up, declining the drink. If they are trying to change their mind, then I need to be sober for this. "It's your wife's Inking Ceremony. You need to be waiting for her to present herself," my father says, throwing back the drink. Since I haven't been to any of these, I don't know what to really expect. I do know that she is expected to kneel to me. After that, most husbands leave their wives on the floor or even allow her to stand next to him. That will not be how it goes for my wife. I have doubts she will even kneel. Iris is too strong and independent to bow to a man.

Not noticing my hands are still in a fist, waiting to be used. "You need to calm down, Gio. I brought some cigars if you want one," Angelo says, just like a child in a candy shop. He is the only guy I know who likes cigars at 26. We all smoke them, but he actually enjoys it.

"That's a great idea, Angelo. We will all take one," my father proclaims. "Also, you need to look more family," waving his hand over to my suit, "for this."

"What do you mean?" I question my father.

"Lose the suit jacket," walking across the room to me, he takes my collar into his hands. "Unbutton a few to show off the gold." My father and grandfather both think like the original bosses. The more gold you have, the higher up you are in the family. The new generation thinks differently. We try to blend in and look like businessmen.

With my jacket in a new home on the back of a chair in the corner of the room, I lose a button and roll up my sleeves. Now showing my chain, my watch, and the tattoos on my chest and arms, I hold my palms to the ceiling. "Is this better?" I cough over the cigar smoke. Angelo and Leonardo have already started puffing on theirs.

All in unison, "much," tilting my head to the side, I put the cigar in my mouth, taking a puff on the cigar. The ashy taste of the tobacco makes me choke on the smoke.

A small knock on the door. I'm told to take a seat on the small, makeshift stage at the front of the room. My father and the other three men take their seats. "Come in," my father says in a deep voice.

Cecilia enters the room with her hands together at her front. "I present Iris Benedetti," stepping aside behind Angelo as the doors open.

Play Women By Emmit

The smoke falls around her like she is an angel walking through the rubble of a purged earth. Her head held high and shoulders back, just like the queen she is. Her arms behind her back, walking painstakingly slowly. She passes Leonardo and Francesco, looking at each other; their eyes go wide in shock. Angelo is next to gasp and whispers to Cecilia, who stands to his side. Sam says nothing, just stares at my father and back at me. Cecilia has a smile pasted on her face. Walking to my father, she looks down on him. One side of his lips turns upward. Accepting it, he escorts her to me with his hand on her back. She turns slightly to make sure I can see it all. Taking up her entire side, from her breast to her hip, I see it's a replica of the dagger they used on her—just white, wrapped with red flowers and green leaves, our oath down the blade. It's the Italian flag. My little Irish girl is marked by Italian colors. I haven't seen any other wife with such a big and detailed tattoo to prove they are truly all in. Looking up to her, I grin in approval. Her head dips and her knees bend, touching the floor. My teeth grin. I know it's to show they will obey, but my wife will not be a servant meant to obey; she will help me build. The moment her knee hits the floor, I grab her hand and pull her into my lap, making sure her tattoo is on display, proving she is now one of us.

When she shifts in my lap, I can feel my cock flexing against my zipper, begging to be set free. Wrapping my hand in my hair, I tug it softly, getting her attention. "My wife will not bow to me. You will always be at my side, never below me." She smiles, knowing I am pleased. I put my hand on her back once again, tracing where her panties should be, only to find she isn't wearing any. My balls fill with pressure, needing release. Needing to be inside her. "Good job on the tattoo, Mia Firoe. I'm proud of you," I whisper into her shoulder. My father claps his hands, inviting Iris to the family by calling her his daughter. I take a sharp breath, knowing this is over. I'm not going to have to worry about if they will let this wedding happen. In the eyes of the board and my father, once an Inking Ceremony is done for someone to enter the Family, they are now married. In the eyes of every person not only in this room but the people who took our oath, Iris is and will forever be my wife.

My heart thumps against my chest, feeling it vibrate against my bones, sending a chill down my spine. Listening to the chants filling the room, I feel a surge of power. This will all someday be mine... ours. Iris will be seen as a sort of queen amongst the wives and women of the Family. They must show her the same respect the men show me. All the thoughts of what could go wrong come rushing forward. She is already in with the guys; they all see her as a part of us, my other half. Will the women test her power in some kind of way? Even if they did, she would tell me. Right.

Rising from the chair, I pull Iris to my side, proudly showing her off. My hand settles in the small dip of her waist. Brushing her hair off her shoulder, making it flow down her back, I rest my chin on the crevice of her neck and shoulder. Pushing my lips to her skin, a growl escapes my lips: "I can't wait to tie you up and have my way with you, Fiore."

"You won't get me until tomorrow night." She smirks, still making eye contact with the room.

"That's okay. That just means I have more time to figure out how to punish this ass," planting my hand on her ass cheek.

We exit the room with Angelo and Cecilia at our heels. The girls go to the room to change back into her other dress, hiding her tattoo from the rest of the people. My jacket and shirt are just as they were before the Ceremony. I spot Iris across the room talking to Avery and Lexi. For some reason, I think Lexi doesn't buy our whole story from the other night. With Angelo at my side, "Hey, look into that one for me," I say, nodding to Lexi. "I just don't think she believed the story." Crossing his arms, he gives me a slight nod.

Walking over to my wife, I rest my hand on her back. She continues her conversation with the girls about the plans for tomorrow. I feel a palm on my back. Dax stands at my back, facing him, my hand grazing her ass. "Yeah, what's up?"

"Are you really going to let her practice while you're still active?"

I swivel my head. Even though the people here have either taken the oath or are associated in some way, we still need to be careful.

"You know I can't go inactive until I'm dead, right?" Looking him up and down, "I don't get the choice of when I'm active." I take the small jab at him, knowing even though he is inactive, he still does help; he takes our cases, even makes sure some of them never see the light of day. Once he becomes a judge, we will need a new person in that spot.

"Well, you have my number. Tell me when she is ready. I'll take her in. I'll show her how to cover the tracks." With that, he vanishes.

About an hour later, Iris and I are saying goodbye to the last of the guests. My father decides he will stay in his room here. We find Angelo in the kitchen, pouring us all shots of some kind of clear liquor—my guess, vodka or tequila. Cecilia, Avery, Lexi, and even my father stand around the kitchen island. My father was never one to turn down a drink. Refusing my drink, Angelo takes it easily. Some of the liquid misses Iris' mouth, spilling down her chin and dripping to her chest. Give it one more night, and it will be a different kind of liquid dripping down her chin to that full chest of hers. I feel the grin that stretches to my lips at that thought.

My attention is brought back to the island when my father slams his third shot onto the counter. "I'm going to bed. I don't want to intrude on your young people's party," he says, pushing off the counter to walk over to Iris. My body tenses at the thought of him touching her. He raises his arms. "Welcome to the family, Iris." What the fuck? Is he going to hug her? I have never in my thirty years of life seen that man hug anyone. Iris is three drinks deep. She meets my father halfway for the hug. Pulling her in, I see his lips move and her eyes widen. She then turns her head, and he chuckles. I couldn't hear their exchange from here. Releasing her, he walks out of the room without saying a word. Finding her place next to me, I lean into her. "What the fuck did he say?" Tilting her head up, she replies, "I'll tell you later."

Everybody went to bed about an hour ago. I couldn't sleep, so I decided to go for a soak in the hot tub. Walking across the hall, I knock on her door, hoping she is still awake. I put both my hands on either side of the frame, leaning in. The door swings open, her legs bare, wearing only one of my black t-shirts, plump lips open yawning, rubbing her eyes. A smile crosses her face. Her voice falls to the sultry one she uses when trying to get me to play with her. "Yes."

"Were you sleeping?"

"No," she says, holding the last letter on her lips.

"Get your bathing suit on. Meet me in the hot tub."

"I can't go into the chlorine for the next two days," her face twists.

Running my hand over her bare legs, I say, "But these can…"

Walking down into the stone hot tub, I felt the sting of the hot water on my skin. Fully submerging my bottom half, my muscles begin to relax. Sitting with my back to the wall, Iris dips her legs in on the other side. The moonlight shows her porcelain skin, contrasted with the bright red string bikini pinned to it. From here, I can see her tattoo, and my chest fills with joy knowing no other women have dedicated themselves like she has. Grabbing her feet, I begin to massage them. She was in heels all day. I bet they hurt. Her head falls back, exposing her throat to the crisp night air. Rolling her head shoulder to shoulder, she lets out a low groan.

"Are you going to tell me what my father said to Mia Fiore?"

"No, because I have it handled."

Tightening my grip on her feet, moving up to her smooth calf, her eyes shoot to mine.

"I wasn't asking."

"Actually, you did."

"What did he say to you, Iris?" My voice deepens, and my head tilts.

"He hopes I don't end up like your mother," she pauses, "dead."

"Why the fuck would he say that?"

"I don't know, but he didn't like my response." A small smile crosses her lips, and her eyebrows jump.

"Which was?" She needs to be careful. He is a tyrant and can basically get away with anything.

"Something about how I'll be fine," she waves her hand in front of her.

"Iris actual words" I grind my teeth.

She sits forward, putting her elbows on her thighs. "I said, 'I'm marrying Giovanni, not you. I'll be just fine.'"

*Play: I feel like I'm drowning By Two feet

I throw her knees over my shoulders, kissing a trail up her thighs. I cup her ass in my hands, my thumbs circling the strings on each side of her bottoms, grabbing the ends. I pull the string, and the knot comes undone. "No sex until tomorrow," I say, using a finger to lift my chin for our eyes to meet. "Who said I was having sex with you?" Tugging her bottoms, they fall, freeing her smooth pussy. She's already wet. I can see her juices running to her ass. Looking up into her eyes through my eyelashes, I wait for any sign of approval. Her finger entangles in my hair, pulling my head to her. Pulling her body forward, her lips meet mine. The sweet smell of her arousal makes my cock stand to attention. I suck the bud into my mouth. Throwing her head back, she lets out a small breathy moan, "Fuck." Laying her body flat on the cool concrete, I slide two fingers in her as her breath picks up. Her grip on my curls tightens. Her hips buck to my face. My free hand dips under her swim top, pinching and pulling her nipple. I can feel my balls tighten, wanting to shoot my load in her. It feels as if I haven't had sex with her in a month. I'm that pent up, and I need a release. Her breath picks up, a cry falls from her lips, "Fuck Gio. Fuck me." Pulling my head free from between her legs, my fingers still at work in her, eyes closed, painting. "You said no sex until tomorrow, Mia Fiore." Her eyes pop open, pulling my watch into her vision. "It's past twelve." Swiping her tongue across my lips, "It is tomorrow, so fuck me." That is all this woman had to say to leave my body on edge. She pushes my swimming trunks just far enough to free me. Pushing me to my back, she puts a knee on each side of my hips. If she wants to be in charge, I'll let her. Just this once. She sinks onto me, and her head dips back. "Oh my fucking god," she moans out, moving her hips up and sinking back down on me. The way she rides me is an addiction I never want to free myself from. Her walls start to tighten around me; I know she is close. My hand makes its way from her breast to her throat, tightening around her neck as I sit up, holding her body to mine. "That's right, fucking cum for me, baby," she starts to shake and cry out. Her cries push me over the edge, and I explode in her. I grunt, forcing my hips to meet her mid-fall. I feel her still pulsing on me, kissing a trail from her chin to her nipple. I take it into my warm mouth, biting down on it. She begins pulsing and shaking on me again.

CHAPTER 30

IRIS

"IT'S YOUR WEDDING DAY." I'm awakened by the girls jumping on me and screaming. Avery and Lexi are both bright-eyed and staring at me. My pussy is sore from last night. Gio and I had sex, but this time I was dropping all my weight on him as I came down. I wanted every inch of him inside me. Sitting up and stretching, I feel the ache the tattoo leaves in its movement. I've only had this one tattoo, but it makes me want more. The pain isn't that bad to have something so beautiful on your body forever; also, it's kind of therapeutic.

Smiling, I cough out a "Good morning," looking to the clock on the desk. I see it's 10 a.m. I must have been so tired from last night. Gio walked me back to my room and put my body through complete euphoria, not once but two more times after the hot tub. I fell asleep in his arms around three. At some point, he must have gone back to his own room.

McKayla told me my makeup and hair artist would be getting here at 11. I had an hour to brush my teeth and eat breakfast. Just then, there is a knock on the door. "Who is it?" Avery yells out, trying to shove my head under the blanket.

"Angelo," the voice behind the door calls back. My heart drops. Is everything okay? Freeing my head from the blanket.

"What's wrong?" I yell out.

"Ugh, nothing. Gio just made you breakfast but can't see you. So he asked me to bring it." Lexi gets up from the bed to open the door. Angelo is already partly dressed. He is wearing the bottoms of the suit that Gio picked out and a dress shirt. He has muscles I didn't see before. His sleeves are so tight I think they might burst if he moved his arms much more than he already has. Walking over to the bed, he sets the tray down on the side where Gio once was, holding out his hand. I look to him. "What, no tip?" he jokes out. Eyeing him from the top of his head to his feet, I watch him bring a piece of bacon to my lips. "I would zip up my pants, but that's just me." His hands fall to his sides, then slide to his crotch. I had never seen an Italian turn so red before.

I eat all of the breakfast that Gio made. I really should let him cook more often. I brush my teeth and run a brush through my hair, even though someone will be doing it in about 20 minutes anyway.

Cecilia set up the formal dining room as a space for us girls to get ready. The dining room has a pocket door that we can close to make sure no prying eyes see us. It matches the rest of the house—white with large windows. Sitting in the room feels like a summer's day with a nice breeze, bathing in light. A small scent of fresh laundry floats through the air. The photographer stands in the corner, shooting photos. She stands far enough that I don't actually notice her. She doesn't pose us; she just takes candid photos.

There is something relaxing about somebody else doing your hair and makeup. My hair is pulled low and messy, with a few of my curls falling out and bangs swooped over on both sides of my face, tucked behind my ears. I have little clear stones placed all throughout my hair. While my makeup was being done, it hit me. In a couple of hours, I am going to be someone's wife. Not just anybody's wife, but a Mafia boss's wife. I will no longer be Iris O'Malley; I will forever be Iris Benedetti.

"OK, ma'am, I am done. What do you think?" the lady says, turning me in the chair. I see myself for the first time truly as someone's wife. My eyeliner makes my eyes pop. The black line falls just above and below the white of my eyes, my lashes on full display, making my eyes look wide open and bigger than they did before. My liner and eyelashes are accompanied by shades of almost rose gold to complement them. My cheeks are a peachy pink. My lips are plump and full with just a clear gloss for a top coat. I have gotten my makeup done professionally before, but this is by far the best. "Oh my god, I love it. Can I just keep you in my pocket?" I laugh out.

"I wish, but you can get my number from McKayla. I live in Boston and will do your makeup anytime you have any event you need to go to." Packing her things, she is on her way out. Avery and Lexi put on their dresses in my room. I hurry and have Cecilia help me put on my dress. Once it's on, I have her leave it untied; I want Avery and Lexi to help me with that.

Gio and I talked about our vows and decided that our vows in front of everyone would be the generic ones most people say, but behind closed doors, we would write a letter to each other and write our real vows down. I finished mine two days ago. I did rewrite it about twenty times; I wanted it to look good as it was handwritten. Pulling it from my wedding dress bag, I give it to Cecilia. "Can you run and give this to Gio?" I ask.

"Of course!" she says with a smile. I know people like weddings, but she seems so much happier than normal. Taking the red envelope, she skips out the door—literally skips.

After I am alone, I turn and stare at myself in the floor-length mirror. My dress looks so much different than the day I decided on it. It has long white see-through floral lace sleeves, a sweetheart neckline, but the same lace to my throat. The skirt is a two-in-one; the first part is for the ceremony, flaring from the waist and has a train. After the ceremony, I can remove the big skirt by unclipping it. It turns into a form-fitting gown that free flows after my thighs. The same gem pattern covers the entirety of the fitted dress; it looks like the string of gems that go from one point to another on a chandelier. Running my hand down the dress, it becomes so real. My nerves shoot into overdrive. I take deep breaths, rubbing my thumb in my palm. Taking a deep breath, as my lungs can't intake any more air, I slowly release it, and my nerves settle.

I catch Avery and Lexi's reflection in the mirror. They both wear the same dress—a maroon floor-length gown with off-the-shoulder straps. Their hair flows in curls down their backs, half pulled up into a braid around the crown of their heads. I smile back at them. "Can you guys tie me in?" Lexi is the one to answer; Avery has tears in her eyes.

"Of course we will."

A black envelope slides under the door. I immediately know it's from Gio, but why would Cecilia slide it under the door? Avery grabs it, looking confused. "What is Mia Fiore?" she says, pronouncing it wrong. Trying to correct her, I say, "Mia Fiore—it's Italian for my flower. It's what Gio calls me." I explain, a smile falling on all of our faces. "We decided to write our own vows, but in a letter. Can I get a minute, please?"

"Of course. We will see you walk down the aisle. We love you."

They each kiss one of my cheeks.

Opening the black envelope, I see a piece of black thin paper with a gold design around the edge. Looking at it, I see it suits him. It represents him.

Mia Fiore,

From the moment I met you, I knew you were special—not only to me but also to this world. Your light is brighter than any darkness the world could produce; you are my beacon in this life. I promise to be your biggest supporter, your partner in all things big and small. Last and not least, I promise to love and cherish you and sustain you for the rest of my days. I have told you I love you, but I don't think you understand the importance of me saying those words. I have never said it to anyone. You may not understand my monstrous side, but you embrace it. You embrace me. Every minute of every day you are on my mind. Your laugh, your smile, and your love. You are a marvel that I proudly get to call mine. My personal beauty.

In times of joy I will laugh with you. In times of sorrow I will be your shoulder to cry on. I will stand by you and at your back if you need.

I love you always,
Your Husband

Tears come to my eyes. I know he says he loves me, but he has never put it into words like this. My body fills with the warmth of the sun to my back. Not wanting to mess up my makeup, I grab a tissue next to the chair and blot the tears that fall from my eyes. I haven't had a man give me this kind of love before. Most girls can say that their father is their first love. Mine was only my first monster. Gio will forever be my monster.

Gio may call himself a monster, but I know his truth. He has to be the monster the family sees and needs. I can't say I was never scared of him. That would be a lie. When he told me the whole truth about the family, I cried not because he lied to me, but because I thought they were going to kill me. I should have known better; he would not hurt me. I wonder how many people say that right before they are killed.

Planting a kiss on the paper, in hopes he can feel it. This letter makes my heart grow for him even more. My mind runs to how the day would go. I walk down the aisle, we say our generic vows, and we kiss, then we party. My breathing picks up when I realize that I'll be his wife, meaning he'll fuck me as much as I ask. My center turns into the sun itself.

CHAPTER 31

GIOVANNI

Forcing my arms into this suit jacket is unbearable. The tailor made the suit just right, or so I thought. If I moved my arms past 90°, these things would rip right off. Angelo stands across from me wearing the same suit as mine—navy blue pants, grey shirt, and a navy blue coat with a maroon tie, or at least that's what I was told the color is called. If it's not black or grey, I don't really wear it. Angelo may fill his suit out more, but let's be honest, I'm much more handsome.

Angelo leans over the counter, fixing his hair. When Iris started planning, she informed me I was going to have to find friends or at least one. I have friends. Well, at least I thought I did, but when I sat to actually think of any for some reason, I couldn't. I— If I'm being honest, I only asked Angelo when we were drunk the other night. Angelo reminded me yesterday that he didn't have a suit fitted for him. We ran to the nearest tailor and had them whip something up as fast as they could; cost wasn't a problem. I just didn't want my wife to kill me before she actually married me. Problem though, Iris has two bridesmaids. Oh well, we will have to make do. Yesterday, we walked them both down, and it was fine.

About twenty minutes ago, Cecilia dropped off a purple envelope with flowers on it, saying that I wasn't supposed to look at it until she left. Iris knows that my vows to her in public can never be more than my vows to The Family. She said that she sees it all over social media where couples write love letters or their vows and have them delivered the morning of.

Iris sent Cecilia to drop her off but doesn't trust anybody with any kind of ammunition against me. People knowing she loves me? Yeah, sure. Someone knowing just how much of a hold she has on me can't happen.

Feeling a hand slap my back, "Ready, dude?"

"Ready as I'll ever be." Angelo walks out first. "Give me a minute?"

He walks past, disappearing behind the bedroom door. Once again alone with my thoughts, I pull the tab open and slide the light purple paper free. It's soft like her—her skin, her heart, her body. Thinking of her makes me want to be in her every moment of every day.

Gio,

I marvel at the simple fact that we found each other. You found me when I was lost in this world. You showed me how to love myself and brought me to life again. I love you for everything you were, everything you are, and everything you have yet to become.

I knew that my life would never be the same the night you took me home. I will do anything for you. I will allow you to push my limits in this life. My heart calls to you and only you. I chose you today and everyday. I promise to you that I am yours and only yours.

Always and forever.

Il tuo Fiore

My breath hitches in my throat. She really does love me. I didn't really have any doubt when it came to that. When she cried for a whole day after she was told everything, I thought that was going to be it. I thought she was going to run in the middle of the night. If my father had told me to kill her, I wouldn't be able to. That would be the one contract I couldn't finish. I know her marrying me was a survival mechanism. I accepted that. I accepted that I would have to spend the rest of my life trying to convince her that I am in love with her. We may have started out unconventional, but it has morphed into something true. I thought I was going to be stuck with someone my father picked out—someone who just wanted power, to stand at my side and reap the benefits. Iris wanted nothing to do with this life, but she wants me, and I want her.

My breathing returns to normal when I hear Angelo knock. "Time for the show." I tuck her letter in my pocket, trying to preserve those words and feelings, knowing they will fade when she is fully submerged into this life. The grip on my letter leaves me worried. What if she reads it and doesn't believe it or, worse, realizes what she's getting into and runs? My throat constricts, barely getting air. I feel as if I have a hand wrapped around my throat. "I'll be out in a minute," I cough out, taking a knee. I roll to my back, trying to open my chest. Is this a fucking panic attack? I don't have these. What the fuck? "Iris is ready, let's go!" Angelo yells back. Her name brings memories to flood my brain. Flashes of her come to mind: her smile, the way her lips curve slightly more on her right side, the way her nose wrinkles when she doesn't like something, and my favorite of all, her laugh—the echo plays in my mind, quieting my heartbeat. As if nothing happened, her name brings me to a peace only I know with her. Bending at the waist, I test the water of my breathing, coming to my full height—nothing hitches.

Walking down the hallway, Angelo starts talking to me. I hear nothing, focusing on the long hallway ahead of me. Cecilia told me where Iris was going to be getting ready. Coming up to the door, I pull my jacket open and slide the black envelope from my inside pocket. Looking down, I see how well the black and purple complement each other—just like I know Iris and I will complement each other.

I slid the envelope on the floor and walked to be greeted by Angelo at the end of the hall. "Let's go, it's time for you to walk down already," he barks out, looking at me. Avery and Lexi are already standing on each side of Angelo.

Violins start to play in the near distance, calling my mind to focus. I straighten my back. One step in front of the other, passing faces of people I have known my whole life. People who think they know me. People who think my loyalty lies with them. I pass my uncle, who sits just behind my father. He doesn't even look at me. My father wears a cheap fake smile; what he told Iris comes to mind, and my hands fist. I hate this man—the man who beat me, the man who killed my mother. The man that ruined my life. I pat my breast pocket where I know her picture lays, my hand going to my wrist, thumbing over the gold band around it. My father's eyes follow my hand. His eyes widen when he sees the watch, then he shoots to my uncle's jaw, lips tghtening.

Angelo stands at the end of the white aisle with Avery to his left and Lexi to his right. Their arms intertwine as they walk down to "Perfect" by Ed Sheeran. All three smile and nod at people. Angelo knows every single person, but the girls don't. I'm sure it looks odd with no one Iris knows. There isn't a bride side, just a groom side. When they get to the top of the aisle, Angelo helps the girls up the three stairs I didn't even notice I walked up.

"Please stand for the bride," the man behind me says. The crowd stands. I pull on my sleeves to adjust them. Looking back, my gaze meets her bold eyes. I feel my chest rise and fall. Staring at her, her lips rise to a smile. Walking toward me, I don't think I am breathing until Angelo pats my back. A deep inhale fills my lungs. Her eyes shoot to the crowd of basic strangers around her. It isn't until she sees Cecilia that she nods her head in the slightest, making her look through her eyelashes at me. Her smile widens even more when she sees me leave my space at the altar, moving to meet her and walk the rest of the way. A few gasps come from the onlookers.

I take my wife's hand and walk. My father goes to stand to hug the both of us. My eyes lock to his, and I continue to walk with her hand in hand. I don't want him to touch her, even if it is just to acknowledge her to The Family present—he did that at the inking ceremony last night. I guide Iris to her spot on the makeshift stage. The man at our back speaks, but I hear nothing. Looking into her eyes, the world vanishes, leaving just us.

"Do you, Giovanni Matteo Benedetti, take Iris Marie O'Malley to be your lawfully wedded wife, to have and to hold until death do you part?" The question pulls me from our private solitude that only we stand in. Licking my dry lips, a slight cough falls from me. "Yes, I do," I try, holding in the smile. I'm pretty sure I failed; I feel my lips widen and my teeth show.

"Do you, Iris Marie O'Malley, take Giovanni Matteo Benedetti to be your lawfully wedded husband, to have, hold, and obey until death do you part?" I flinch when I see her eye twitch at the word "obey." Opening her mouth, I wait for her to say no. "I do," she says. "You may now kiss your bride."

Leaning into my wife, our lips crash into each other as the people around burst into cheers and yells. Trying to leave our kiss, I pull her back into my ear. "Remember, you're going to let me push your boundaries." A breath, "Yes," is moaned into my ear. "Good, that starts tonight," I groan into her, feeling her legs clench. I walk back down the aisle hand in hand with my wife. When we get to the end, I pull her close, closing the ceremony with a lasting kiss.

We eat, drink, and party the night away. My wife has no idea what I have planned for her. Tonight I might go easy on her, but tomorrow I will push every boundary she has.

CHAPTER 32

IRIS

Feeling the beat of the music rattling my bones, my husband standing at my back. Our bodies are grinding against each other, he wraps his arms around my waist, pinning my arms to his back "Are you ready to leave Mrs. Benedetti?" his warm breath hits my sensitive neck. It may be the alcohol but my body has been on fire since our first dance. His hands rested on my hips swaying my hips from left to rest. His hands putting pressure on my hips made me think of him driving into me. Remembering he asked me a question "Yes" I replied licking my lips.

My husband grabs my hand pulling me from the tent where the reception is being held. The guests are still dancing and drinking; I doubt they will even notice if we leave. The crisp cold air hits my exposed chest as I'm pulled from the crowd' goosebumps pepper my skin. A smile crosses my face when I see what is waiting for me. It is the largest boat I have ever seen. no not a boat, a yacht. Pulling my back to his front I feel him already hard for me. Just the feeling of him against me makes my center pool.

His lips touch my ear "a whole week just you" he plants a kiss to my neck "me" placing another kiss "no interruptions." I toss my head back with a moan leaving my lips. "Nobody to hear you scream" his whispers hit me "Or cry" I feel his lips curl on my neck.

We are greeted by what I assume is the captain and one stewardess, they both wear white shirts and black pants. I see how the women stairs up at my husband through her lashes when we walk pass. Skipping the introductions Gio pulls me onto the boat and shows me to our room. The walls are a light grey, the bed white but something catches my eye. A big mirror hangs at the headboard of the bed reflecting the room. I can see my husband standing at my back, there is a devious smile plastered on his face as his eyes roam my body. His hand shoots to my hair tugging my head to look up. His front touches my back. "i'll go easy on you tonight," his eyes locked on mine. "but tomorrow your ass is all mine." I feel my body tremble. Not with excitement but more with fear at the thought of him fucking my ass. It's work for my vagina to take him my ass is much tighter and has never been used.

Gio kicks the door closed behind us. His hands slide down my back untying the corset of my dress. A breath I didn't know I was holding escapes when the dress hits the floor. He releases my hair and my head drops, my eyes hit the floor. His hand wraps to the front of my body rubbing the edge of the tender skin that was tattooed just two days ago. Trailing down my side to the sweet spot between my legs, he runs his fingers up and down my thighs. One hand dips between my legs "you are so wet for me aren't you?" nodding my head he dips his head to my neck while plunging one finger in "use your words."

I blink catching his eyes in the mirror watching my knees bend slightly. "I'm always wet Gio" I rush out breathing "I can't help it I'm sorry". Dipping another Finger into me my breath hitches in my throat, my head falls back to his shoulder. His hand runs from my hip to my throat.

"Why are you sorry? It just means I can fuck you as much as I want" tightening his grip "which is everyday all the time" Forcing my chin up I look into the reflection of his eyes. His head dips to my shoulder and I see him open his mouth and bite down. The burn his teeth leave makes me putty in his hand, my hips begin to buck to his hand. His tongue licks the pain away up to my ear "isn't that what you want?" his voice vibrates through my body. His jaw rubs the sensitive skin under my ear making my core tighten. I can't cum yet I want to ride out this feeling until my body breaks.

"Gio i need you in me" i huff out. His eyes darken in the mirror.

"Then get on your knees and beg for me *Mia Fiore*"

My knees hit the floor. I am kneeling bare for my husband to use me as he needs, to push me to the brink of what my body can handle and even further. Looking at him through my lashes, "Please, Gio, fuck me."

His finger grazes my back from shoulder to shoulder as he walks to the suitcases on the side of the room. Pulling something from his bag, I see him in the mirror standing behind me. His hand comes to rest on my head. "Head on the floor, ass in the air." My chest rises. Is this it? Is he going to fuck my ass? I can feel my wetness leaking out of me, running down my thighs. My forehead falls to the plush bed. I feel him kneel between my legs, spreading me wider. A cool breeze glides across my ass cheek. I have never tried anal. I fist my hand, waiting for the pain I hear is accompanied with it, taking deep breaths in through my nose and out through my mouth.

I hear the click of a cap, a cooling sensation of lube hitting my back, making me arch to him. His finger runs through the lube to the rim of my puckered hole. "Relax," his hand runs up my spine, his thumb circling each vertebrae. His touch makes me moan, the pillow not able to muffle the sound as it escapes my mouth.

His finger slowly presses against my back opening. I can feel my body pushing back against him. "Big breath," his voice is the only sound that fills the room.

I reach up and grab the pillow, burying my face into it. Taking a deep breath, I fill my lungs until I can't fit any more air in my body. His finger pushes its way inside. I bite down and cry into the pillow, tears running down my face. The pillow is ripped from under me. I look to see my husband staring back at me in the mirror. "I want to hear every sound you make while I fuck this ass," he growls, really growls, as if possessed by an animal. Black streaks run down my face from my tears.

He retreats and re-enters a few more times, returning with more lube each time. Keeping eye contact with me, he works another finger inside. My body starts to not hate the feeling. A moan leaves my mouth. My body is moving back to him, bucking against his fingers, inviting him in. His fingers leave without re-entering. My body slumps from the missing pressure. His hands wrap around my biceps, pulling my arms to my back, putting my hands on each of my ass cheeks. "Spread your ass cheeks," he demands.

I grip my cheeks, pulling until I feel my skin on the verge of ripping open. I feel so vulnerable and embarrassed in front of my husband. He squirts lube again on what I don't know. Looking to the mirror, I see him holding up a silver butt plug with a bright red gem. My eyes widen. Looking to him, he just smiles. "You're going to want to take a deep breath for this one."

His hand pushes my Stomach flat to the bed., forcing my ass up in the air again. I grab the pillow, pulling it back to my face. Gio doesn't let that happen, pulling it and throwing it across the room. I take in a deep breath, holding it, when I feel the cold metal at my entrance. His two fingers dip into my pussy. The familiar feeling makes my body relax and awaken for him, basically crying and begging for him. The more he pushes the butt plug inside, the harder and needier his fingers become inside me, working the spongy spot that makes me whimper and shake with pleasure.

With one final push, the plug is in. "My good fucking girl!" tears stream down my face dripping to the blanket.

His fingers withdraw from me, replaced by his cock. With one thrust, his hips hit my ass, dragging a gasp from me. The fullness I feel doesn't seem real—it feels like I'm about to be torn apart. I can't stop myself from crying out, "Oh fuck," reaching my hands back to feel for his body. Grabbing my arms and bringing them together at my back, he holds them with one hand, not letting me move.

"OH MY FUCKING GOD," I scream out before I know what I am saying. My ass begins to vibrate. Seeing my husband smiling, I know what is happening. Planting a smack on my ass and pushing forward, he pulls me back full force onto him, making me cry out. "You like that, don't you, baby?"

My core tightens, and I feel a rush coming from within me. "Not yet, Iris," he barks at me.

"I can't stop it," I plead. Releasing my hands, he pulls my back to his front, placing his hand on my throat. I thought he didn't want me to come yet. I could live the rest of my life getting fucked just like this. He knows how to push my pain into my pleasure. Forcing my face to look at the mirror, I notice this isn't for me—this is for him. He likes taking my ability to breathe just as much, if not more, than I like not being able to breathe.

My hand finds his, and I tighten his grip. "Oh fuck, baby girl, yes, take my cock," he rasps into my ear. "All of it, every last drop." Thrusting harder into me, he makes both of us ride the edge. One cry is the only warning I get before he is pulsing inside me. He keeps his rhythm, carrying me over the edge. My walls flex around him, accepting every last drop from him.

I fall to our bed as he slides out of me. He falls onto his back, pulling me into him. "Are you tired?" he asks. I shake my head slightly, letting out a long breath.

"Wait until you see what I have planned for you tomorrow night," he says, planting a kiss on my neck. Snuggling in, I hear the quiet snores that fall from him, followed by mine.

CHAPTER 33

GIOVANNI

Opening my eyes to the dimly lit room, I blink a few times, seeing Iris cuddled up next to me. Her red hair is spread across my shoulder, her hand splayed on my chest. I lean down and kiss her forehead, leaving the room while it's still dark outside. The clock at the top of the stairs shows it's only 2:30 in the morning. Nobody is up on the boat, not even the crew. I pace the length of the boat. Looking at my phone, I see my father called. Placing the phone to my ear, it only rings twice.

"Where the fuck did you go?"

Letting out a breath, "My honeymoon. What do you mean?" I instinctively roll my eyes. I always show him respect in front of others, but he knows how I feel about him. Behind closed doors, he knows I could easily kill him. His body is too frail to fight me off—honestly, it's too frail to fight off the common cold.

"Well, you have a contract. You better come home. It needs to be done soon. Don't take too fucking long on vacation."

My teeth grind. I am not cutting my wife's honeymoon short just because of a stupid hit. When did he get this hit? We only left six hours ago. It takes weeks to get a contract approved. I get called the minute one is even proposed to the board, and since I wasn't called, I assume this is one of his secret ones that didn't go to the board. It doesn't happen often, but once or twice, my father has called me to do a job he didn't get approval for or even petition for.

"Since when did I have a contract? Is it one of your little jobs?"

I hear glass shatter on the other end.

"You don't get to ask questions. You get a fucking name and an end date. That's how this works, you ungrateful little shit."

I cut him off. "I'll be home on Thursday. Just have it sent over to the penthouse then." I click the end button.

Walking out to the deck, I lean over and drop my phone right into the ocean. The boat has lights on the outside, making the water shine blue in the dead of dark. I watch the phone float down until the light can't reach it anymore.

"What are you doing out here?" a soft voice calls from behind me.

I slowly turn to see my wife standing in the dark with our white sheet draped over her small-framed body.

"I couldn't sleep. Why are you awake? You were just sleeping ten minutes ago," I ask, running my hand to my face, running it through my hair.

Her full lips part slowly, puckering to let out a slight breath. "I tried to cuddle with you, but you weren't in bed anymore. I laid there for a little while, thinking you would come back to bed." She looks from me to the water and back to me. "Why did you throw your phone in the water?"

I say, leaning my forearms on the banister, looking at the water. "My father called. I have a contract."

Padding over to me, her hands rest on my back.

"Do we need to head back early?" I can hear the sadness in her voice.

I turn to take her in my arms. "No. It will be delivered to the penthouse on Thursday when we get home." I didn't even think about how she would feel about that. I would most likely be coming home covered in blood or even bringing my target back to the penthouse. "Is that okay? I can keep the business away from the penthouse if you want." I run my hand to her face, thumbing her chin and tucking her hair behind her ear.

Looking up at me, her eyebrows shoot up. "You and I both know that's a lie. The business will always come to the house," her hands run to my chest, running up and down.

"If you want, we can buy a house, and I just keep the penthouse for business. That way, you won't have to be exposed to it that much," I suggest, cocking my head to the side.

"Hey, I know what I got myself into, and even if we did buy a house, we both know it would follow you there too," she says, looking up to the sky. "Can we lay out here to watch the stars?" she asks, looking up at me.

"I'm sure we could. It's our boat until Thursday, my love," I look to the floor, "but I am not laying on the floor. My back will be fucked up for a month." She starts laughing as she walks to the deck just below. I can still hear her giggle while she is gone. She walks back up the stairs with cushions in her hand.

Laying on a makeshift bed, her head rests on my chest, rising and falling with my breath. I know I am supposed to be looking at the stars, but I can't take my eyes off my wife lying with me. My hand rests on her lower back.

"I used to look at the stars when we lived in Alaska. It was the only thing that actually calmed my mind. I had hoped for years that I would just die." I hold her tighter. "When I was younger, I thought that when you die, you become a star in the sky. I know it's dumb." She says, shaking her head on my chest.

I cut her off. "No, that's not dumb. It's a beautiful thought," I rush out, not wanting to stop her story but needing her to know it was beautiful. I feel her fingertips through the thin fabric of my shirt, drawing shapes

"He found me one day, though, and dragged me back to the camp. When we got there, he told them I was trying to run away. I spent the next week bound to a bed, 24 hours a day. I wasn't even allowed to go to the bathroom." My hands fist at the picture it brings to my mind. Her father is lucky he isn't alive. He would hate to be locked in a room with me—only one of us would come out alive, and it wouldn't be him.

"Then the week after that, when I finally told them I was just looking at the stars, they covered my eyes and made me be blind. I learned really quickly not to look at them anymore. Once in a while, I would catch a glimpse of them for just a second and then act like I never saw them." Her breath becomes ragged, and I feel her shake.

"When my mom and I ran to North Dakota, we settled in such a small town there were no street lights. She knew I loved seeing the stars and made sure I got to see them every night. It's what I have missed most since moving to Boston. It always brought me peace, and I haven't really been able to find that since." She pauses. "But laying here looking at them with you, I feel grounded again."

I hug my wife closer to my body. I need her to know she is safe and that she can trust me with anything. "Let's get you to bed, baby. You're cold," I say, rubbing my hands up and down her body, trying to transfer warmth to her. I feel her head nod slowly, but she doesn't move. I stand, placing my arms under her knees and around her back. I carry my wife to bed. She is asleep before her head hits the pillow. I fall next to her, rolling her into my side, planting a kiss on her forehead.

"I love you, Iris Benedetti."

"Mr. and Mrs. Benedetti, breakfast is ready for you," the stewardess announces from outside the door. I stir awake, my wife lying next to me. "Thank you," I shout back. I roll over, kissing my wife's temple.

"Wake up. Breakfast is ready." Her arms stretch to the headboard and her feet to the bottom of the bed as a yawn escapes her mouth.

"Five more minutes," she asks.

I roll out of bed, going to the en suite bathroom. After quickly showering, I walk out of the bathroom with a towel wrapped around my waist. Through the fog, I see that my wife is still lying in bed with nothing covering her. I walk next to the bed, running my hands through my hair shaking my head flinging water onto her bare skin. Her arms flail as she rolls to her stomach.

What I see makes my lips turn into the devil's smile. The bright red gem still sits at her tight ass.

"Fiore, why is that still in you?"

Rolling onto her back, her breast fall free and her eyes lock onto mine. "You didn't tell me to take it out. I thought I was supposed to keep it in."

Leaning my body against the doorframe, I cross my arms. "Oh, playing sub today instead of brat, are we?"

"I always do. I'm a good girl," she lets out a sarcastic laugh, her shoulders moving up and down. Her hands go to cover her face.

"We should get that out of you, though. I don't want you sore for tonight." Padding over to her naked body in bed, I lift my finger and spin it, indicating for her to turn around. My little whore doesn't need any further instruction. She gets on her knees, ass in the air, spreading her ass open with her hands. Her training has only begun, but she caught on so very well, very fast.

She lets out a loud gasp just as my hand hits her cheek. I pop the lid on the lube. The fact that it went in lubed up and has been in there for the last six hours means it will need to be wet to pull it out. Running the lube across the gem, I spin the plug, getting it covered. I can see her biting her lip to quiet herself.

"Big breath," I say, rubbing her back. Her breath becomes ragged as I pull little by little. It's free, followed by the POP it makes when it's out. Her body relaxes, and she falls into the bed.

We did nothing for the rest of the day but lay out by the hot tub, getting sun. One of the good things about being Italian is that I don't need sunscreen. My wife, on the other hand, needs sunscreen more than anyone else I know. Her pale skin turns red in just a matter of minutes. I had to reapply her sunscreen after only three hours. She insisted on going for a swim. Me, on the other hand, would rather not get eaten by a shark. I know it's an irrational fear, but in my defense, when someone goes swimming, they normally don't have a gun on them. So I will sit my happy ass right in this chair and do nothing.

"Are you really not going to do anything? Just lay there and be a boring old man?" she asks from the water.

I move my sunglasses to the side with my index finger. "Well, Iris, you did marry an old man."

"You're 30"

"Yeah, but I feel like I'm 60."

Hands wrap around me, falling to my chest. For the first time in daylight, I actually get to see her stack of rings that sits upon her dainty finger. Her chin hits my neck. "You don't fuck like a 60-year-old man," she plants a kiss on the sensitive spot just below my earlobe, "at least I don't think so."

Pulling her into my lap, her wet body settles between my legs. She lays her head on my chest, going limp and relaxing fully into my chest. My body accepts every curve of hers. The quiet sounds of her soft snores fall from her lips. She must be tired from the wedding yesterday and last night. I'll let her nap for a bit; she won't be sleeping tonight. Throughout the next hour of her nap I reapply sunscreen to her limp body.

We sat down for dinner three hours later. Steak, asparagus, and roasted potatoes filled our plates.

"When you were little, what did you want to be?" It feels odd asking my wife these questions—this is something you would ask on a first date. I'm now just realizing I have never taken her on a date. I will need to change that.

"Well, when I was younger, I wanted to be an archaeologist," she puts her fork down, sitting further back into her chair. "Although I didn't know what that was called, so I called it 'a dino doc.' After the whole dad thing, though, I didn't think I had a choice in what I was going to be. I knew he would have forced me to be bound to someone. It's kind of like marriage. The day I figured that out, I had made a plan—I wasn't going to be alive to be forced into that." Her hands go to her lap under the table. "When I finally got free, my mother and I lived in a one-room apartment. I had a good friend whose dad was a lawyer, and they had the biggest house in town. It was even bigger than the mayor's. That's when I decided I was going to be a lawyer. I wanted to make sure my mom was set for life." She looks to the floor. "It's sad I haven't even talked to her in a while."

"Do you want to see her? Has she reached out to you?" I want to reach for her hand, but it's not there. I want her to have her mother in her life. I think every day about how my life would be different if my mother were still alive.

"Of course I do, she's my mother," she replies, sitting taller in her chair. "But no, I haven't talked to her in about eight months. I've been a little busy."

I see tears forming in her eyes. "After things settle down, do you want to go see her?"

She looks at me with joy in her eyes. "Can we do that?"

"Go on a vacation?" I say, looking around at the cabin where we sit eating our dinner. "Isn't that what we're doing now?"

"I thought that with our lifestyle we wouldn't be able to leave and go on vacation, really."

I let out the loudest laugh I think I've ever done. "Oh, honey, even the mafia knows people need vacations." I take a bite of the steak from my fork, the metal scraping against my teeth. "I'll arrange it when we get back."

I stand from my chair, walking around the table, planting a kiss on the top of her head. "Did you eat enough?" She just nods her head without saying anything.

Placing my hand on her shoulder, she stands, facing me. Her eyes drop to her feet. I push her to the wall, placing my hand on her throat. Her chest rises and falls against my arm. Her breath deepens, her lips get sucked in between her teeth.

"Remember when you said I could push your boundaries?" I growl into her ear. Her head moves slightly; she can't shake it fully with my hand around her throat.

"Oh, good. Remember that, because in about five minutes you're going to forget your own fucking name."

I throw her over my shoulder, carrying her to our room. She hasn't seen the surprise I've set up for her yet. I tied two ropes from the ceiling. I plan on tying my wife up and fucking her until the sun comes up.

Throwing her on the bed, her eyes widen when she sees the ropes hanging just above her face. Her hands grab at the ropes, exploring the feeling of them against her skin. The light in the cabin is dim, but I still see her eyes widen when I tell her to get on her knees. She leaves her arms to hang at her sides. I take her small, fragile arms in my hands, lifting them to the ropes.

Pulling her to her knees, her hands rest on my shoulders. I wrap the rope around one wrist. Her eyes go wide and shoot to mine. Her lips part, her breath falling. A whimper escapes her mouth as the rope ties against her skin. She's tied up. I'm free to do whatever I want to her. Sliding her pants off her smooth legs, I see she's wearing no underwear for me. She knew what was going to happen after last night. Her white tank top is the only thing standing between our bodies. My hands grope her breasts. Fisting the fabric, I pull, and the shirt comes away from her body in rags.

"Gio, that was my shirt," she yelps out.

Play: Like you mean it by Steven Rodriquez

My hand flies to her mouth after the last word. "I'll buy you more," I growl. Her body is exposed in her truest, most beautiful form. I can't take my eyes off her. My cock stands at its full length, straining against the zipper of my jeans. Freeing him, he bounces free. Her eyes don't leave mine.

I turn her to face the mirror behind our bed. Getting on the bed behind her, I see her eyes on me. Pulling all her hair to her back, I whisper, "Don't worry, you'll like what I have planned for you," nipping her ear. Her head falls to my chest. Bringing my cock to her ass, I run lube up and down the shaft.

"Breathe, Mia Fiore," I say. Her breath becomes ragged. With one thrust, I'm inside her. A cry escapes her lips. She's trying to hold her noises back from me.

"I want to hear the noises you make," I demand.

Her body starts to meet my hips in a needy motion. She wraps the ropes around herself once more on her own. Her head falls as her breath picks up. My hand flies to her hair, pulling her head to make her look at the mirror. Tears run down her face, leaving behind black streaks.

"Do you see what I do to you when I fuck you, Iris?" I moan out. She feels so good wrapped around my cock. I need to be deeper. My hands run to her pussy, plunging one finger in. Adding to the sensation, I pinch her nipples, knowing she will be pulling me over in just a matter of seconds. I refuse to cum without making her cum at the same time.

"Oh fuck, Gio," she swallows. "Please make me cum," she begs.

"Ride my cock," I hiss. "I need to cum in you. To claim you."

Her hips rock, slapping my waist, pushing me closer to the edge. I dip another finger into her, moving them faster and faster against the spongy part of her walls. Her breathing picks up.

"Harder, baby, please," she cries out.

"Which part, baby?" I ask, hoping she wants me to fuck her ass harder.

"Both," falls from her lips in a yell.

I move my fingers faster, with my palm hitting her clit, pushing my hips harder and faster into her. I feel her walls tighten around my fingers. Her head falls back as I start to push her body to its breaking point. Biting down on her shoulder, I make her look at the mirror.

"Watch me make you cum," I demand. Her eyes lock to mine, and we ride that edge with each other. I spill every last drop my body has to offer in her.

CHAPTER 34

IRIS

Walking into the penthouse on Thursday, it feels nice being back home. Don't get me wrong, our honeymoon was amazing,, but I missed just being home, having my own clothes. I wore Gio's T-shirts most of the time—I didn't bring a lot of clothes, and all the ones I did bring ended up being torn by Gio when he 'needed' me.

"What the fuck do you think you're doing?" Gio asks from behind me.

Turning, I see his hands are empty. "Going into the house," I reply, confused. Did I do something wrong? "Are you supposed to go first?" I remember the rules that the family has, but was this a rule Gio had? Did he have to walk in before me to a place?

"What? No," his face scrunches together. "I'm supposed to carry you over the threshold. All newly married people do it." A small laugh follows the last word.

"That's not really a thing anymore." I turn to walk away, but my feet leave the floor, and a yelp escapes my mouth. "Put me down," I yell, hitting his back playfully.

"No, Mrs. Benedetti," he demands, and I settle into his shoulder when his hand hits my ass. Putting me on my own feet, he leans down and places a kiss on my lips. "I'll go get the rest of the bags. Be right back."

Stacks of colorfully wrapped boxes cover our living room. I'm guessing they're from the wedding. We didn't do a registry, though—we have everything—so I'm not sure what's in all these boxes. Gio and I can tackle that after we unpack from the honeymoon. Walking to the closet, I find my husband kneeling on the floor with a free-floating floorboard placed behind him.

"What are you doing?" His shoulders jump a bit when I ask the question.

He doesn't turn to me. "Hiding the watch and photo from my father."

I fall to my knees next to him. "He doesn't live here. You could put that stuff out if you want." I rub his back as we speak. "We could hang the photo up."

"No," he says, turning to face me. "I don't even want to risk him seeing it. He's supposed to bring me my contract today." He covers the hole back up with the floorboard.

We finish unpacking, and he doesn't bring it up again. I can't get the photo out of my mind, though. It was a woman with long black hair standing in front of the water fountain at the Meeting House with a baby—who I assume is Gio—on her hip. She at least looked happy, but from what Gio told me, she was miserable.

Gio used my phone to call his dad about twenty minutes ago. Apparently, his contract got canceled—whatever that means. After the call, we leave the house to get him a new phone. Thankfully, the store was able to transfer his old contacts and everything over, even his number. His phone started blowing up after leaving the store.

Walking down the sidewalk, he takes my hand, making sure he's the one next to the busy street. "Want to get lunch while we're out?" he squeezes my hand to get my attention.

"Sure, any place in mind?" I say, looking up at him. The sun hits my eyes, making me temporarily blind. He slides his sunglasses off and puts them on my face.

"Sam's Deli is up here—they make a mean chicken parm sandwich." He wraps his arm around my shoulders, pulling me closer to him.

"Wait, Sam your uncle?" I ask.

"Yes," he laughs in response.

"Okay, sounds good to me."

We walk for a few more minutes before we come up to 'Sam's Sub Shop.' Well, that's a tongue twister. Angelo stands behind the glass counter filled with meats and cheeses. It looks like an old diner, with red booths, black checkered floors, and old Boston signs from the different sports teams around: Red Sox, Bruins, and the Patriots. The deli is empty, though, even during prime lunch hour. Angelo looks up when he hears the bell ringing at the top of the door.

"Yo, Gio, I've been texting you the last two days," Angelo says as he rounds the counter to give Gio one of those half-hug, half-handshake things.

"Yeah, sorry, I lost my phone on the honeymoon. I just got a new one. What's up?" Gio says, releasing Angelo.

Next thing I know, Angelo is hugging me tight. My arms stay down at my sides, squeezed into my body.

"Angelo, I can't breathe," I huff out as loud as I can, which is barely a whisper.

"Oh shit, sorry. Sometimes I forget my own strength," he says, pulling away.

"It's okay."

"That fight I told you about got moved to tonight. Do you guys still want to come?" he asks, turning to Gio. But Gio turns to me.

"I don't have anything planned." I'm not sure if they're waiting for me to say yes.

"Alright, we'll be there. Just text me the address. Same number."

"K, cool. You know what to wear, Gio. Iris, gotta wear a club dress," he says, winking at me. Gio's hand tightens around mine.

"Why, so you can see what only your cousin gets?" I shoot back at him. He lets out a loud laugh.

"Gio, I like her. She can dish shit right back," Angelo says.

Gio's shoulder nudges mine.

Two hours later, we are finally walking back into the penthouse. Angelo's fight is at nine tonight. I have about six hours to do nothing. Wrong—I have four hours to do nothing. It'll take me about two hours to get ready. Until then, I plan to lounge on the couch and do absolutely nothing. The living room is empty; the boxes are gone.

"Where did the boxes go?" I turn to see Gio texting on his phone.

"I had the staff move them to the spare room while we were gone."

Shrugging my shoulders, I lay on the couch with a blanket draped over me. I can feel Gio's eyes on me.

"Stop looking at me. I'm gonna nap," I say. As my eyes finally drift off, I hear the sounds of the news in the background.

"It wouldn't be my first time watching you sleep," he murmurs back.

Sometime later, my body is woken up by the smell of what I think is pasta. I sit up, looking toward the kitchen where I see my husband over the stove, steam covering his face.

"What are you cooking? It smells good," I say, rubbing my eyes until I see spots in the corner of my vision.

"Chicken fettuccine. It was Angelo's favorite, and I know his ass doesn't eat before fights, so it's for after," he says, putting some in a container. "I made extra for you though, if you want it."

Is this man joking? Of course I want it.

"Oh, thank God. I'm hungry—I don't know why; we just ate," I say, rubbing my stomach. His eyes go to mine. I know what he's thinking.

"I'm not pregnant," I shout back.

His hands shoot up. "I didn't say you were pregnant, baby." he says, shaking his head.

Grabbing the bowl, I go back to the couch. I want to eat my food in peace. He may not have said it, but I know what that look meant. I know it's my job to give him his heir, but I'm not ready for a baby yet. At least, I don't think I am.

I slurp the last noodle from my bowl. Going to get ready for the fight, I drop my bowl into the sink with a slight attitude. Not meaning to—I know he wasn't really pushing for the whole baby thing—but sooner rather than later, he'll want one. Or four.

The hot water hits my hair, rushing down my body, leaving the spots not yet wet to shiver from cold. My hair is full of suds when I hear the shower door open. His hands run around me, meeting at the front of my body.

"I didn't mean to suggest you were pregnant. That wasn't why I looked at you like that," he says, rinsing the soap from my hair. "Okay, it is. But if I'm being honest, it's because I don't know if I'm ready for a baby yet or even if I'd be a good dad. I didn't really have a good role model in that department."

I turn to him. "You would make an amazing dad." I hold up a finger. "When that time comes. I'm not really ready either."

His head dips down to claim my mouth, and my hands run to his cock. He grabs my hands, lifting them to his chest.

"I don't want sex from you right now. I just wanted to tell you I didn't mean to upset you, if I did." He turns me again so his front is to my back.

We stand there for a good while, just swaying in the warm water cascading down our bodies.

Ahead of schedule for once, we pull up to the warehouse where Angelo's fight is, at eight-thirty. Gio picked out my dress for tonight—a gold silk dress that hangs from my shoulders to just above my knees. My hair falls in curls, just as it always does.

Gio gives our name to the guy at the front door. We spot Angelo and Lorenzo in the corner in what looks like a heated argument.

"Everything good over here?", Gio asks, with me standing at his back knowing he wouldn't want me in front of him or even next to him. Angelo's eyes widen at Gio's face. Lorenzo is the first to break the silence.

"Yea, Gio, we are all good."

Gio's hand tightens in my grip. I dig into my purse slung over my shoulder, pulling out the clear glass container. "Angelo, we made you chicken Alfredo for after the fight," I rush out before they can start an argument.

Angelo thanks us and disappears behind a door guarded by two big guys dressed in all black. I catch myself looking at their knuckles—or really everyone's knuckles. I want to know who around me is affiliated with my new family. Not many people around us have any kind of tattoo at all, at least not visible ones.

We find our seats in the front row, between Sam and Cecilia. Cecilia compliments my dress, and Sam refuses to make eye contact with me or Gio. Gio doesn't sit long before he is up at the ring with Angelo. A half-naked woman walks around the ring with a card above her head with a big number "1" on it. The girl makes googly eyes at Angelo, who just smirks at her. Oh yeah, Angelo is gonna get laid tonight, although I don't think he has a problem in that department.

I don't know much about boxing, but I can tell when someone is kicking someone else's ass—and Angelo was definitely kicking this guy's ass. There is blood flying; I'm pretty sure I saw a tooth roll across the mat. The bell dings to signal the end and beginning of each round. By round three, Angelo has a bloody lip and his eyebrow is bleeding, but other than that, he doesn't have a mark on him. The other guy has one eye already swollen shut, is missing a few teeth, and I'm pretty sure I heard fingers break. Angelo lands punch after punch, not letting his opponent land a single hit.

The ring of the bell is louder than normal. A deafening yell breaks out from behind me as another bell rings. Gio is on me faster than I can turn.

"Stay down!" he yells at me, his body covering mine. Screams erupt from all around. I'm able to turn my head just enough to see Lorenzo hunched over in his chair, blood pooling on the floor. Gio's yells continue to echo. He screams for Angelo to get me out. Before I know it, Angelo has me wrapped up in his arms, pulling me away from my husband. Gio is dragging his father to the ground while people run in every direction.

I just keep repeating the same thing over and over again: "What's happening?"

By the third time I say it, I think Angelo hasn't heard me. This time, I scream it at him. "ANGELO, WHAT THE FUCK IS HAPPENING?"

Once we're outside, he sets me down.

"Look, I can't let you go back in there. Understand?" he says, grabbing my shoulders.

"What happened, Angelo?" I ask, tears streaming down my face.

Running his hands through his curls, he says, "Lorenzo was shot. And until we know what's happening, Gio's in charge."

"You have to go in and get him out. Now," I demand screaming.

"No, Iris. He has to stay with him just in case."

"What if the guy who shot him is still in there? He isn't safe!"

My heart skips. Is Gio next? What would happen to me if Gio died before he came to power? A million questions run back and forth in my mind. I fall to the ground, wrapping my knees to my chest. Tears pour from my eyes as I start hyperventilating. I can't catch my breath.

"Please," I try to beg, air refusing to fill my lungs, "you have to—" breathe, try to breathe—"go get him."

I close my eyes as tight as I can.

The sounds behind me make me think Angelo went in to get Gio. A loud thud makes me turn. I see Angelo on the ground, eyes closed, body limp.

"Hey there, Iris," a deep voice says behind me before I'm hit over the head. Black. All I see is black—no shapes, no colors, just black.

CHAPTER 35

GIOVANNI

My father lays on the floor of the warehouse, covered in blood. There isn't anything I can do—he has no pulse. He's already dead. The hole in his forehead gives it away. He won't be back, no need to call for an ambulance. The blood runs from his body to a small drain just a few inches from his limp lifeless body.

"Somebody call for an ambulance!" Sam yells.

"There's no use," I say, closing his eyes with my bloody fingers. "He's already dead."

"What? No, he's still The Boss! Do something! Anything!" Sam screams.

Wiping his blood on my white shirt, I stand. "Enough." I take Sam's arms in my hands. He may be my uncle, but he's old, frail, and small. "He's dead. We need to leave."

"We can't just leave his body!" he protests. Sirens wail in the distance.

"They're going to arrest every single one of us if we don't FUCKING LEAVE!" I grab his arm, leading him to the back door where I told Angelo to take Iris. Except Iris isn't there. Angelo is on the ground, unconscious, and alone.

Rage fills my mind and body. "Angelo!" I yell, trying to wake him up. He doesn't move. Thinking he's dead, I go over to his body and turn him onto his back. No blood, no holes—he's just knocked out. I would smack him, but I'm sure that won't do anything. He's used to getting hit and punched for a living. It may not be the living he does for the family, but it's a living.

Pulling him into the back seat of the SUV, I grab a smelling salt from the glove box, breaking it under his nose. He sits up abruptly. "Iris."

I look at him. "That's my FUCKING question too. Where is she?"

Rubbing the back of his head, he says, "I'm not sure. I was hit with something from behind."

"What about your dad?" he asks.

I shake my head, not needing to say anything. Sitting up straighter, he grunts and bends his neck. "Boss, what's our next step?"

I've known my whole life I was meant to take over for my father, but I thought when he died it would be of old age, not murder. I don't care about any of that right now. I need to find my wife.

I'm not proud of what I had Cas do, but right about now, I'm pretty fucking happy I did. We pass the cop cars heading to the warehouse. All they'll find is an empty ring and my father's dead body in a pool of blood. Watching in the rearview mirror, I make sure none of them turn to follow us. Thank God they don't—my shirt is covered in blood that isn't mine. I free my phone from my pocket, shooting off a text to Cas.

Me: *Lorenzo's out of commission. Penthouse in 15.*

Doc: *10-4.*

Walking in the door not even fifteen minutes later, Cas is already inside and has a whole OR set up. His eyes shoot to mine.

"Holy fuck, where are you hit?" he asks, trying to touch me.

"It's not mine," I pause, looking at him. "It's Lorenzo's."

"What am I doing here, then? You said he was out of commission," he says, crossing his arms. "I can't heal a dead body."

"No, but you can track Iris," I growl bunching his collar in my fist.

Angelo turns to face me, mouth open. I shoot daggers with my eyes, telling him to fuck off. She's my wife. I will track her to keep her safe if I want.

It takes another twenty minutes to pull up the tracking on Iris. Angelo keeps telling me I need to go clean up. Ignoring him, I keep my eyes locked on Cas' computer. His screen never changes. Angelo keeps looking at his phone, biting his nails. I've never seen Angelo bite his nails, not once.

Cas looks up at me. "I'm guessing she isn't pregnant."

"No. Why the fuck would that matter?" I ask, anger lacing my voice.

"I told your father when he picked out the tracker that it would only signal with the baby's heartbeat."

"What the fuck do you mean, 'when my father picked it out'?" I growl.

"Your father picked out her tracker. That's how I knew to bring it. I thought you knew. that's why they stabbed her stomach that was planned by your father."

"No, I didn't fucking know," I say, throwing the things on the counter to the floor in one solid motion.

The men talk in the kitchen as I sit on the couch, not hearing anything. I know they're talking to me, but I'm in a trance. It's Angelo who breaks me out of it.

"Were there any cameras around the outside of the warehouse?" Angelo asks no one in particular.

Sam left about fifteen minutes ago. Matteo, the guard from the fight, turns to him. "Yeah, on each door. Why?"

Angelo steals Cas's laptop. "Because I can hack into the cameras. Maybe we'll get a face, and if he took a car, we can track it with traffic videos."

I jump up from the couch, walking to the counter. It takes a few seconds before he has some blotchy camera footage up.

"See?" Angelo says.

"No, Angelo, I don't see anything. Put on your damn glasses—it's shitty footage," I bark back.

"Hold on, let me enhance it, fuck," he snaps. "And I don't need glasses."

I decide to drop it. If we don't find my wife, I'm killing every person who was there tonight, even if they had no part in taking her from me. Whoever took her made a mistake. That woman is the only thing that can check my ass, keeping my dark side at bay.

Angelo's screen clears. "See."

There's a man who stands just taller than Iris, dressed in all black. I don't recognize him. Iris looks scared. I may not know him, but she does.

"Do you think it's the Irish again?" Angelo asks.

"I don't think so," I answer honestly. If she knows him, then he's not part of this world.

My thoughts are cut off by the phone across the room. "BLOCKED" flashes across the screen. Hoping it's a ransom call for Iris, I quickly find that's not the case.

"Mr. Giovanni Benedetti?" the voice on the other end asks. I can hear her clearly, but in the background, I catch the sound of a police radio. I remind myself—I don't know anything about my father to me he is still alive.

"Yes, this is Giovanni," I say, softening my voice and calming my breathing. Most of the cops know that we own a personal security company and multiple apartment buildings around town, with some even out of state. The higher-ups know what's really going on, they are paid to have everybody else look the other way.

"Hello, this is Detective Stephanie Parsons with Boston Homicide. Would you be willing to come talk to me at the precinct?"

Knowing exactly what this is about, I play dumb. They can't know I was there. "Of course. Does this have to be right now? I'm not dressed for an outing," I reply, dropping my voice to the one I use with the public.

"It would be best, Mr. Benedetti," she says, coughing. It almost sounds like she's crying or about to. Please tell me this bitch isn't a newbie, or better yet tell me she is.

"Okay, I'll be on my way."

"Thank you, sir."

Hanging up the phone, I turn to Cas, Angelo, and Matteo. "That was the cops. They didn't tell me he was dead, but they want to talk to me at the precinct. That's where they're going to tell me—I'm sure of it." I grab a hoodie and throw it over my new, clean white T-shirt. The hoodie matches my all-black sweatpants.

Pulling into the station, a scream rips from my lips. I'm pissed—not about my father. I didn't love that man like a son should love a father. It was the opposite. I hated him. I'm pissed about my wife. I should have protected her better. I just don't understand. If she was able to protect herself from her father and during her initiation, why not during this? Who was this man she didn't want to hurt?

When I watched the video, she seemed scared. But he hit her before she got a real, honest look at him. My lungs burn from the lack of air. My face is red, and my hands sting from gripping the steering wheel.

How the fuck did my father know I was going to put a tracker in Iris? And who makes a tracker that only tracks the heartbeat of a baby and not the mother?

Pulling my shit together for the next half hour, I step out of the car and walk to the station. I pull my hood up, covering my face to get into character. I don't want anyone taking a photo of me right now. My eyes feel heavy, like they want to close and stay closed for the night.

But I can't, and I won't, fall asleep until I bring Iris home.

"Hello, I'm looking for Detective Parsons," I say to the man sitting at the desk. I don't think he's a cop—he isn't in uniform.

"Okay, and what's your name, sir, so I can let her know you're here?" he asks, grabbing the phone on his desk.

"Giovanni Benedetti," I answer simply.

"Have a seat; she'll be right with you, sir," he says, pointing to the seats in the lobby.

I shoot off a quick text to Angelo.

Me: *Be back soon. I want a plate on the car, if not the damn car itself.*

Angelo: *Working on it.*

I hear the sound of heels clicking against the floor before I see her. Standing up, I meet her gaze.

"Mr. Benedetti, I hate to do this here," she says, looking around. She places a hand on my shoulder. "We found your father's body tonight in a warehouse."

I take a seat, looking down at the floor. I know it would be suspicious if I didn't cry. I try to flood my mind with memories of my father to get myself to tear up, but none come to mind. Shit. Instead, Iris fills my thoughts. The idea of never seeing her, never touching her again, brings tears that don't fall but sting my eyes enough to appear genuine.

"Do you know of anybody who would want to cause your father harm?" she asks.

The real answer is yes. Everybody. But the police won't be solving this case. The Family will take care of it.

"No," I say, adding a sniffle to make it more believable. "How did he die?"

The detective takes the seat to my left. "He was shot," she says in an apologetic voice. She holds out two business cards. "One has my number on it. If you think of anyone or anything, please call. The other is for the coroner where his body was taken. You'll be able to have a funeral home arrange pickup"

Back at the penthouse, Angelo sits at the island counter with his eyes glued to the laptop, talking on the phone.

"I gotta go. I'll swing by later tonight," he says, hanging up as I walk in.

I throw my hoodie into the front closet. Reaching for my gun, I remember I didn't bring it with me. Of course I didn't—who brings a gun to a police station?

"Dude, you can go home. I'll be fine," I say to the wide-eyed Angelo.

"You sure, man? I don't mind."

211

Crossing my arms, I stand firm. I don't need any witnesses for what I'm about to do. "Yeah, I'll be fine. I gotta come up with a plan to track Iris down. I think better on my own."

Angelo packs his things faster than he can ask another question. "I'm a call away if you need anything—or if you find her somehow, okay?" he says, looking at his bag. His head springs up to me. "Do not leave the house by yourself. We just lost our boss; we can't lose the new one too," he says, his voice deep like he's giving an order.

I run my hands through my hair. "I know. I won't." I hold my hand up. "You have my word—Scout's honor."

"Your ass wasn't in the Scouts," he laughs, closing the door.

Finally alone, I peel my clothes off and walk down the hallway. Passing the bed we both shared—just last night—I hang my head. Will she ever lay in our bed again? I will never stop looking for her until she's found, dead or alive. My stomach turns almost making me sick when my mind thinks of Iris as dead.

Twisting the handle, steam fills the bathroom before I step into the hot water. Grabbing her body wash, I bring it to my nose, taking in her scent. It's the first time since I was a kid that I've been truly scared— scared she'll be lost to me forever.

Tears fall from my eyes, mixing with the water streaming down my face. Every memory I have of her—of us—replays in my head like a movie. Morning coffee on the balcony. Soaking in the bath together. Eating dinner and hearing the noises she makes when the food touches her tongue. It's the small things.

A scream rips from my throat, echoing off the tiled walls. My body slams against the shower as I slide to the floor. The water runs over me, tears burning as they streak down my face. Eventually, the water turns cold, the chill biting against my skin. Shivering, I turn off the shower but remain on the floor until I'm dry.

Crawling into our bed, I choose to lay on her side instead of mine. I need to smell her scent. No—what I really need is her here with me, in my arms. To know she is safe. I held her in this bed, telling her no one would hurt her. I lied to her. Pulling her pillow into my chest, I scream into it, wishing she were here.

I go the night without sleep. The morning light breaks through the curtains, stinging my eyes. I have no will to leave our bed, but I have to. I have to try and find my wife. Throwing the blanket off, I get dressed in something easy to clean. Before I know what I'm doing, I'm grabbing my gun from the lockbox by the front door.

Throwing open the door to O'Flannigan's, I start twirling the bat I found in my car around my palm. The bar is filled with most of the Irishmen in the Boston area.

"RONAN, WHERE THE FUCK ARE YOU?" I scream out.

All heads turn in my direction. I even catch the face of who I thought was my wife sitting at the bar—same red hair, same pale skin. My breath hitches in my throat, only releasing when my mind realizes it's not her.

A man my height stands at the back of the bar. "You've got some nerve coming onto our side of town, Goombah," he says, pulling a beer to his mouth.

I hate that fucking term. All Italians do. Is it true in my case? Sure—I'm in a crime family. But he must not know yet: I'm not just *in* the family. I'm the boss now.

"I know you have her. Where is she?" I demand, making eye contact with a man to my right before turning my full attention to Ronan.

"Who?" he asks, feigning ignorance.

"My wife," I bark, walking toward him. "Don't play dumb with me."

"Why would I have your wife?" he questions, walking around the table to confront me. The men around the bar all turn their backs to the wall, lining the room.

"Don't fuck with me, Ronan. You sent someone to my house three weeks ago to kidnap her." My teeth grind at the words as they spill from my mouth.

His shoulders move up and down in silent laughter. This motherfucker is *laughing*. I'll cut his fucking throat.

"I haven't sent anyone to your house—ever. Why do I care who you marry?"

"SHE'S IRISH," I huff. "So if you didn't send him, who did?"

This time his laugh is audible, ringing in my ears, echoing through the bar. "Well, the only person who cares about who you marry would be your father. Go ask him."

It hits me like a ton of bricks—the world doesn't know he's dead yet. If Ronan had my father killed, he wouldn't have told me to go ask him. He didn't do it, and I doubt he had anything to do with taking Iris. Don't get me wrong—we have plenty of enemies in this town. It's not just the Italians and the Irish.

"Who's Kallum McKenzie?" I ask, the name lingering in my mind. Saying it makes my back ache where the whips hit me.

His eyes dart around the room. "Anybody know the name?" he asks aloud. The room erupts into murmurs.

"Shut up!" he barks, and the room falls silent again. "If you know the man, raise your fucking hand."

Not a single hand is raised. Ronan looks around the room. "He's not with us. Sorry, Benedetti—we don't have your wife, and we never sent anybody after her," he says, slowly walking toward me, his hands in his front pockets. "I hope you find your wife, but you're not invited here anymore. Leave."

He says it with sorrow, a softness in his voice, like he knows what I'm going through.

"I apologize for assuming it was you. Thank you for some clarity."

I walk out, but I don't give them my back. I know I'm not myself, but I'm not that out of it.

Getting into my car, I punch the steering wheel, screaming into the air. The anger I feel fills the confined space. I scream until my lungs burn and no sound comes out anymore.

The long drive home feels dreadful. That place isn't really my home— not anymore. Not when she's not there. That's it. My mind is made up. When I find her—not *if*—we're leaving the penthouse. I will not sleep until I find her and hold her in my arms again.

Rain hits my windshield, bringing me back to the task at hand.

FINDING MY WIFE.

CHAPTER 36

IRIS

My eyes open to the dim light swinging above me, they feel heavy and tired. I try to rub my head, but I can't move my arms. Opening my eyes as much as I can, I see that I'm strapped to a chair in the middle of a concrete room with no windows. Stairs lead up from the corner. A basement?

Is this another initiation? I was told I was done, but even Gio said his dad... *Gio.*

My mind races back through what feels like an hour ago. Was Gio alive? *Angelo—oh my God—he was lying on the ground next to me, not moving. Was he dead?*

If they're alive, I know one person who isn't: Lorenzo. I saw him bleeding out, his blood pooling on the floor in a red waterfall. The memory of it turns my stomach. Then I remember the person who hit Angelo and me. My throat burns as vomit crawls up, desperate to be set free. Leaning as far over as I can, I let it spill onto the floor.

I need to get out of here. *Now.* This isn't another initiation.

Rocking back and forth on the chair, I hear a door creak open somewhere above me. Heavy boots stomp down the stairs to my right. I close my eyes as tightly as I can, willing him to think I'm still unconscious. Reminding myself that Gio will come for me—*he won't let this man stand in his way of taking me home.*

SMACK.

A sharp hand slides across my face, making my eyes shoot open. My breath is heavy. I can't let him win.

Blinking, I look to my side. A laugh cuts through me as I feel a sharp poke on my arm. I look down and see him pushing the plunger of a needle, forcing a clear liquid into my veins.

"MY HUSBAND IS GOING TO FIND ME, AND WHEN HE DOES, HE'S GOING TO SKIN YOU!" I scream at him, my voice cracking just as I hear the door slam shut at the top of the stairs.

My eyes flutter shut, then close for the final time of the night.

CHAPTER 37

GIOVANNI

I feel like I haven't slept in six days. My house has been empty for six fucking days. Not really empty—Angelo has been crashing on my couch. He insists I can't be left alone in case someone tries to kill me. As if I'm not a trained killer myself. After he found out about me going to O'Flannagian's.

Yesterday was my father's funeral, and I felt nothing for him. No sadness that he was gone. Only anger. Anger at the person who took my wife. I will get her back. Tears came to my eyes when the grave was filled—not for the bastard in the coffin, but for the thought that one day it might be my wife if I don't find her soon.

I lay in our bed with her pillow pulled to my chest, as I've done every night since she was taken. Running my hand down my face, the stubble pokes against my palm. I can't shave. I can't shower. I don't want to eat, but Angelo basically shoves food down my throat. I pull myself from the bed that's memorized my body all too well.

Walking to the living room, I find Angelo lying on my couch.

"Is everything okay?" he asks, sitting up.

"Yeah, why wouldn't it be?" I whisper back to him in a monotone.

"Well, it's before noon, and you're out of bed without me pulling you out of it."

"You're not my keeper, Angelo. You can go home," I hiss, pouring a cup of coffee.

"Dude, are you sure you're okay? Your dad didn't even act like this after your mom died," he questions.

Throwing my cup into the sink, it shatters. "THAT'S BECAUSE HE FUCKING MURDERED HER!" I scream, not looking at him.

Finally turning to meet his gaze, I see his face is frozen. "What do you mean?"

Walking toward him, I start to tell the story, leaving out the part about him whipping my back. That's my secret. The only person I ever told was Iris, and that's where it ends. Nobody else will know the damage he did to me—my body or my mind.

Angelo wraps his arms around me. "I didn't know. I'm sorry," he says, taking a step back to sit in the chair at the island. "You should sit down. I have something to tell you."

I take a seat across the counter from him. "My dad had him killed," he says, his tone even and emotionless.

"Killed who?" I ask, leaning forward and gripping the counter.

Angelo looks up at me, his eyes wet but no tears falling. "Your dad."

"How do you know that?" I demand, my hands tightening on the counter.

"I walked in on him talking to some guy about it. The guy wasn't even affiliated. That's what you saw—we were arguing because I didn't want him at the fight. I knew it was going down, but I didn't know when or where. I couldn't come out and tell him word for word yet."

I pace back and forth in the kitchen, rubbing my hands together. So my uncle had my father killed. But why? "Why? Why did he do it?" Not that I care. He's dead—I wouldn't change that even if I could. I never needed him, and I don't need him now.

"That, I don't know. He didn't say. After i left here that night I went to his house to confront him but he wasn't there" he paused slightly "and I can't find him."

"But wait," I pause, the pieces clicking into place, "your dad gets nothing when he dies. *I* get it all. Me and Iris." I walk toward him, pinning him against the wall, my forearm goes to his throat. "Did your father take my FUCKING WIFE?"

The last words rip from my throat, raw and painful. My voice feels shredded from yelling so much these past few days. "I swear to God, Angelo, you better fucking tell the truth, or I'm going to kill your dad and make you watch,then kill you"

Angelo's hands claw at mine, wrapped tightly around his neck. His face begins to turn blue. Loosening my grip just enough, he starts coughing. "No," he rasps, gasping for air. "His plan... was to kill you both."

"Why?" I demand, releasing his throat.

He hunches over, clutching his knees, still rasping for air. "I think he wants power," he finally chokes out.

So my uncle wanted to kill me for power. But why is Angelo telling me? "Why are you telling me this?"

He looks up, laughing bitterly. "You're not the only person who hates their father. I saw how you were at his funeral. You didn't care about that fucker."

I mean, he isn't wrong.

"I don't care that he killed him," I say, pausing, "but you know I'm going to have to do something in retaliation, right?"

"Oh, I know. I want him dead, and I want to be the one to kill him." he says standing at his full height,

They always seemed close to me. Sitting on the chair, I ask, "Why do you want him dead?"

"I never asked you why you don't care if yours is dead. Don't ask me that."

I put my hands up. "Fair enough," I say, dropping the conversation.

We spend the next two hours talking about how we're going to do it. Angelo wants to handle it off the books, but if the board finds out, they could send someone after us. Angelo stops talking when I bring up the board, his eyes locking with mine.

"I'll do it so it can't get back to you," he says.

"What? No. We do it together or not at all," I reply to his back as he turns to grab a drink. "Plus, he may not have taken her, but he knows who did."

Coming back to my side, he hands me a glass of amber liquid.

Angelo falls asleep on my couch, while I, once again, just lay in bed, not sleeping. I can't help it. I think about the things she's been through. I *know* she's alive. I have a gut feeling, but nothing can settle my mind. My thoughts drift to us sitting on a porch, watching our two kids play outside. The boy with her hair color but my curls. The girl, a splitting image of her. For the first time in days, I feel my lips turn into a smile.

I wake up to the rattling of Angelo's fist on the door. "Yo, you up?"

Throwing the blanket off me, I walk to the door and throw it open. "Do you need to do anything today?" I ask him.

He looks around, confused. "No, why?"

I know what I need to do. "Want to go house hunting with me?" I ask.

When I bring my wife home, I want her to have a space where the business is not allowed for any reason—unless she invites it.

Angelo looks around. "What do you need a house for? You have the penthouse."

"I want a house just for me, Iris, and the kids—when we have them," I explain simply.

Angelo looks at the floor before glancing back up. "What if she…"

I stop him, knowing what he's going to say. "Stop. She is alive, and I'm going to make sure we have a home when she gets back."

"Okay," he says, nodding.

Two days later, we've seen every house suitable for my wife and future kids. Angelo tagged along but didn't have much to say. His eyes were glued to his phone the entire time, texting.

I finally settled on a house with six bedrooms and seven bathrooms. It's large enough for her to entertain people if she chooses. It's missing two things I had in mind—a porch and a surprise for Iris. I already called Marco, our head construction guy, and he knows what I want. He'll send over the plans soon. One good thing about being the boss is that when I want something done, it gets done first.

It's been two weeks since she was taken. I managed to get an hour or two of sleep lastnight. I still haven't shaved, but Angelo forced me to shower. He said the house was starting to get a "funk," whatever that means. He literally sat in the bathroom to make sure I actually showered. Of course, he saw me bring her body wash to my nose. Not only did I smell it, but her pillow had started losing its scent, so I used it to wash the pillowcase. I need her scent to calm me. I even debated washing my clothes in it.

Angelo hasn't left my house since he told me about his dad going for power. We've decided to focus on one thing at a time, and my wife comes first. We haven't made a solid plan for Sam yet—just pieces of one.

I lay on the balcony connected to our room, looking up at the stars, praying Iris is looking at the same sky. The bedroom door opens, and I see Angelo walking toward me. He doesn't look like himself. He looks... sad.

"Do you want to watch a movie?" he asks.

"What do you want to watch?" I ask back.

"I don't know. Something funny, maybe," he answers.

"Sure. I'll make popcorn. You can pick whatever one you want."

CHAPTER 38

IRIS

I don't know how long Michael has kept me down here. I have no clock, no windows, and he wouldn't tell me if I asked. The only time he comes down is to hit me into submission, force food down my throat, or drug me. What's the point of taking me if he doesn't actually *do* anything? He slaps me around a time or two, but he did that before. It doesn't affect me anymore.

I need to find a way out. I overheard him on the phone upstairs, talking to a man he called Sam. I only know one Sam—Gio's uncle. I heard Michael admit the whole plan: Sam had him kill Lorenzo, and Gio is next. As for me, Sam doesn't care. Nobody would follow me if Gio died.

I may be his wife, but I don't know how to run the family. Even I know that. Plus, I don't have any heirs for Gio. I was worthless when Michael took me. Sam wants power, and he's going to kill us for it. But I *know* Gio isn't dead—I keep hearing them make plans for him.

The basement door creaks open.

"Iris, are you awake yet?" Michael calls down.

"Yup, just down here contemplating ways to kill you when I get out," I chuckle back. If he wants to play crazy, I'll play too, and beat him at his own game.

His dark, almost black, eyes burn holes into my soul as he glares at me. "You think you're smart, don't you?"

He pulls a knife from his back pocket and runs it down my side. "I'm going to carve that tattoo off of you," he sneers. The blade pokes through my shirt, and I squirm, pushing my body as far into the chair as I can. My stomach turns violently, and I vomit all over him, spitting it onto his chest and face.

"You dirty bitch!" he yells, backhanding me.

My head snaps to the left, blood dripping to the floor. I taste copper as I reply, "Funny enough, my husband has called me that"—a smile spreads across my face, blood coating my teeth—"but for many different reasons." I add a wink to fuel the fire.

Michael stomps up the stairs, slamming the door behind him. I hear the locks click—one, two, three, four times.

Left alone with my thoughts, I imagine the things Giovanni will do to him when he finds me. They call him a monster, and I *can't wait* to see him let that side of himself free. Maybe he'll even let me help. I've never wanted to torture anyone before, but the idea of helping my husband brings a certain joy, torturing him the way he tortured me.

Michael brings food down to me, allowing me to eat with one hand uncuffed from the chair. Today, it's tomato soup, noodles, and a piece of bread. I manage to keep down some noodles and bread, but the drug he keeps pumping into me is messing with my body. Throwing up hurts more and more the less I eat.

My whole body aches. I haven't moved in—I don't even know how long. I haven't slept. My body forces me to stay awake. I've pissed on myself, knowing he won't let me up to use the bathroom. I'm terrified of him, but I refuse to show it. I refuse to give him that power.

I've taken control of my life before. I've turned it around. I won't let Michael ruin it, again I know Gio will find a way to save me—or I'll save myself, just like I did all those years ago.

Tears roll down my face. I suck in as much air as my lungs can hold, trying to sob quietly. My chest burns with every cry, every ragged breath leaving it. I begin rocking back and forth again, hoping the chair's screws are loosening, but I have no luck. Throwing my head back, I scream. The sound echoes in the bare room, building pressure in my head. Shaking my head does nothing to ease the pain—it only makes me lean over and vomit everything I just ate.

What feels like an eternity later, he comes down the stairs again. He injects me with another clear liquid. Every time he does this, my body betrays me. I begin to sweat and shake uncontrollably, almost seizure-like.

The drug does its job. Before I can fight back, my body is limp. My eyes remain open, but my mind is an endless void. I can't speak. I can't yell. I can't move.

I'm paralyzed prey, waiting to be eaten.

CHAPTER 39

GIOVANNI

A frantic knock on the door scares the shit out of Angelo and me. He had just put on his movie of choice, *The Nun*. Jumping up from the couch, Angelo saunters to the door. Looking through the peephole, he turns back to me, his face twisted in confusion.

"Did you call Cas?" he asks.

Adjusting myself on the couch, I reply, "No, why would I?"

Angelo takes his hand off his gun—I didn't even know he had it on him. Swinging the door open, Cas doesn't give Angelo a chance to speak.

"She's alive," he rushes out, running into the living room, "and I know where she is!"

I jump from the couch. "What the fuck do you mean? Where is she?" I demand, a growl ripping from my throat.

His chest heaves as he catches his breath. "I kept checking the tracker, just in case it popped up as a heartbeat. It takes three to five weeks for a baby to develop a heartbeat." he says leaning over heaving.

My breath catches in my throat. "Wait, stop. She's *pregnant*?" I ask, my voice a mixture of joy and concern. My heart pounds, and my emotions are all over the place—joy, excitement, and terror. Joy and excitement at the thought of us becoming parents, of my dream from the other night coming true. But terror rips through me at the thought of the things she's probably been through in the last two weeks. The pain. The fear.

"Yes, but that means we can track her and, better yet, *find her*," Angelo says, grabbing my shoulders.

My eyes lock onto Cas's. "Where the fuck is my wife? I need her with me *tonight*," I demand. Not waiting for their response, I storm toward the bedroom to get dressed, grabbing something I've planned for whoever took her.

"I have coordinates. That's all I've got," Cas says.

"I'll put them in my GPS—it'll get us there," Angelo offers.

Pulling up to an old, run-down cabin three hours outside of Boston.

"I see movement in the kitchen," Angelo coughs out. We may not have been in the military, but we trained as if we were—we are, in our own way. Angelo, Cas, and I sit in Angelo's SUV, watching from a distance. My body itches with impatience, overwhelmed by the waiting. Glancing at the clock on the dash, I see it reads 2:00 AM.

"I can't do this. We need to go in," I say, my voice nearly a scream.

Cas stays in the car—that's for Iris. I don't know what state she'll be in when we find her.

We have no idea what or who we'll find in this house with Iris. We have to be prepared for anything. Pulling on black hats and leather gloves, we silently move out. Angelo takes the left side of the house, and I take the right, leaving Cas in the car for now.

Standing on a wooden box under a window, I peek over the trim, trying to get a sense of the layout—or anything at all. To my surprise, I catch a glimpse of an older man about my height walking into the kitchen from an adjacent room. Angelo comes up behind me.

"Nothing on my side," he whispers.

"One guy in the kitchen," I whisper back.

Checking the door to my right, I test the handle. It moves but doesn't fully turn. Angelo whistles softly to catch my attention, then points to the open window just above the kitchen sink.

Angelo pulls the screen off the window and tosses it aside. Stepping up, he balances one foot in the sink and one on my shoulder. Once he's sure the coast is clear, he throws his hand out to help me through the window. Together, we move silently from the kitchen to the living room. The house feels eerily empty until we pass a door propped slightly open.

I swear I hear whispers coming from behind it. The moment her voice reaches my ears, my heart jumps into my throat, stopping my breath. I *know* that voice—it belongs to my wife. There's no mistaking it.

I start toward the stairs, but Angelo grabs my arm, pulling me behind him.

The conversation below echoes up the stairs, growing louder in my ears.

"What I don't understand is why *you*? Why would Sam hire you to kill Lorenzo?" Iris asks.

"I told you to shut up, bitch," I hear the man snarl, followed by the sickening sound of his hand hitting her face. My body tightens, and every fiber of me wants to rush in there and cut that hand off.

Angelo creeps down the stairs slowly, making sure the old wood doesn't betray us with a sound. The dim light swings over the two figures in the dark, damp room. My eyes lock onto my wife tied to a chair in the middle. The metallic smell of blood fills my nose. Her face and body are bruised. My breath catches in my throat. Rage and pure hatred consume me. Plans form in my head—detailed, violent plans of what I'll do to this man once she's free.

This man dared to put his hands on my wife. My *pregnant* wife. I doubt she even knows yet.

I pass Angelo without a word, my eyes locking onto hers. Iris's eyes widen when she recognizes me standing behind her kidnapper. Her lips curl into a slow, faint smile, her shoulders relex.

"You know," the man growls, "your mother smiled just like that right before I killed her."

Tears well in her eyes. "You killed her?" she whispers, her gaze pulling from mine to meet his.

Who is this man? I think, my mind racing. *How did Sam find him? And why would he kill her mother?*

I press the barrel of my gun against the back of his skull. "Who the fuck are you?" I demand.

He says nothing, standing straighter, matching my height almost exactly.

It's Iris's voice that breaks the silence. "Michael, this is Gio," she says, her voice filled with quiet venom as she locks eyes with him. "My husband."

Then she looks at me, her voice soft but firm. "Gio, this is Michael. My father."

Her words hit me like a freight train. Did she just say her *father*? I thought he was dead. He turns his back to her, but before he can speak, my gun slams across the side of his head, and he crumples.

I rush to untie my wife as Angelo ties up her father and drags him to the corner of the room under the stairs.. My knife cuts through the ropes quickly, and I don't even bother freeing her legs before her arms are wrapped tightly around me. I pull her into my chest, and for the first time in weeks, I can breathe. She's safe. Nobody else can touch her. Nobody else can harm her. Angelo disappears up the stairs.

"How did you find me?" Her soft, sweet voice fills my ears, stopping my racing thoughts.

I spread my hand across her stomach. "I followed the baby's heartbeat," I say quietly.

Her head shakes slowly, and she pulls back slightly to look at me. "I'm not preg—"

I cut her off. "You *are* pregnant, baby," I say, holding her gaze. "Don't get mad when I tell you this, okay?" I interlock my fingers behind her back. She nods hesitantly.

"I had Cas put a tracker in you the night he stitched you up." I take her hand and guide it to the small incision on her abdomen. "I didn't know it was one my dad picked out. It only tracks a baby's heartbeat, not yours. That's why it took us so long to find you. The baby didn't have a heartbeat until yesterday."

Her eyes drop to her stomach, where our hands are still interlocked. "I'm going to be a mom," she whispers, her voice trembling. "We're going to be parents, Gio," she says, tears spilling from her eyes.

I cup her face, wiping away the tears. "Are these good tears or bad tears, *Mia Fiore*?" I ask, my hands trailing to her neck. I silently pray they're happy tears. When Cas ran into the penthouse not even eight hours ago, I was terrified—terrified I'd fail as a father, a husband, and a boss. They say having a family in this line of work makes you want to do the right thing instead of what needs to be done.

"They're good, happy tears, Giovanni," she says, placing her hand on my cheek and circling her thumb along my jawline. Her arms wrap around my neck, pulling me down as she crashes her lips into mine.

"Hey," I murmur, gently pushing her back. "We need to get you checked out. Cas is in the car. I'll have Angelo take you."

"I'm not leaving. If you're taking care of my father, I'm helping," she says, her bruised eyes wide and determined.

My eyes widen in response. "I don't think that's a good idea, Iris," I say, my hands resting on her mid-back. "You can't unsee what I'm going to do to him."

"First of all, I can handle it. Second of all, you're not going to tell me what I can and can't do," she says, pulling her hands away from me and gathering her hair at the top of her head, securing it with a hair tie. "And third, *I'm* going to be the one to do anything to him. He is *my* monster to kill," she barks out, adding a bite to her tone on the final words.

Her eyes go dark as she scans the room. I can imagine the scenarios running through her mind, ideas forming of what she wants to do to him. I had my own plans—to tie him to a chair and make slow, deliberate cuts to his body, over and over, until he bleeds out. Of course, I'd record everything to get his confession to killing my father and Sam being the one who hired him.

"At least let me be down here when you do it," I ask, looking her up and down, weighing whether or not I should let her take the lead. "Listen, though." I pull her back into my arms. "If shit goes south, I'm pulling you out and finishing the job myself." I press a kiss to the top of her head. "Got it?"

As I turn to walk away, I stop myself. "And remember—you're pregnant. You can't overwork yourself."

Her head tilts back as a laugh bursts from her lips. "I can only be about a month along at most," she says, resting her hand on her stomach. "We'll be fine." The way she emphasizes *we* sends a rush of joy and love through my chest.

"Actually, you're only three to five weeks," I correct.

"How do you know that?"

"The tracker, remember?" I tap her head lightly. "Pregnancy brain already?"

"Oh, shut up," she replies, rolling her eyes. "Get everything set up, please. I'm going to go shower." She starts up the stairs. "Love you. Thank you!" she calls down.

I hear Angelo greet her with a warm hug through the floor above. I'm not sure if I should feel happy or nervous about her decision to handle this without me. She clearly has her own plans for dealing with her father. I don't know if they've been simmering in her mind for years or if they've only formed during her time chained in this makeshift cell.

As far as I knew, she thought he was dead.

CHAPTER 40

IRIS

The red water ran down my body to the white shower floor. The sight of it churned my stomach, forcing me to stumble from the shower and vomit. Hunched over, I barely hear the knock on the door.

"Are you okay?" Angelo asks.

Arching my back as the last of it leaves my mouth, I manage to reply, "I'm fine" I shout

Getting off my knees, I finish my shower. The shampoo stings the fresh cuts on my scalp. As I lather my body, I look down for the first time and see the bruises blooming across my skin where his fists landed. Once the water runs clear, I turn the knob, wrapping my hair in a towel and draping another around my body.

Wiping the fog from the mirror, I see my face free of blood. My index finger gently traces the bruise covering my left eye and cheek. When I reach my jaw, I wince in pain. Curious, I carefully reach into my mouth and feel a loose molar. Gritting my teeth, I pull it free and spit the blood into the sink below.

As I open the bathroom door, I nearly walk into Cas.

"Gio sent me to check on you. Let me look at those cuts," he says, digging into a bag I hadn't noticed until now.

"I'm fine. I've had much worse from him," I reply, running my hand over one of the bruises I saw in the mirror.

Cas lets out a disapproving sigh. "At least let me give you a shot of antibiotics?" pulling a syringe from his bag. It brings back memories of Micheal drugging me, then I remember it's Cas he wouldn't hurt me.

Reluctantly, I roll up my sleeve, but he shakes his head. "It doesn't go there," he says, holding up a finger before motioning for me to turn around.

"Sorry," he murmurs, pushing the needle into my ass cheek. I grunt at the sting.

"Let's not tell your husband I just saw your ass, okay?" he jokes, zipping his bag shut and walking to the living room.

Pulling open the basement door, I walk downstairs. The darkness feels oppressive compared to the brightness of the upstairs. As I reach the last step, my eyes adjust, and I see Gio and Angelo stationed on opposite sides of the room. My father is strapped to a restraint chair in the center, the single light swinging above his head. Each pass of the bulb reveals fresh bruises on his face, and a small smile curls onto my lips.

"I'm glad you got the chance to meet my husband before you die," I say, running my hand across his shoulders. "And better yet, I finally get to do everything I ever wished I could do to you."

"I'm not scared of a little girl," he sneers.

"You killed that little girl a long time ago," I reply, walking to the table where Gio and Angelo have laid out knives, metal pokers, scissors, pliers, and ropes. Picking up a knife as my first tool, I turn back to him. "You know, the only good thing about you torturing me is that I learned what *truly* hurts a person"

I run the knife over his strapped-down hand, letting the blade kiss his skin. Applying pressure, I watch as red liquid pools beneath the steel. He grits his teeth, a low grunt escaping his lips.

"You think I care if you break my bones?" he hisses.

"Oh, I'm not just going to break your bones." I drag the knife from his hand to just below his elbow. Leaning close to his ear, I whisper loud enough for Gio and Angelo to hear, "I'm going to break your will to live." Slapping my hands onto his shoulders, I squeeze the nonexistent muscles. "And then I'm going to grant that wish and end you." My voice deepens as I emphasize the last three words.

I walk back to the table and pick up a pair of pliers. Behind me, I hear him cough, followed by a pained laugh. "You think I'll be that easy to break?"

"Even if I don't break you, I'll still end you," I reply coldly. For a moment, I feel the urge to glance at Gio for approval, but I stop myself. He's *mine* to kill, and I'll do it my way. And right now, I want to make him bleed.

"Do we have anything to hold his mouth open?" I ask, scanning the room.

Gio steps forward and points to an open-mouth gag. Forcing his jaw apart, I secure the leather straps tightly behind his head. He pulls against them, the edges rubbing his raw skin. Drool pools at the corners of his mouth, and I wait patiently for it to start dripping down his chin.

The first drip hits his chest. I grab the pliers, twirling them in my hands. "Open wide," I say, mocking him just as he did to me years ago. I begin to sweat—it's the first time since I started. I'm nervous. Stabbing is pretty easy, just stay away from the big organs. But I'm about to pull teeth. I don't know if there's a right or wrong way to do it. Can it kill him if I do it wrong? What the fuck was I thinking? He's going to die either way, so why does it matter?

I insert the pliers into his mouth and tuck the scissors into my back pocket. His lips try to move but can't. He begins to yell, but I can't make out what he's saying. I never knew until now just how much you need your lips to actually talk. Getting a hold of one of his teeth, I start to wiggle and pull at the same time. Just when I think I'm going to give up, it pops free from its place. Blood starts to flow from the new hole I made. I repeat the process a few more times before I get annoyed with his tongue getting in my way.

I look up at Angelo across the room and see his eyes partly closed. I guess he doesn't do the same thing Gio does, that's for sure. Gio stands against the wall, nodding in approval of the things I do. It brings me joy to see that I have a professional's approval on the things I'm doing.

I pinch his tongue with the pliers. "Do you remember when you would tie a bandana so tight around my mouth that I couldn't talk?" I ask. He just shakes his head, acknowledging the things he did to me for the first time out loud. "Well, I'm going to do something similar to that." I pull the scissors from my pocket, showing them to him. His eyes go wide. "But mine is going to be a little more permanent." Using all my strength, I pull his tongue as far as I can out of his mouth. *Snip.* It cuts through just like it's a piece of tender steak. He starts to yell to the best of his ability, but I just took that ability away. Sitting forward, blood flows from his mouth down his body to the drain on the floor.

"It's not fun, is it?"

We leave him to get Cas to cauterize his tongue. I wasn't ready to be done with him yet. After Cas exits the living room, Gio looks over at me.

"How did you come up with these ideas on what to do to him?"

"Do you want the truth?"

"Yes, always."

I turn to him, smiling. "Most of it I got from TV shows or books. Why, am I doing bad?"

"No, it's actually scary good," he says, calming my nerves for this final one.

"Good. I'm going to need you to find me a few things for this last part."

Cas walks up from the basement. "I got his mouth to stop bleeding, but hey Gio, take it a little easy on him. He's basically dead," Cas says, looking at Gio with sad eyes.

Gio raises his hands. "Oh, none of that is me," he says, pointing at me. "All my wife."

Cas looks at me, about to say something, but I cut him off. "Don't tell me how I can and can't treat my father. He is getting everything he deserves." My hands clench into fists at my sides. "I want him to want to die. Just like I wanted to."

I turn from them, walking down the stairs, but I hear Gio say one last thing to Cas before he follows me. "She needs this.

Play: Jokes on You BY Charlotte Lawrence

I see his body slumped over, his chest barely moving with each breath. "Wake up. You don't get a break." I kick the chair, and his eyes weakly open. His wrists pull against the straps, cutting into them more with each movement.

"One thing we're all still trying to figure out is *how*. How did Sam reach out to you? How did he even know about you?" I backhand his face, waiting for an answer. A guttural laugh leaves my body when I remember. "I guess I should have asked that before I took your tongue. Oops." I pat his face. "Oh well, we'll figure it out without you, I guess."

Looking at Gio, I nod my head. A plastic bucket is shoved over Michael's head. "Remember when you used to put me in a coffin and sometimes bury me?" I turn on my heels, grabbing the blowtorch from Angelo's hands. "Well, this is kind of like that—except it's much hotter."

My finger presses the button, and the hissing of gas echoes through the quiet room. *Click.* The spark ignites, and the gas transforms into a yellow flame, ready to devour anything it touches. Bringing the flame to the bucket, I watch as he begins to buck against the heat now engulfing his head. He lets out a muffled scream—garbled, like someone yelling underwater.

The bucket starts to melt, conforming to the shape of his head. His hands strain at the straps, desperate to pull free. I walk around his body, keeping the torch just far enough away to slow the melting. I don't want the plastic to liquefy too quickly. His body eventually goes limp, but I don't stop. I know he's dead, but I refuse to let history repeat itself. I'm going to make sure he *stays* dead.

By the time I'm finished, the bucket has lost its shape completely, plastic running down his body to where his arms meet the chair.

Walking out of the basement, we're met with the soft glow of sunlight streaming through the windows.

"It's one-thirty," Cas coughs out from the living room. "And judging by the smell, I'm going to guess he's dead and burned?"

"He's dead," Gio replies. "But only his head is burned. You might want to go take a look and figure out how we get rid of the body."

"Why don't we just call Luka?" Angelo suggests.

"We don't know how deep this goes," Gio responds. "Yeah, it could just be your dad, but we don't know that."

Too tired and hungry to focus on their conversation, I rummage through the cabinets until I find a box of clubhouse crackers. "Why don't we just soak him"—I point toward the basement—"in acid, then burn the house down?" I ask.

"Mia Fiore," Gio says, brushing my hair back behind my ear, "do you just *have* acid lying around?"

"No, but he was going to soak me in it. At least, that's what he said. Did you check the shed?"

The three of them exchange glances, shrugging. "And you call yourselves a crime organization," I say, pointing accusingly at each of them. Holding out my hand, I demand, "Now give me the keys. I'm going to take a nap."

Gio looks at Angelo, nodding in my direction. Angelo rolls his eyes as he digs into his pocket and retrieves the keys. Pulling them free, he dangles them in front of my face. Snatching them from his hand, I announce, "You three have fun. Me and Baby Gio"—I rub my still-flat stomach—"are going to lay down. Bye."

I throw one hand in the air as I walk off, giving them a dismissive wave.

Crawling into the backseat of the SUV, I let out a scream as tears stream down my face. The scream morphs into laughter. I just killed the man who not only ruined my life but also my mother's. When he told me he killed her, I made up my mind right then and there. I wished him all the pain and suffering he caused us over the years.

My mother and I weren't allowed to speak unless spoken to directly, and even then, sometimes not at all. So, I made sure he'd never speak again. When he used to bury me in the woods, leaving me there so long I thought I'd suffocate, I made sure he felt that same pain and panic.

Does that make me a monster? Maybe. But am I truly one if I killed the biggest monster I know? No. It was a fight, and I won.

I took the life of a man who did me wrong, and it felt... *freeing.*

CHAPTER 41

GIOVANNI

Angelo finds the acid right where Iris said it would be. Throwing Michael's body into the bathtub and filling it to the brim, the liquid begins to bubble, eating away his flesh and muscle. The smell is unbearable—worse than when Iris melted his flesh and the bucket together. Angelo, Cas, and I head to the basement to retrieve all the tools she used.

"Did you know she had a side like that?" Angelo breaks the silence with his question.

Letting out a loud breath, I lean up against the table. "No, but is it bad that I'm proud she does?" I ask honestly.

Cas, his back to us, is the next to speak. "No, it means she can take care of herself."

Without another word, we finish the task at hand.

I'm just as shocked as they are. I knew she might be capable of something like this, but even so, I'm impressed. I never thought to melt a bucket onto a man's head—and I've killed people for the past twelve years of my life. She said she was going to break his will to live, and it's safe to say she did just that. Who knows if he was begging to die or to live? He couldn't speak—she made sure of that when she cut out his tongue.

An hour later, all that's left of Michael's body is his bones. I rinse them to remove the acid, knowing that if I don't, my hands will look just like his. Shoving the bones into a bag alongside the tools that killed him feels poetic. We drench the house in gasoline and set it on fire, ensuring we cleanse the space of any evidence of the crimes that took place there.

Iris is asleep when we get back to the car. We climb in quietly. I join her in the backseat, pulling her head onto my lap and running my fingers mindlessly through her hair. We watch the house crumble, the flames devouring the wood. I stroke her face, silently hoping that what she did truly helped her, and didn't hurt her more in the long run. At this moment, we're more alike than ever before—both killers, both orphans. No real family. Few friends. only each other

It's been four days since we got Iris back, and I haven't slept once until she falls asleep first. I've kept her hidden in the penthouse, wanting Sam to think he's won something—for a little while, at least. Even if it means I have to keep up the act I put on when she was gone.

I gifted Iris a gun when she came back. One night, we went out to practice, and I must say, I wouldn't want her pointing it at me.

We lay on the couch, Iris's head on my lap. She gets more beautiful every day. I'm not sure if it's the pregnancy or just the fact that I lost her and never want to go through that again, but I've become so possessive. I don't let anyone touch her or even see her—not even Angelo, who was there when we found her. Cas is the only exception. I have to let him see and touch her when he checks on the baby. He's been here every day since she's been home. Cas has determined that Iris is now seven weeks pregnant.

We share a bowl of popcorn while watching some movie. Our attention is pulled away by a knock at the front door.

"Are you expecting someone?" she asks.

"No." I pull out my phone and switch to the camera app, checking the front door feed. "It's Vinny."

"Who is Vinny?" she asks.

I forget for a moment that she doesn't know. He was forced out just before she joined the family. "Angelo's brother."

Her eyes go wide. "Wait, I didn't know Angelo had a brother."

"Mia Fiore, we'll talk about this later. Go to the room and hide," I say firmly.

Hearing the worry in my voice, she obeys without question.

I pull the gun from the lockbox by the door. I don't know what Vinny is doing here. It could be revenge—my father did exile him. If that's what he wants, I'll be ready for him.

Propping the door open, I put my foot behind it so he can't push it open further than what I allow. Opening it, I'm met with Vinny's face, but something is wrong. He has dark circles under his eyes, as if he hasn't slept in a month, and dirt covers his face.

"Vinny, what's wrong?"

Tears start to fall from his eyes. "Oh, thank God you're alive. He didn't get to you," he says, taking a deep breath.

"What are you talking about?" I gesture for him to come in.

"My dad—he has a plan to kill you and your dad," he coughs out.

"Wait, you knew?" I ask.

"Wait, *you* know? How?"

"Well, he had my dad killed and then had my wife taken. I guess he just hasn't gotten to me yet," I say, tucking my gun into the waistband of my pants at the back. "Plus, Angelo told me. He overheard him talking on the phone about it. How do *you* know?"

Out of the corner of my eye, I catch a glimpse of Iris in the hallway. She never listens to anything I say. Goddamn it. Vinny isn't a danger, but she doesn't know that. He could have been out here killing me, and she would have been next. My eyes dart to her hand, where I see her gun perched, ready to fire. At least she came armed to help if I needed it.

"I was with him when he ran into some guy who said he needed his daughter. I'm guessing that was your wife. So wait—your dad is dead, and your wife is missing? I know where she is."

"Yeah, so do I." I take a sip of my drink. "She's behind you with a gun ready to shoot."

Vinny's hands slowly raise in the air. "Put it down, *Mia Fiore*. He's not an enemy," I tell her.

She lowers her gun. "For now."

I slide Vinny a glass of water, and he gulps it down in one drink.

"Where have you been?" I ask.

"I've been hiding from him in a homeless camp since he threatened to put out a contract on me—and have you fulfill it," he answers.

Was *that* the contract I was supposed to have when I got back?

I walk to the fridge and pull out meat and cheese from the crisper. Iris hands me the bread and disappears into the pantry, returning with a big bag of chips. "What about your girlfriend and baby?" I ask.

"What girlfriend? Better yet, what baby?" he says, confused.

"Your dad told my dad that you knocked up a girl and were being exiled to leave with her."

"No, that's a lie! When he met up with that guy, I told him I was going to tell Lorenzo everything—his plans to kill all of you, his thirst for power, and even what he did to Angelo and me growing up. Then he tied me up and took me to a house in the middle of nowhere, expecting..." He looks at Iris. "I guess your dad to kill me. But instead, he told me to run and never stop—that I wasn't his problem to clean up anymore."

I place the sandwich and bowl of chips in front of him. He eats like a wolf, tearing at the food and barely breathing between bites. He isn't a danger to us. He came here to help save me.

"Why are you only coming out now?" I ask, my voice more skeptical than I intended.

He looks down at the floor. "I was scared to find you. Then I saw Angelo walking into the deli, and I knew I couldn't hide forever. I needed to face my fears. I wanted my brother back."

"You'll stay here with us in the guest room until we sort all of this out." I thought those words, but Iris is the one who says them. It's like we share a mind.

I love that she's already sliding into the role of a mafia wife. She puts the family first, knows what needs to be done, and sometimes even sees it before I do. She may not have been born into this life, but she was made for it.

We settle Vinny into his new room. The first thing he does is shower and change clothes. Iris throws his old clothes into the washer and hands him a pair of sweatpants and a shirt to wear until we can get him some of his own.

Iris and I find our way back to the couch to finish up our movie and popcorn.

"Are you going to tell Angelo he's here?" she asks.

I assume Angelo knows the truth regarding Vinny, but I'm not sure. "I don't know. Maybe we let Vin decide if we tell him or not."

Iris takes Vinny out of the house while I call Angelo for a meeting. We need to finalize the details for dealing with his dad. I know we're going to call for an admissions hearing, where Sam will be forced to confess to the things he's done and pay for all of it. Rage courses through my body, shaking me as the memories of how I found Iris resurface—her black and blue face, the blood on her split lip. I want to know why. Why the fuck would Sam go after Iris and me? For all I know, I never did anything to him. But I'm almost positive he's hiding more than what will come to light during the hearing.

"What else is he hiding?" I ask Angelo, who sits across from me at the kitchen island.

His head lifts just enough for our eyes to meet. "I'm not sure. He doesn't tell me anything."

"Angelo, you aren't stupid. Tell me the things he doesn't want people to know," I press, my voice harsh.

It looks like tears are about to fall from his eyes. "He isn't the man everybody thinks he is."

"None of us are, it seems."

An hour later, I have more ammunition on my uncle than I'd ever need. I also know why Sam forbade me from hanging out with Angelo. When this comes out, they won't just accept his death—they'll demand it. Angelo leaves, letting the door close with its own momentum.

Walking out of the hallway, I'm greeted by Iris and Vinny, each carrying a mountain of bags.

"What did you buy?" I ask, holding up a finger. "Actually, the better question is, what didn't you buy?"

Iris turns to me, her face scrunched in mock concern. "Are you mad?"

"No. I don't spend money, so you might as well."

"Oh, good, because I bought a bunch of stuff!" She grins, dropping the bags to the floor and pulling items out one by one. "I bought stuff for me—I'm going to be growing soon—and some stuff for the baby." She looks up at me, smiling.

"That's good, baby. I'm glad you had fun. How was Vinny?"

"He was fine, but he didn't like spending money he said he didn't earn."

Opening my laptop on the island, I think aloud. "Most men don't." I pause before calling out, "Yo, Vinny, come here."

Iris gives me a puzzled look.

Vinny's voice rings out before he appears in the room. "What's up?"

"Do you want to make some money?" I ask.

"Yes, of course I do!"

Looking at his eager face, I nod. "Good. You started yesterday. You're going to act as Iris's bodyguard when she goes out. I assume you have a gun and know how to use it."

"Yeah, I always have one," he confirms.

"Plus, I have mine too, you know," Iris chimes in from the living room, surrounded by bags.

"Then that's your job," I say, crossing my arms over my chest. "Until we get this sorted, feel free to use our cards as your paycheck for whatever you need."

"Yes, boss. Thank you." He nods, then turns to leave, leaving Iris and me alone.

"Can you really straighten all of this out?" she asks, her face scrunching as though she knows I can but doesn't want to think about how. I follow her down the hallway to our room.

"Yes," I reply, running my hand up her arm to her shoulder, pushing her hair back. My thumb traces her jaw. "But I'm going to need your help."

"Anything," she says softly. Standing at the window of our room, she stares outside. "But I have to be honest," she continues, her voice tinged with worry. Her hand rests on her belly. I take a seat on our bed "I'm scared for the future of this baby with our life. I don't want anything to happen, that's all."

*Play: Love is Gone By: Camylio

Fear flashes through me. Is she going to leave me? Am I going to wake up one day and find her gone?

This can't happen. I cannot survive without her in my life. That baby isn't even born, but I already know I would do anything for them both. I know it's hard, but I wouldn't be able to breathe if anything happened to either of them.

My body jumps out of our bed. Tears don't just drop, they run from my eyes " You are my angel in this life of monsters and demons" I look up to her, not even realizing my knees hit the floor. "please I can't lose you either of you" My arms snake around her legs forcing her knees to bend.

She takes my face in her small trembling hands forcing me to look into her bright eyes wiping away my tears with her thumbs "Hey my vows were family above all else" her knees starts to bend hitting the floor, face to face with me "you are my family and I stand by those vows" she brings her forehead to mine "always and forever"

My mind stops racing once she reassures me that she is in this with me. I know she says it all the time but it just feels different every time " I have a surprise for you. I will take you to it after the hearing. I promise you'll love it. It will help settle your mind on all of this" I said to her as she held my head to her lap.

Iris lays in my arms tonight her body flush with mine, turning us into one physical body. My mind runs through the possibilities of what's going to happen tomorrow. I know Sam is going to die whether the board approves or not. My body shivers with the possibility of the board siding with Sam and not me. It's an uneasy, scary feeling., but this space right here is where I feel the safest. Once I hear the little snores leaving her parted lips, my mind silences. Her scent hanging in my nose calming me to sleep.

Angelo meets me at the Meeting house. Vinny and Iris are just behind me in her car. I didn't want Angelo to see Vinny just yet. From what I gathered he really does believe that he was off living in Pennsylvania with the so-called pregnant girlfriend, starting a life. It is plausible that he never knew. Once someone leaves we never hear from them again, plus Sam told everybody including Angelo he left in the middle of the night with the girl. I see Angelo out front in a suit similar to mine, black pants, black jacket, the only difference is my shirt is red where his is a dark blue. We walk into the house not saying a word to each other, the house feels far too quiet, there are always people here. The board is well aware of the meeting, they know part of the true reason why they were called here, but Sam has no idea he thinks im gonna have him be my right hand man just like he was to my father. He also doesn't know I found my pregnant wife yet. What a surprising day this will be for him.

Entering the boardroom I find all the men who served with my father including my uncle. Angelo follows in short behind me. Angelo was never privy to be in the room during meetings so he looks a bit out of place. All eyes turn to me as I start the meeting seated in the chair where my father once sat. "Good morning everybody" Angelo stands in the corner at his fathers back. Interlacing my fingers on the table in front of me "Most of you know why i called this meeting im sure." I stop and make eye contact with every single man sitting at this table, only skipping Sam. I can feel the tension thicken in the air, seeing his body tense from the corner of my eyes. "I call for an admissions hearing" finally making eyes contact with Sam, Angelo leaps forward grabbing his father forcing him to stay glued to the chair "against Samuel Aldo Benedetti" Then men sitting on either side of Sam move their chairs in opposite directions.

"This is absolutely insane. What is it you think I have done?" Sam asks, struggling against angelos grip on his shoulders. "Boy you better get your hands off of me"

"Sam it's what I know you did not what I think you did." my voice remains calm and steady. Lifting my hand it rattles off the thick wooden table, knock. knock. pause knock. Just as my hand raised from the table Iris enters the room leaving Vinny in the hallway Finding her spot next to me. she rested her hand on my right shoulder, I take her hand in mine, pressing my lips to her knuckles. My eyes stay glued to his during the whole show she puts on by planting her hand spread on her belly, straightening her back to stand at full height.

Her voice smooth and calm, Iris says, "Hello, Uncle Sam. I think you may know my friend here." She lifts her arm, gesturing to the door she just walked through. "Please, come in."

Both Sam and Angelo's eyes widen as the door opens and Vinny walks into the room, wearing the same suit as Angelo. He takes the spot on the other side of me, opposite my wife. Angelo looks from Iris to Vinny, then finally to me. I lift my eyes to Angelo, and when they meet, I shake my head. He returns the gesture with a nod. Sam tries to wiggle his way out of Angelo's grip—unsuccessfully, of course.

Sam's voice cuts through the silence that has fallen over the room. "Iris, I'm glad to see that you are safe and back." My body trembles with rage as he welcomes her home. "I'm still unaware of what this has to do with me, though."

"Cut the bullshit, Sam," Iris snaps, taking the lead. The room falls even more silent. No wife has ever spoken to any of these men this way. I'm glad mine will be the first. "We know everything."

"You might as well confess, Father," Angelo says, his knuckles whitening as his grip tightens. Sam lets out a hiss, looking at Angelo.

"I have done nothing! Let go of me," Sam demands.

"You had my father killed by my wife's father in exchange for her." My fist slams against the table. "You wanted power. Power that is not yours to take."

A man on the board speaks up. "Do you have evidence on this, Gio?"

My mouth turns up into a smile. "As a matter of fact, yes, I do. I have witnesses who heard you speaking on the phone with Michael about the plan." I slide my hand into the inside pocket of my coat and retrieve my phone. "Plus, before my wife killed Michael, he confessed to everything. His confession and death were recorded."

I hear Iris' breath hitch in her throat. I never told her that Angelo and I got Michael to confess with very little torture—just a few hits and some electrical questioning.

Sam's head falls to his chest as he looks at me through his lashes. A small laugh escapes him. "Your father had it coming. He was never fit to run this family. And you will be the same. If it's not me, someone else will take you out."

Iris's hand tightens on my shoulder, then releases to rest on her belly.

"You think you are more fit to run this family?" Angelo asks from above Sam.

"Of course I am. I'm the one who has basically ran this family while your father had his dick stuck in every whore in this city. I was focused on this family. I had no distractions. I wasn't screwing random women every night," Sam yells.

"NO, YOU JUST RAPED YOUR SONS EVERY NIGHT," Angelo yells back, looking at Vinny.

The room grows silent. I look at both boys. They both shake their heads, tears threatening to fall. I nod silently, letting them know I stand by them and think nothing different of them. Angelo's voice is low, but it echoes off the walls for everyone to hear. "And when this is over, I'm going to run my knife across your throat and watch you bleed out." weather they agree or not.

"We are going to," Vinny adds from behind me.

Sam's facial expression doesn't change. He knew he was going to die before, so it doesn't matter what he says to them now—his fate is already decided. The men in the room begin to murmur.

"Do you have anything to say, Sam?" one of them asks. Sam sits there, saying nothing, his eyes locked on mine.

"Then we vote. Everybody who finds him guilty, raise your hand."

Every hand shoots into the air. It's unanimous. He will die.

"We give you free reign on his death," the man says to me.

"Thank you, but I give that task to his two sons if they agree to it." Without saying a word, Vinny saunters over to Angelo, who holds a knife in his free hand. Vinny grabs a hold of Sam's hair, forcing him to make eye contact with me. Of course, we all know what's coming.

Thinking Iris would turn away, she doesn't; she looks at Sam, who then looks at her and smiles.

"Remember, I won't be the only one," Sam says, letting out a low, raspy laugh.

Angelo flicks the blade open, placing it on Sam's throat. With one swift movement, the blade slices through, coming away covered in red. Sam coughs, blood running from the table to the floor as it pours from his neck. He whimpers quietly, his vocal cords severed, rendering him unable to speak. Angelo hands the knife to Vinny and takes over the grip on Sam's hair. Angelo pulls Sam's head up so far that the blood spurts from his neck, splattering across the table and landing halfway to my chair.

Vinny takes the knife and cuts an X over Sam's lips and eyes.

Sam's body finally goes limp after a minute or two. Angelo and Vinny may not have been trained as our hitmen, but I approve of their form of torture. It's something I would have done. Although, after hearing what he did to them, I personally would have started by cutting his dick off.

Play: Noble Blood By Tommee Profit

We all stand as the room shifts to silence. One by one, the men turn to Iris and me, bowing their heads. In unison, they say, *"Il nostro erede."*

Standing tall, I take my wife's hand, placing her in front of me as I slide my hand around to her belly. My chin lands on her shoulder.

"They just acknowledged us as their rulers, Mia Fiore," I whisper.

Both of our backs straighten, and our shoulders square. We are now in charge. We now hold all the power. I am seen as a king, and she as the queen.

CHAPTER 42

IRIS

Gio drives me in his car back to our home. It's a slow realization, but I am now seen as his queen and he as my king. It's hard to think about what our life is going to be like after this. I fear it will be more dangerous, but with Gio by my side, we can handle anything and everything. Angelo and Vinny are in my car, following us to the penthouse. Vinny is coming back to get his things; he's going to stay with Angelo for a bit.

Gio takes my hand in his as we enter the parking garage. "Are you okay? You didn't say a word the entire way home."

"Yes, just a lot to take in, that's all." Turning to him in the seat, I ask, "Did you know?"

He looks at me with confusion, his eyebrows pulling together. "About what he did to them?"

I can see his jaw tighten. "No, I would have killed him a long time ago." He looks around the garage before continuing, "But I think my father knew, and I think Sam knew he knew. I wasn't allowed to hang out with Angelo much. When Angelo was about 12 and I was 14, his dad didn't let me come over, and my dad didn't push it. So I'm sure he knew. And he didn't do anything."

My hand flies to my mouth. I see Angelo and Vinny pulling into the garage, and I quickly wipe away the few tears that have fallen from my eyes. "I feel bad for them."

"I do too. But they killed their monster just like you did. And I am proud of both of you for that," Gio says, planting a kiss on my wedding ring. "Let's go." He exits the car, rounding to my side. I've learned I don't get to touch my own door handles anymore, so I wait until he opens it for me.

Meeting the boys at the elevator, I ask Angelo, "Do you have clothes in the car?" when I see he is dirty.

He looks down at the dried blood clinging to his clothing. "No."

"It's okay. You can borrow some sweats and a shirt from me," Gio says from behind me.

Turning to face him, I smile. "I love you, but I don't think he"—I pause to look at Angelo, who is the same height but significantly broader—"is going to fit your shirts, baby," I say, patting his chest.

A guttural laugh escapes Angelo's mouth. "I like her."

Gio looks at Angelo in warning.

"Don't worry. I have a regular shirt on under this—it didn't get through. But thank you, Iris, for admitting I'm bigger."

Gio leans forward, pressing his mouth to my ear. "I'm going to punish," he murmurs, laying his hand on my ass, "that tight ass of yours for that."

My cheeks flush. "Good. Just what I wanted," I reply.

"Ew," Angelo and Vinny say in unison, pulling laughter from both Gio and me as we all enter the elevator to the penthouse.

It only took Angelo and Vinny thirty minutes to get his things, but they stayed for two hours. We all made dinner together. The boys had spaghetti, but I just had buttered noodles. I have such bad heartburn from the pregnancy that I can't eat anything with tomatoes. Sitting down, I realize something.

"Your real name isn't just Vinny, is it?" I ask.

He looks up from his bowl. "No, it's Vinicio, but nobody calls me that—like, ever."

"And yours is really Angelo?" I ask.

"Yeah, I don't have a nickname. It's a pretty easy name, so no need for one," he replies, slurping his noodles. "Other than 'King of the Ring,' but that's just for fighting."

"Why do you ask, Mia Fiore?" Gio asks me from the head of the table.

"Oh, I'm just thinking of names, that's all," I reply. They both perk up slightly.

"I am not naming the baby after either of these two," I add. Vinny and Angelo slump back in their seats.

I laugh. "Oh, God, no! I was just thinking and realized I didn't know their real names." We all laugh together.

After the boys clean up dinner, we walk them out, leaving Gio and me alone for the first time since he promised to punish my ass. He turns to me, his back to the door. I know what's coming, and I'm going to make him work for it. I playfully run down the hallway to our room. He doesn't run after me; he stalks after me, not running but still keeping up.

I get to the room and close the door behind me, thinking it will give me some form of advantage over him, having to open the door. I run to the bathroom, shutting the door and turning the shower on. Stripping down as fast as I can, I jump into the shower. My body barely hits the water before he kicks through the door, finding me.

He doesn't remove his clothes before stepping into the shower. His hands are around my throat, cutting off my airflow. "I told you I was going to fuck that ass, but God, I really want to be in my wife's pussy," he whispers, his voice a deep growl beneath the sound of the water and the closeness of our bodies. "I'm going to fuck you so hard, you'll beg me to let you cum."

My pussy tightens at just his words. My hands run the full length of his body, from his broad shoulders to his cock. His clothes still in my way, I rip his shirt open, sending buttons flying around us. I feel his muscles go rigid as his dominance flares. He turns me, forcing my face to the wall. "Do you remember the first time we had sex in the shower?" he asks, his lips grazing the sensitive shell of my ear.

My body responds in a way that only Gio can command it to. It roars to life, an inferno burning at its hottest, his hands stoking the flames with every touch. Every place he touches feels as if it's igniting a new fire. My back presses against his front, fire meeting ice. My head falls back onto his shoulder, finding its home in the crook of his neck. His lips press against my temple as his hand snakes around my body to cover my mouth. I can only breathe through my nose, my lungs filling with the intoxicating scent of him.

His pants must be gone—I feel his cock sliding against my ass cheeks. Sucking in a deep breath, I brace myself for him to bury himself inside me.

"Not yet, baby. I'm going to play with you first," he whispers, his teeth grazing my skin.

The hand covering my mouth drops to my throat, forcing me to look forward into the flow of hot water streaming down my face. I surrender control of my body to him entirely. His inked hand trails from my belly to my knee, lifting it to rest on the stone bench. His fingers slide against my clit, rubbing me until the heat becomes unbearable. My pussy tightens and throbs; it must be the pregnancy because I'm already ready to cum without him even being inside me.

257

"Please, Gio, I need you," I rush out, desperation thick in my voice.

"Does my wife want to cum?" he asks, his fingers hooking under my chin. I answer him by sucking his thumb into my mouth, teeth grazing the pad of his finger.

Without warning, he pulls me out from under the steaming water. His arms lift me, carrying me into our room and leaving me kneeling at the edge of our bed. My mouth hangs open instinctively, knowing what's about to happen. His hand caresses my chin and cheek. "Good girl," he says, his voice so deep and dark it's almost unrecognizable.

He doesn't move closer to me, so I lean forward, taking him into my mouth. My tongue swirls around his head, and he throws his head back, letting out a loud moan. Has he gotten bigger since the last time I had him in my mouth? Before, I could take him just fine, but now, drool pools at the corners of my lips, dripping free. My hand works the length of his shaft while my tongue teases his sensitive head. His groans, low moans, and sharp hisses tell me I'm doing everything right.

Lost in the rhythm of our bodies colliding, I take his full length into my mouth. "Oh my fucking God," he rasps, his voice low and sultry as he fists his hand into my hair. My free hand slips between my thighs, seeking relief for the ache radiating from my pussy. I'm already so wet that my fingers slide in easily. I take his full length again, reveling in the way his body jerks in response.

A yank on my hair pulls him free from my mouth. "You keep doing that, and I'm going to cum down your throat," he growls.

I shake my head frantically, trying to pull him back into me, but he grabs my arms, forcing me to my feet. He backs me up until my ass hits the edge of the bed.

"That's not fair," he murmurs, his lips curling into a wicked smile. "I want to make you cum."

His hands push my back onto the bed, pulling my arms above my head and securing them into smooth leather cuffs. I yank and pull, trying to free myself, but it's no use. I feel the bed dip to my left.

"Don't worry, you'll get my cum," he grunts, his voice low and demanding. "You're being so needy tonight."

With a thrust, he buries himself inside me, forcing me to pull harder at the restraints, making the wood creak under the strain. I don't know how much more I can take; I was already so close from my own hand before he took over. Words refuse to form, only low moans and panting escape my lips as thrust after thrust pushes me closer and closer to the edge.

"I need you to cum for me, Iris," he demands, his voice an intoxicating growl. "Cum for your husband."

His hand wraps around my throat, applying just enough pressure to send my vision fading at the edges. My body responds instinctively, my pussy throbbing as jolts of electricity ripple through me. I fall over the edge, surrendering to pure bliss and ecstasy, my body trembling from the force of the orgasm he commanded from me.

Not even a second later, Gio thrusts deep inside me, his cock throbbing as my pussy milks every last drop he has to give. He lets out one final grunt, collapsing to my side. Running his hand to my belly, he brushes my hair behind my ears and lets out a long breath.

"I love you," he whispers, placing a tender kiss on my stomach. "Both of you."

Rolling me to my side, his front pressing against my back, he plants a kiss on my temple. "Sleep tight tonight," he murmurs. "I have a surprise for you tomorrow."

After a solid ten hours of sleep, a refreshing shower, and breakfast, Gio drives me out of the city. The familiar brownstones give way to fields of trees and open land. We turn into a long, winding driveway surrounded by rows of apple trees, their branches hanging low with ripe fruit. The sight makes me want to reach out and pluck one.

I tried to pry the surprise out of Gio this morning in the shower, but he kept his mouth shut, repeating the same thing over and over: "It's a surprise, and I'm not ruining it for you."

As we crest a small hill, the trees clear, revealing a stunning white colonial house with blue shutters. A three-car garage stands beside it, and a wraparound porch complete with two matching rocking chairs beckons invitingly.

I turn to Gio, sitting in the driver's seat, my confusion evident. "Whose house is this?"

Putting the car in park, he takes my hand. "It's ours. I bought it while you were gone. I kept thinking about how I could keep you and our kids safe. I bought this house for us to live in. The penthouse can be for business, and the meeting house will stay as it always has been."

Tears prick my eyes as his words sink in. My chest tightens with joy. I want to say something, anything, but no words come. My heart overflows. I knew Gio thought about me while I was gone, but this is beyond anything I imagined.

"This isn't your only surprise," he continues, smiling softly. "I had something else built alongside the house."

"Wait, you had this house built?" I ask, my voice cracking slightly with emotion.

"No, I had it renovated.. It's perfect for our growing family—five bedrooms, six bathrooms, and even a basement I turned into a movie theater."

The tears in my eyes spill over. My voice rises slightly as I ask, "Can we go inside and see?"

He chuckles. "Yes, of course."

I don't even wait for him to open the door for me. Flinging it open, I jump out of the car before he can even turn off the engine. Taking the small three steps up to the front porch, I find the door unlocked. Pushing it open, a wave of calm washes over me.

This house is ours. We'll raise our children here, make memories here. This place is ours. The penthouse was his, the dorm was mine, the meeting house belonged to everyone. But this house? This is ours to do with as we please.

Gio stands in the doorway waiting for me to step in further. I only got to the entryway, a large room with an accent table with Iris' placed on top next to stairs. Following the hallway we enter the Kitchen. I can tell now that the kitchen will be my most favorite part of this house. The lower cabinets are navy blue and top are pure white. It's all pulled together by the white and almost blue marble. The Kitchen floors are white while all the fixtures are gold.

"I hope you like it," Gio says from the kitchen opening.

"Like it. Baby I love it. It's so beautiful. Can I ask with the blue?"

"I don't know the designer said it was 'the hip thing to do'" he says, holding his fingers in the air bending them to quote. "But the real surprise is right through those doors" he points to a door on the other side of the connected living room. Following his finger he comes up behind me covering my eyes with his hands. "I want you to actually be surprised"

Running my hands along the wall the texture is so smooth it feels as if there is nothing there. His hands keep me from peeking. I hear the slight creak of a door open. When Gio moves his hands I see my surprise and the memories of the boat flood back to my mind. I love to look at the stars and Gio made sure I can see them from here. It's almost like a greenhouse, the walls are solid but the roof is a clear material letting us see the sky in shine and rain.

Epilogue 1

6 Months later

Giovanni

I push the white doors open, hearing them hit the walls as I run out the hospital hallway. Angelo, Vinny, Cecilia, Lexi, and Avery line the waiting room. We didn't even find out the gender; we wanted to be surprised when it was born. Iris only had one scan when Cas confirmed the pregnancy 7 months ago. Iris said she didn't want to put the baby at risk. Every time Cas asked if she wanted to know anything, she always said no. Cas made sure to check her often, every week, taking her vitals and doing blood work. I feel my blood drain from my face.

"Oh my god, what's wrong? Is she okay?" Avery rushes out as they all walk toward me, crowding me.

I look at all of them, ripping the hospital gown off my body. "It's two," I pause, hearing them gasp, "a boy and a girl." Angelo is the first to hug me, patting me on my back with an open hand.

Iris

I lay in the hospital bed with both of my babies in each arm, looking at the beautiful little masterpieces Gio and I made together. One wrapped in blue, one wrapped in pink. It may have been a surprise to both of us, but a good surprise.

They both coo at almost the same time, scrunching their noses just like their daddy does. They both look just like a perfect mix of Gio and me.

She has my hair, copper curls, but Gio's eyes; he has my blue eyes and Gio's dark curly hair. I can tell now they are both going to be heartbreakers.

The door slowly creeps open. Gio pokes his head in. "They all want to come in." His face is still pale; he might need to sit down and eat something.

"Bring them in." Gio ushers everybody in. All of our friends file into the room, hugging the wall. The girls, of course, are gushing over the two small human beings in my arms, while the boys try to keep their composure, but they aren't very good. I see the tears scratching to get out of Angelo and Vinny's eyes.

"Everybody meet Matteo James Benedetti and Isabella Grace Benedetti," I gesture to each one when I say the respective names.

Gio comes to my side, taking her in his arms. "You named her after my mom?" he asks, a tear falling down his cheek.

My hand goes to his face, wiping the free tear away. "Of course I did. I know I didn't know her, but it's a beautiful name for such a beautiful baby." Gio rocks her in his arms, walking around the room showing her to everybody.

Gio and I ask if we can speak to Angelo and Cecilia alone for just a moment. After we are alone, Gio takes a hold of my hand, squeezing it, giving me a signal to talk. "Gio and I would like to ask you both to be their godparents. We know it's a big ask, especially with two instead of just one. Take time to think about it, please."

The two look to each other. "We don't need time," Cecilia says, holding her hands over her chest.

"Of course we will do it," Angelo says.

They both walk to the bed, taking the babies from our arms. They look so natural with them, like it was always meant to be them to watch over our babies.

Epilogue 2

16 years later

Iris

My house has fallen into absolute chaos and madness for the last two weeks. I told Gio last year that I wanted the twins to have a sweet sixteen party and let me tell you, I didn't know how much that would entail. I swear I am not doing this again... Well, that's a lie. Leo will get a party too, but he's only eleven, so I have five years to plan. What I should have done was hire a planner, but no, Cecilia and I thought we had it handled.

My phone dings, pulling my attention. It's Cecilia.

Cecilia: *Hey girl, on my way. I have all of my hair stuff.*

Me: *Oh thank god I don't have that stuff.*

"Isabella, hurry up! Your aunt is coming to do your hair!" I yell up the stairs.

Gio and Angelo took Matteo to the tailor to get his suit. I have no idea what they put him in. I trust Gio a hundred percent, but those two turn from adults to teenagers real quick when they are around each other. Eight years ago around Christmas, Matteo was going through a *Star Wars* phase. I found a drunk Angelo and Gio fighting in the backyard with lightsabers. Then, five years ago, I found the two idiots playing bumper cars with their ride-on battery cars. They were supposed to be cleaning out the garage. Angelo sat in a princess Jeep, and Gio sat in a

Jurassic Park Jeep. This time though, they were sober. I can't wait to see what this year brings us now.

Giovanni

"You can't tell your mother at all or I swear to God, Matteo, I'll tell her about the girl sneaking out of the house the other morning," I say. Matteo sits in the chair in front of me, Angelo to his left and Cecilia behind him.

"Yeah, kid. Don't tell your mom I did it either. I like breathing," Cecilia says while my son hisses from the burning.

Matteo originally wanted to get his FAAE tattoo today, but Iris and I decided to push all the kids' inking ceremonies to eighteen—not just ours, but everybody's kids. Not everyone waits, though; some still follow the old tradition. So today, Matteo is just getting a lion on his back, positioned just where his shirt collar can hide it. It will eventually be part of his entire back piece. I'm fine with the kids getting tattoos, but I want them to think about it. Matteo has been asking for a lion since he was fourteen.

Matteo grunts and moans as Cecilia finishes, turning off her tattoo gun. "Okay, kiddo, you're done. I gotta get going to do your sister's hair. Go look in the mirror. Do you like it?"

Looking over her shoulder, I see a black-and-white lion, its eyes the color of the Italian flag, framed in a black-lined triangle with shading.

Walking into the house, I realize Iris wasn't kidding when she said it was going to be chaos. She runs by with Isabella's dress in her arms. "Hi, love, I have a hundred things to do. Did you guys get Matteo's suit? Where is Matteo?"

Knowing the urgency, I rush out the answers in order: "Yes, got the suit. He's riding back with Angelo. Do you need me to do anything?"

"No, just make sure Matteo is dressed and at the venue at eight," she says.

Looking at my watch, it reads 6:30. We've got time.

I don't see Iris again until we get to the hotel ballroom. "Giovanni Benedetti, it is 8:15. You are late," she says, strutting toward me in a long, tight black gown. "You're lucky we're around people, my love," she adds, planting a kiss on my cheek and leaning in for a hug. "I might hit you," she whispers into my ear.

"I'm sorry, Mia Fiore, but Matteo didn't know how to tie his tie, and he wouldn't let us help," I say, kissing her cheek. "But don't worry, we found Cecilia in the parking lot. It's tied now."

"Oh, thank God. Your daughter decided she was going to try to fight the balloon lady earlier for putting them too far over—by three inches. I think she's worse than me."

My arms meet at her lower back. Pulling away slightly to see her face, I raise my eyebrows. "There is nobody worse than you."

A small smirk falls from her lips. "We are definitely hiring someone for Leo's. I'm not doing this again."

I look over her shoulder and see Isabella walking down the hallway to the entrance of the ballroom. She's wearing a gold gown that shows too much for my liking. "Speaking of... here comes your little mini-me. And who let her wear that dress?"

She gets to us before Iris can say anything. "Hi, Daddy," she says, getting on her tiptoes to plant a kiss on my cheek. "How do you like my dress?"

"It shows a little too much, Bella."

"She isn't a child anymore, love," her mother cuts in. "Go on in, have fun."

"Thanks, Mom and Dad. I love you," Isabella says.

We both take a big breath as Matteo and Isabella disappear into the ballroom arm in arm, greeted by smoke and loud music.

After a few hours, we gather everyone outside to give the kids their gifts. They knew they were getting cars; they just didn't know which ones. We got them both a BMW 3 Series—one white for Isabella and one black for Matteo. We thought about getting Matteo a car with a bigger trunk to fit all his hockey gear, but Ryan assured us it would be big enough.

Watching the twins get into the cars with their friends, a sudden sadness hits me. They really aren't babies anymore. Isabella is a young woman, and soon she'll be off to college. Matteo will be working for the family soon. Hell, the boy just got his first tattoo—something, thankfully, my wife knows nothing about. The kids drive away as Iris and I scream in unison, "Be careful!"

All the guests are gone, leaving myself, Iris, Angelo, and Cecilia behind, cleaning up some of the decorations. The girls are across the room, picking up the empty cups the kids left behind.

"So, how did his tattoo turn out?" Iris calls out.

My arms go numb, and my breath hitches in my throat. **FUCK. FUCK. FUCK. FUCK.** She is going to kill me tonight.

"What tattoo?" I cough out, avoiding looking at her.

"Gio, don't play stupid with me. You haven't been able to do anything without me knowing in the last sixteen years. Matteo asked me before he asked you." I look up to see her with her hand on her hip. "I told him yes and that he should help you keep it a secret from me."

"Why the fuck would you do that?" I say, walking to meet her in the middle.

"I like making you nervous," she says with a smirk.

Cecilia and Angelo both let out a laugh from their sides of the room.

"You and the kids are going to give me a heart attack," I mutter.

"No, we won't." She pauses, tilting her head with a mischievous grin. "Actually, yeah, we might."

"I love you, baby," I breathe into her neck, pulling her into my arms.

Taking a final look at her, I understand how I've been able to survive this long. She settled into her crown all too fast. I'd be lying if I said the men weren't scared of her. To be honest, she probably scares them more than I do.

When they doubted her all those years ago, she personally called a meeting, making sure every single person showed up—men and their wives, everyone affiliated. She sat them all down and made them watch the video Angelo and I made of what she did to her father. People ended up throwing up. They stopped questioning her that day. She's even done a few jobs here and there for us.

I'm just glad that she has been able to stay so loyal to the family. I meant it all those years ago—I will never be like him.

We are nothing like our fathers.

www.ingramcontent.com/pod-product-compliance
Lightning Source LLC
Chambersburg PA
CBHW021518240626
47154CB00002B/687